MURDER AND MAYHEM IN MUSKEGO

MURDER AND MAYHEM IN MUSKEGO

EDITED BY
JON AND RUTH JORDAN

Down and Out Books, LLC
3959 Van Dyke Rd, Ste. 265
Lutz, FL 33558
www.DownAndOutBooks.com

The characters and events in this book are fictitious. Any similarity to real persons, living or dead, is coincidental and not intended by the author.

Cover design by JT Lindroos

ISBN: 193749537X

ISBN-13: 978-1-937495-37-4

CONTENTS

CONTENTS

Welcome to Murder & Mayhem in Muskego
(M&M, the convention not the candy)

I've often been asked how M&M began. My story has always been that I blame a late night, a fully loaded pizza and one too many bottles of mediocre wine. While that's a colorful story, in reality, only one part of it is marginally true, alcohol was involved just not wine. The reality is Jane Genzel, my friend and partner in crime at the library and I were commiserating about not being able to attend all the mystery conventions we would like. Financial and time constraints were weighing heavily on us. We felt our only option was to bring the mystery community to us! Sounds simple enough, we would select some of our favorite authors, invite them to Muskego Public Library, share the event with other mystery readers and have a great time! It was a Mountain to Muhammad moment. The problem had been solved!

In the cold clear light of Monday morning, when common sense is said to prevail, we still knew we had a great idea. We really were brilliant! But brilliance only lasts until you actually have to make the idea work. Two months later our collective brilliance was on a downward spiral and gaining momentum, when Jane and I attended the local MWA dinner meeting. We were assigned the table with friends Jon and Ruth Jordan and somewhere during the second course I scraped up enough courage to ask if a day long library event with selected mystery authors might work. Before dessert was served we had mapped out a plan and the rest is history.

In November 2012, Muskego Public Library will host the 8th Edition of Murder & Mayhem in Muskego. Has it been easy? Well, no. We've had our share of bumps and bone jarring pot holes, but it has been a spectacular adventure. Nothing can compare to welcoming 350 mystery readers and knowing you've brought these people a one of a kind program. Seeing the authors everyone knows, reads and enjoys actually in my library gives me goose bumps every single time.

M&M has hosted the most incredible list of authors, far too many to list, the number is well over 400. Without their generous gift of time and their unbelievable talents, Murder & Mayhem would not exist. To each and every one, I say thank you.

To the Friends of Muskego Public Library, I owe a huge debt. They said yes to the vague plan for this event and every year since, they say yes again. The Friends spend all year raising money to support Murder & Mayhem. Thank you, thank you and thank you. Support your local library and Friends group, they need you.

And you, Dear Reader, thank you!

Penny Halle
Muskego Public Library
May 2012

Hollywood Lanes
Megan Abbott

The way their banner-blue uniforms pressed up against each other, the wilting collar corners, her twitchy cocktail apron and his regulation pinman trousers—I was only a kid, but I knew it was something and it made my head go hot, my stomach pinch. Eddie worked the alley, made the lanes shine with that burring rotary machine. Carol slung beer at the cocktail lounge, heels digging in the heavy carpet, studded each night with peanut skins, cigarette ashes, cherry stems.

They were there every day, at 3:30, in the dark, narrow alley behind the pinsetting machines. And I saw them, saw them plain as day as I sat just outside the machine room on a metal stool, picking summer scabs off my knee. First time by accident, just hiding out back there, where it was quiet and no one came around.

Eddie'd been there a month, he and his wife, Sherry, who ran concessions with my mother over by the shoe station. He had blue-black hair, slick like those olives in the jar at the Italian grocery store. When he walked through the joint, coming on his shift, everyone, the waitresses, even old Jimmy, the sweaty-faced manager, lit up like a row of sparklers because he was a friendly guy with a lot of smiles and his uniform always finely pressed and the strong smell of limey cologne coming off him like a movie star or something.

No one could figure him and Sherry. Sherry with the damp, faded blonde features, eyes empty as the rubber dish tub she was always resting her dusty elbows on. Cracking gum, staring open-mouthed at the crowds, the families, the amateur baseball team, the VFW fellas, the beery young marrieds swinging their arms around, skidding down the lanes, collapsing into each other's laps after each crack of the pins, Sherry never moved, except to shift her weight from one spindly leg to the other.

Just shy of thirteen, I was at Hollywood Lanes every day that summer. Husband three months gone, my mother was working double shifts to keep me in shoes, to hear her tell it. I helped the dish washers, loading racks of cloudy glasses into the steaming machine, the only girl they ever let do it. Some days, I helped Georgie spray out the shoes or use Clean Strike on the balls.

But I always beat tracks at 3:30 so I could be behind the pin racks. Eddie and Carol, his hands spread across her waist, leaning into her, saying things to her. *What was he saying? What was he telling her?*

Sherry's face looked tired in the yellow haze of the fluorescent pretzel carousel.

"Kid," she said. "You're here all the time."

I didn't say anything. My mother was stacking cups in the corner, squirming in her uniform, too tight across her chest.

"You know Eddie? You know him?" Sherry gestured over to the lanes.

I nodded. My mother spun one of the waxy cups on her finger, watching.

"I know what's what," Sherry said, looking over at my mother. I felt something ring in my chest, like a buzzer or school bell.

"You don't know," my mother said, looking at the rotating hotdogs, thick and glossy.

"I got eyes," Sherry said, gaze fixed on the lanes, on Eddie, running the floor waxer over them jauntily. He liked using the machine. He kind of danced with it, not in a showy way, but there was a rhythm to the way he moved it, twirled around on it like he was ice skating. Billy, the last guy, twice Eddie's age, looked like he would fall asleep as he did it, weaving down each lane, hung over from a long night at Marshall's Tavern.

His hands always shook when he handed out shoes. Then he threw up all over the men's room during Family Night and Jimmy fired him.

"Don't tell me I don't got eyes," Sherry was saying.

"We all got eyes," my mother said. "But there's nothing to see." Her brow wet with grease from the grill, her eyeshadow smeared. "There's not a goddamned thing to see."

I didn't say anything. I never said anything. But something was funny in the way Sherry was looking at Eddie. She always had that blank look, but it used to seem like a little girl, a doll, limbs soft and loose, black buttons for eyes. Now, though, it was different. It was different, but I wasn't sure how.

Back there in that space behind the pins, it was like backstage and no one could see even though all eyes were facing it. As soon as you walked in a bowling alley that was where your eyes went. You couldn't help it. But you never thought that could be going on behind the pins, so tidy and white.

And each day I'd watch. It was a hundred degrees or more back there. It was filled with noise, all the sharp cracks echoing through the place. But I was watching the way Carol trembled. Because she always seemed so cool and easy, with her long pane of dark hair, her thick fringe of dark lashes pasted on in the Ladies Room one by one. ("They get her tips, batting those babies like a raccoon in heat," Myrna, the old lady who worked dayshift concessions, said. "Those and the pushup brassiere.")

Carol was talking to Diane, the other cocktail waitress. Diane used to work at the Stratton but, to hear her tell it, the minute her tits dropped a half-inch, they put her out on her can. She hated the Lanes. "How much tips can I get from these Knights of Columbus types," she always groaned. She worked at Whitestone Lanes too and had plenty to say about the customers there as well.

I was sitting at a table in the cocktail lounge, looking at pictures of Princess Grace in someone's leftover *Life Magazine*. I wasn't supposed to be in there, but no one ever bothered me until Happy Hour.

"She can jaw all she wants," Carol was saying, eating green cherries from the dish on the bar. "It's all noise to me." She was talking about Sherry.

"She should take it up with her man, she has something to say about things," Diane said.

"I don't care what she does."

"What I hear, she can't show her face in Ozone Park. They all remember her family. Trash from trash."

"I'm going to haul bills tonight, I can tell. Look at 'em," Carol said, surveying the softball team swarming in like bright bumble bees.

"Yeah, good luck," Diane said, then nodded at Carol's neckline. "Bend, bend, bend."

In the bathroom once, right after, I pretended to be fixing my hair, snapping and resnapping a colored rubber band around my slack ponytail. I knew Carol would be in there, always went in there after. When she came out of the stall, I looked at her in the mirror. Her face steaming pink, she brushed her shiny hair in long strokes, swooping her arm up and down and swiveling a little like she was dancing or something. She was watching her own face in the mirror. I wondered what she was watching for.

I saw the dust on her back, shaken between her shoulder blades. I wanted to reach my hand out and brush it away.

Eddie was oiling the lanes and saw me watching, eating French fries off a paper plate at the head of Lane 3.

"And there's my girl," he said. He said it like we talked all the time, but it was the first time he'd ever said anything to me. "Stuck inside every day. Don't you like to go to the Y or something? Go to the city pool?"

"I don't like to swim," I said. Which was true, but my

mother didn't want me to go there by myself. When summer started, she let me go once to a pool day with the kids at school, but when I got home, she was sitting on the front steps of our building like she'd been waiting for me for hours. Her face was red and puffy and I never saw her so glad to see me. That was the only time I went. Besides, she'd never liked it. Mr. Upton, before he left, was always telling her I'd get diseases at the public pool.

"All kids like to swim, don't they?" Eddie was saying. He tilted his head and smiled. "Don't girls like to show off their swimming suits?"

I ate another fry, even though it was too hot and made my mouth burn, lips sting with salt.

"I always liked to go, just splash around and stuff," he said. "You got no one to take you, huh?"

"I don't really swim much," I said.

He nodded with a grin, like he was figuring something out. "I get it. Well, I'd take you, but I guess your daddy wouldn't like it."

I felt my thigh slide on the plastic seat. I looked at the far end of the lanes. I felt my thigh come unstuck and slide off the edge of the seat and it was shaking. "He's gone" I said.

Eddie paused for a flickering second before he smiled. "Then I guess I got a chance."

Fred Upton was my mother's husband. My real old man died when I was a baby. He had some kind of infection that went to his brain.

There were some guys in between, but two years ago it was all about Mr. Upton. We moved from Kew Gardens when she got tangled up with him and quit her job at Leona Pick selling dresses. She'd met Mr. Upton working there, sold him a billowy nightgown for his fiancée and he took her out for spaghetti with clams at LaStella on Queens Boulevard that very night. They got hitched at City Hall three weeks later.

Before he left, times were pretty good. It was always trips to Austin Street to buy new shoes with t-straps and lunch at the Hamburger Train and going in the dress store with the soft carpet, running our hands through the linen and seersucker dresses—with names like buttercup yellow, grasshopper green, goldenrod, strawberry punch. One day he bought her three dresses, soft summer sheaths with boatneck collars like a woman you'd see on TV or the movies. The sales lady wrapped them in tissue for her even when my mother told her they weren't a gift.

"They're a gift for you, aren't they?" the lady had said, her pink cake icing lips doing something like a smile.

Those dresses were sitting in the closet now, unworn for months yellowing, smelling like stale perfume, old smoke. Never saw my mother out of one of her two uniforms these days, except when she slept in the foldout couch, usually in her slip. Some days I tugged off her pantyhose while she slept.

"He said he was going to the Aqueduct," I heard my mother say on the telephone to a girlfriend soon after he left. "But his sister tells me he's in Miami Beach."

It had been three months now and wherever Fred Upton went, he wasn't in Queens. Someone my mother met in a bar told her he heard Mr. Upton was dead, killed in a hotel fire in Atlantic City the same night he'd left. That was the last I heard. I didn't ask. I could tell she didn't want me to. I hoped she'd forget about Mr. Upton and marry a mailman or a man who worked in an office. As it was, I figured us for six more weeks of this and we'd be moving in with my grandmother in Flushing.

"She's got ants in her pants, that one," Myrna was saying to Sherry. Myrna had a big birthmark on her cheek that twitched whenever she disapproved of something, which was a lot. She was talking about Carol, who she called "Lane 30," because that was where the cocktail lounge was. "Thinks she's got it coming and going."

"Don't I know. She better watch where she shakes that," Sherry said, face tight and sallow under the fluorescent light. She looked like a sickly yellow bird, a pinched lemon.

"You got ideas."

"Sure I got ideas. And I'm no rabbit. Maybe she needs to

hear that."

"I'll see she does."

Sherry nodded. Those flat eyes were jumping. That slack lip now drawn tight. Her face all moving, all jigsawing around. She looked different, more interesting. Not pretty. It was all too much for pretty. But you couldn't take your eyes off it.

I wasn't supposed to be back there at all. Once, years before, some kid, not even fifteen-years-old, was working at the Lanes. He got stuck in the pinsetter machine and died. There were a million different stories of how it happened, but ever since, no one under twenty-one was supposed to be back there. But I never got near the clanging machine. I stayed in the alcove where they kept the cleaning equipment.

From there, I could see them and they never saw me. They never even looked around.

Sometimes, Eddie would be whispering to her, but I couldn't hear.

They were just pressed together and, when the machine wasn't going, when no one was bowling, you could hear the rustle of their uniforms brushing against each other.

The more he moved, the more she did and I could hear her breathing and her breath go faster and faster. He covered her and I couldn't see her except her long hair and her long legs wound round. I was too far to see her eyes. I wanted to see her eyes. It was like he was shaking her into life.

"Things are getting interesting," Mrs. Schwartz was saying to my mother, who was resting against the counter, slapping around a washrag tiredly. You can lean, you can clean, Jimmy always said.

"Don't count on it," my mother said.

"She might try harder, wants to keep a man like that," Mrs. Schwartz said. Mrs. Schwartz was the head of one of the women's leagues. She was always there early to gossip with Diane. I think she knew Diane from the Stratton, where Mrs.

Schwartz met her second husband. They liked to talk about everybody they knew and the terrible things they were doing.

"Looks like a singer or something," she added, twisting in her capris. "A television personality. Even his teeth. He's got fine teeth."

"I never noticed his teeth," my mother said.

"Take note," Mrs. Schwartz said, nodding gravely.

Diane walked up, clipping her name tag on her uniform. No one said anything for a minute. They were watching Sherry walk into the Ladies Room, cigarette pack in hand

"She can't even be bothered to put on lipstick," Mrs. Schwartz said, shaking her head. "Comb her hair more than twice a day."

"Her skin smells like grill," Diane said under her breath. The two women laughed without making any noise, hands passing in front of their faces.

Mrs. Schwartz left to meet her teammates surging into the place with their shocks of bright hair and matching shirts the color of Creamsicles.

Diane was watching Sherry come out of the Ladies Room, tying her apron.

"Trash," Diane said to my mother. Then, in a lower voice, "They used to live upstate. Her father's doing a hitch in Auburn. Got in a fight at a stoplight, beat a man with a tire iron. Man lost an eye."

"How do you know," my mother said.

"Jimmy told me. He gave her hell for making a call to State Corrections on his dime." Diane shook her head again. "Mark my words, she's trouble too. Trash from trash."

I looked over at Sherry, leaning against a ball return to tie her apron. She had her eyes on them, on all of us. She couldn't hear, but it was like she did.

"Mark my words," Diane said. "Blood will tell."

That whole summer, I'd lie in bed at night waiting for my mother to come home from her shift waiting tables at the tavern. I'd lie in bed and think about Eddie and Carol. It was like how I used to think about Alice Crimmins, the Kew

Gardens lady who killed her kids so she could be with her boyfriend. I couldn't get her face from the newspaper out of my head. Two, three times a night, I'd run around testing all the window latches, the window gates.

Now, though, it was all about Eddie and Carol. I'd stay under my sheets—cool from sitting in the refrigerator for hours while I watched television and ate Chef Boyardee—and think about how they looked, all flushed and pulsing, how you could feel it coming off them. You could feel it burning in them. It made my throat go dry. It made something ripple in me, like the time I rode the rollercoaster at Fairyland and thought I just might die.

But then I'd start thinking of Sherry standing behind that counter all day. When she'd first started, she cracked gum and looked bored, went in the bathroom twice a day to wash hotdog sweat off her hands and spit out her gum in the sink.

But lately she didn't look bored. And, nights, she'd get into my head. Standing there like that, her head dropping, eyes lowered, watching.

Watching so close I wondered when she was going to make her move. Was she waiting to see it for herself? Hadn't she figured out yet when and where it was happening, right behind the wall of pin trestles she—we all—stared at every day, all day?

Each day it seemed closer and closer. Each day you could feel it in the place, even as the clean and fresh-faced Forest Hills kids pounded their bright white tennis shoes down each alley, even as the shiny haired teenagers hunched over the pinball machines, shoving their hips, twisting their bodies, like they wanted to squirm out of their skin, even as the customers at the bar, steeled behind smoked glass by Lane 30, cocooned from the pitch of the squealing kids and mooning double dates, cool in their adult hideaway of tonic and cool beer, crushed ice and lemon rinds and low jazz and soft-toned waitress with long, snapping sheets of hair and warm smiles and a bartender who understood them and would make them happy, would know just what to do to make them happy...even with all that going on at the Lanes, it was going to happen.

* * *

"I don't like the way they talk about her," Diane was whispering to my mother, leaning over my mother's counter, tangerine nails tapping anxiously. "Sherry and Myrna and Myrna's friends from the Tuesday league."

"Talk's just talk," my mother said, loosening her apron.

"Listen," she said, leaning closer. Looking over at me, trying to get me not to listen. "Listen, she deserves something. Carol does." Her voice even lower, husky and suddenly soft. "Her mom's at Creedmore. She's been there a while. Took a hot iron to Carol when she was a kid. She was sound asleep when it happened. Still a scar the shape of a shield on her stomach."

Diane was looking at my mother, looking at her like she was asking her something. Asking her to understand something.

My mother nodded, eyes flickering as the fluorescent light made a pop. "You got a customer, Diane," she said, pointing toward the bar.

I was thinking they might stop. Might take a few days off, let things cool off. But they didn't. They only changed it up a little. From what I could tell, Carol came in the back way for her shift and met Eddie first. Met him back there before anyone even saw her. But they didn't stop. And one day Eddie came out with a streak of Carol's lilac lipstick on his bleach-white collar, just like in a story in a women's magazine.

I watched him walk across the place, lane by lane, with the stain on him. I looked over at Sherry, who was leaning against the pinball machine and watching him. I thought: *this is it. She's too far to see it*, I thought to myself. But if he moved closer. If she moves closer.

But neither of them did.

When I saw him later, the lipstick was gone, collar slightly damp. I pictured him in the Men's Room scrubbing it off, scrubbing her off. Looking in the mirror and thinking about what he'd done and what he couldn't help but keep doing.

***

The kids from Forest Hills High School were all over the place that afternoon, all in their summer clothes, girls with tan legs and boys freshly showered and gleaming. The rain had sent them already, some straight from lounge chairs at the club, others from lifeguarding or the tennis courts. I always noticed the fuzzy edges of my summer Keds around them. I always wondered how the girls got their hair so shiny, their clothes so crisp, their eyes so bright.

I had a feeling it was going to happen that day. I couldn't say why. Before Sherry even got there. But when she did I knew for sure.

She looked like she'd been running a fever. There was this gritty film all over her skin and red blotches at her temples. Her uniform looked unwashed from the day before, a ring of grease circling her belly.

She was late and I'd just left my post, just left the two of them. *They never took their clothes off, ever, but sometimes he'd lift her skirt so high I could see flashes of her skin. I was looking for the scar, but I never saw it.*

Her fingers pinched around his neck, the rushed pitch to her voice, soft but streaming…it felt different this time. It felt like something was turning. Maybe it was something in the way his hands moved, more quiet, more careful. Maybe something in her that made her move looser, almost still.

I got it then. And then it was for sure when I saw them break apart and each look the other way. She dropped her skirt down. He was already walking away.

I flicked off the last piece of the strawberried scar on my knee. The skin underneath was still tender, puckered.

And now there was Sherry. I was walking from the back and she was right in front of me, talking at me, her voice funny, toneless.

"I saw you sitting over there yesterday. By the machine room."

"No one's at concessions," I said, wondering where my mother had gone.

"It was the same time. I saw you come out from there at

the same time yesterday."

"I guess," I said.

It was ten minutes later, no more, when we all heard the shouting. Jimmy, Myrna, Eddie, two guys putting on their bowling shoes—we all followed the sounds to the Ladies Room.

Carol was hunched over, hair hanging in long panels in front of her. She looked surprised, her mouth a small "o."

At first, I thought Sherry'd just punched her in the stomach.

But then I saw it in her hand. The blade was short and Sherry held it so close to her, elbows at her waist.

The blade was short and it couldn't have gone deep.

Jimmy backhanded Sherry. She cracked her head on the stall door and slid slowly to the floor, one hand reaching out for Jimmy's shirt.

The knife fell and I saw it was one of those plastic-handled ones they used to open the hotdog packages at concessions.

Eddie pushed past Jimmy and knelt down beside Sherry. She had a surprised look on her face. He was whispering to her, "Sherry, Sherry..."

Carol was watching Eddie. Then she turned away and looked down at her stomach and a tiny blotch of red against the banner blue.

"That ain't nothing," Myrna said, birthmark twitching. "That ain't nothing at all."

Myrna taped up Carol with the first-aid kit. Then Jimmy took all three of them to his office. I walked over to concessions, but no one was there.

That was when Diane came running in, shouting for someone to call an ambulance.

"We don't need no ambulance," Myrna said. "I hurt myself worse getting out of bed."

But Diane was already on the phone at the shoe rental desk.

* * *

We all ran down the long hallway that led out of the lanes and up the stairs to the Boulevard.

Someone must have already called because the ambulance was there.

At first, it was like my mother had just lain down on the street. But the way her neck was turned looked funny. Like her head had put on wrong.

Diane grabbed me from behind and pulled me back.

That was when I saw a middle-aged man in a gray suit sitting on the curb, his face in his hands. His car door was open like he'd stumbled out to the curb. He was crying loudly, his whole body shaking. I'd never heard a man cry like that.

Diane was telling everyone who would listen.

"She said she saw him. She said she saw Fred Upton pass by on the 4:08 yesterday. But he'd never take a bus, would he. That's what she said. So she wanted to watch for it at the same time today. See if it was him. You know how she always thought she was seeing him somewhere.

"No one must've hit the bell because the bus didn't stop. And she just ran out onto the Boulevard after it. That car didn't have time to stop."

She looked over at the man, who started sobbing even louder.

"Hit her like a paper doll," Diane was saying. "Nothing but a paper doll going up in the wind and then coming down."

Later, I would figure it out. My mother, nights spent looking out diner windows, uniform steeped in smoke, thinking of the stretch of her thirty years, filled with glazy-eyed men stumbling into her life all with the promise of four decades of union wages like her old man, repairing refrigerators, freezers in private homes, restaurants, country clubs, office buildings for her whole life never stopping for more than one Rheingold at the corner bar before coming home for pot roast at the table with wife and three kids.

Those men came, but never for long or they came and then turned, sometime during the first, second night in her bed into something else altogether, something that needed her, sure, but also needed the countergirl at Peter Pan bakery or four nights a week betting horses at the parking garage on Austin Street or a night watching the fights at Sunnyside Garden even it was her birthday and, yeah, maybe he needed the roundcard girl he met there too.

There was a dream of something and maybe it wasn't even a man like her old man or the man in the Arrow Shirt ad or the doctor she met once at the diner, the one with the big apartment in the new highrises, the view from the bedroom so great that she'd have to see it to believe it, he said. Maybe it wasn't a man dream at all. But it was something. It was something and it was there and then it was gone.

"Hollywood Lanes" originally appeared in *Queens Noir* (Akashic Books, 2007), edited by Robert Knightly.

Pattern Recognition
Dana Cameron

Joel's eyes went straight to her breasts, then lower, where they loitered. The next moment was a blur of arousal, interest and, when his brain caught up with his spinal cord, curiosity, followed by concern and building fear.

Naked, was the first word that came to him. Then *girl, dirty, crazy.*

She *was* naked, save for a scarf draped over her head. She stood on a rickety wooden chair in the middle of the room, skinny arms outstretched wide before her, shaking with the effort of holding them up. Her brown hair was long and tangled and she looked like something out of *National Geographic.*

Joel felt a rumbling beneath his feet; maybe it was the train passing nearby.

Her eyes finally opened, wide and unfocused, as if he'd wakened her from a dream. She glanced around, looked right through Joel as if he wasn't even there, then mumbled something.

"Didn't catch that," he said, wondering if reaching for his cell phone would set her off. *She didn't look like much,* he thought, *but you couldn't be too careful. Not with a killer on the loose.*

"Thought it would work," she said, swallowing. "This time."

He pretended to look around, shook his head. "Nope. I guess not."

He didn't want to know who she was, didn't want her to be his problem. He held out a hand, hoping she'd get down and leave.

It halfway worked. She climbed off the chair, but then sat down.

He stepped toward her and his foot slipped. When he looked down, he saw olive oil covering the floor. All over her arms, dripping down her legs, the empty container in the corner, as if it had been flung away.

Joel tamped down burgeoning panic as he tried not to think of the ridiculously expensive olive oil. It had been one of the last things he and Lenore had argued about before she left.

The anxiety that plagued him so constantly—had he locked the door? Had he been offensive to the waitress? Had he really cut someone off in traffic?—was somewhat at bay because he'd just come from therapy. Maybe this was one of those opportunities his shrink had mentioned, about climbing out of his own head to help someone else. Not her words exactly, but...

"You got a name?" he said, flinching. He hadn't meant the question to come out so brusquely.

"I don't think so." She stood, and to Joel's relief, went over to a pile of clothing on the floor, just out of range of the pool of oil that was being sucked into the hungry, rough wood planks. "This isn't your place." She seemed fine now, blotting herself with the scarf, as if she remembered nothing of standing naked in a stranger's presence. As if she'd suddenly realized how cold and drafty the room was.

"No." The apartment was his cousin's, loaned to him on condition he admit the bead shop staff downstairs every day and lock up at night. "It's not yours either," he said. *Not aggressive, really*, he thought. *Maybe a little nudge, a hint of assertiveness. Nothing anyone could take offense at, surely?*

She didn't seem so dangerous now, in an old pair of cargo pants, a hoodie and Docs. The sodden scarf was wrapped around her neck, forgotten.

"No. I..." She faltered for the first time, looked around her. "I don't know where I am."

"How about we get someone to come pick you up?" Joel was emboldened by the idea of his authority. It had been a while. "Is there someone we can call?"

She opened her mouth to speak, then shut it. After half a

minute, she said, "I don't think so. I think I'm trying to hide."

No shit. I would, too, if I was crazy as you, he thought. He flinched at the uncharitable thought. "Um...okay. We won't let anyone hurt you. I'll call a friend of mine." The more he thought about calling Dr. Steuben, the more it seemed like a good idea. "She'll be able to help you sort things out."

And if not, she can check you into the cracker factory.

"Okay." She went over to the window, looked out into the winter dusk and shivered. "This is Salem?"

Joel fumbled with his phone. *And I'd been so close to taking the doctor off speed-dial,* he thought. "Uh, yeah. Massachusetts. March 14, 20—"

"Yeah, thanks, I got it." She interrupted him with a frown that said "asshole."

"Hey, I'm not the one standing naked on chairs," he said then immediately regretted it. What if he set her off? What if she got violent? He of all people should be more sympathetic. "Sorry. I'm sorry. I just didn't know...what else you didn't know."

She shrugged. "Me, neither."

Luckily, Dr. Steuben answered just then. Joel told his story and after confirming neither one of them was injured—as far as he could tell the woman was perfectly fine, just lost in thought—Dr. Steuben asked, "Did you ask if she knew your cousin? If she'd been given a key of her own?"

"Ummm..."

"It's like we discussed, Joel. Stick with the basics, what's most likely. That will help."

He imagined he could hear her impatience and felt chastened. "Okay, hang on a sec." He covered the phone. "You don't know Diana, do you?

"Who?"

"My cousin, the woman who owns this apartment? And the bead store downstairs?"

"No." That seemed to worry her.

Joel returned to the phone, feeling vindicated. "Never heard of Diana."

"Tell me again what the woman was doing."

He turned away, as if to conceal his words from the

woman herself and described the scene. "It was, I don't know," he finished. "Like something from the History Channel? Ancient looking?"

He felt stupid as soon as he said it and when his therapist didn't say anything, he was sure her concern about him had cranked up a couple of notches. He could hear a keyboard clattering in the background and wondered if she was taking notes. On him. "Can I bring her to see you?"

"Do you think she'll come with you?"

"Sure. She seems—" He turned around to check on the girl—woman, he corrected himself automatically.

She was gone. The door leading to the back alley stairs was hanging open.

He went over and looked down into the alley. No sign of her.

"Hey, it looks like she took off." His relief to be rid of this problem was tinged with regret. He couldn't have said why.

Both relief and regret were short-lived.

"Find her, if you can," Dr. Steuben said, surprising him. "I'll be there in ten minutes."

My sister Claudia insisted on driving, which was fine. She drives at least as fast as I do, if not as cautiously. She's a vampire—with all the speed, agility and coordination that implies—and if she gets pulled over, she can always charm the cop.

I can't charm cops. They shouldn't be allergic to me, but they are. There's a serious mistrust of ex-cops who go to the dark side. Not 'dark side' because I'm a werewolf—most of the guys I know would think that was pretty cool, once they got done pissing themselves. Even cooler if they learned I'm Fangborn, born to a family of supernatural beings dedicated to the protection of humanity and the eradication of evil. No, I went to the dark side when I retired from the force and became a PI. That's when the love got lost.

So I let Claudia drive and tried not to flinch as she changed lanes, slipping into a nearly nonexistent space between cars.

"My patient, Joel Weeks," she said, "is working on issues

with grief, depression and separation anxiety. No real breakthrough, no catharsis, yet—there's a lot of denial there—but it's nothing I can't fix with talk therapy and a little vampire boost. It's the woman he found in his apartment I'm interested in."

"Why? You said he'd never met her before."

"Her posture, the oil, the nudity—it's a hunch, Gerry, that's all."

Claudia's hunches are pretty good—honed by her training as a shrink and vampire intuition—and while I didn't say anything, I agreed with her. There was something about this whole situation that got my spidey sense tingling, too.

"When we get there," she said, "I'll ask him what he saw and distract him while you track the girl. We need to find her."

We arrived at the shop and I didn't need to hear Claudia's gasp to tell me plans had changed.

Outside the construction site for the local museum's new wing, a hapless-looking guy—just a citizen, weedy, remarkably unimpressive—was frozen in his tracks, gawking at another man trying to drag a young woman away. The late winter snow had started again, muffling the sounds outside. The jerk dragging the girl outweighed her by at least seventy pounds and looked like he enjoyed his job. When she actually managed to wriggle out of one of his hands, he cocked his head. Then he stepped in, yanked her by the other hand and gave her a slap so hard it knocked her head into the concrete foundation.

"Gerry!" Claudia warned.

I stopped growling, unfastened my seat belt, then Changed halfway as Claudia stomped the accelerator. The rush came over me as it always does, adrenaline gearing me up for battle. A glance in the rear view showed we were alone. It also revealed my inhuman face: muzzle filled with teeth; furry, upright ears; a wolf's predator eyes. Red Sox cap.

"I'll get Joel," she said, as I unlocked my door. "You get the bad guy."

"Fastball special, coming up." I've had a lot of practice, talking around fangs.

My sister accelerated, then pulled the handbrake, sliding in alongside the sidewalk and blocking the struggling couple from Joel's view with the BMW. I threw myself from the still-moving car, tucked and rolled. Because my reflexes are about a hundred times better than a human's, I landed right at the jerk's feet before he realized it.

I stood up, driving my fist into his chin with all my 200 pounds behind it. When his head bashed into the same wall he'd just bounced the girl against, I thought it had a certain kind of poetry.

Something freaky happened: an overwhelming urge to Change completely to wolfself hit me. It was all concentrated at the base of my skull though, like I'd never felt before, Pop Rocks and Alka-Seltzer buzzing my brain. I was losing control like I hadn't since I was a kid, damn near drunk on the glory of fangs, fur and the pursuit of evil.

Then, a loud, metallic crack, high overhead. I grabbed the girl and threw us both to one side.

A tangle of rebar crashed down from the construction site to the sidewalk. If I hadn't moved, the girl would have been dead for sure and I'd have looked like roadkill for a week, at the very least. The jerk was extremely dead, a mess of metal rods and hamburger.

"Hey, you guys?" Claudia spoke calmly, as if she only wanted to get out of the wet snow. "Let's get out of here. Joel, could you get us some coffee at your place?"

I felt the tug of her vampiric suggestion and wondered why my sister was pushing so hard. Maybe she was afraid the girl was going to run again, but she still seemed pretty dazed, maybe concussed. Maybe she was worried Joel would freak out at what he'd just seen, but he only nodded.

We followed him a few doors down to one of those old brick warehouses converted to apartments and shops. As we entered, something told me to look back down the block.

If I'd been a Normal, I might have told myself it was a trick of the light. I knew better. The rebar on the sidewalk had been twisted into the shapes of perfectly formed snowflakes, as delicate as the ones falling around us.

***

Joel found himself making coffee in the apartment over his cousin's shop. He felt calmer now, probably because Dr. Steuben and her slab of a brother seemed to be taking charge. Fine with him; he'd never been a leader. He was still fuzzy about what had happened on the street.

Dr. Steuben was talking softly with the woman, when he emerged from the tiny kitchen. They looked up.

"Hey." He set down the coffee, glanced nervously at Dr. Steuben. He always felt so...useless...around her. "Um...any luck?"

"Nope." Dr. Steuben smiled and his anxiety vanished. "She seems to have suffered some kind of massive trauma. The first thing she remembers is asking you where she was."

The woman shrugged. "Apparently, I put on quite a show when I've suffered a trauma." She was trying for casual, but fell a mile short, her laugh nervous. She was shaking now.

Joel wasn't sure what to say. Fortunately, Gerry looked up from the smart phone he'd been studying. "There's been an unusual number of missing persons cases lately. I've been keeping an eye on them, and so far, everyone has either stayed missing, or..."

"Or?" the woman said.

Gerry hesitated. "Was found deceased."

Joel stirred his coffee, frowning. "You mean the ones who were macheted to death? It's been all over the papers. Some kind of gang war, I thought."

Gerry shook his head. "Maybe. I doubt it."

Joel felt the hair on the back of his neck stand up and swallowed hard.

"Any luck on a name for our friend here?" Dr. Steuben said.

Gerry tapped the keys on his phone. "I think so: Alexa Thompson, white, age twenty-seven, brown and brown. Sounds about right. Reported missing three days ago when she didn't show up to her IT job at the college."

The girl—Alexa—swept her arm out and knocked her coffee cup to the floor. She took a deep breath, then began to cry.

Joel booked it for the kitchen to find a towel; he had no problem leaving this kind of emotion to a trained professional. When he returned, Alexa was calmer, but Dr. Steuben was downright agitated.

"Gerry, it doesn't work like that," she was saying to her brother. "She's had a blackout—without any symptoms of post-traumatic confusional state—but with no sign of injury. Exhibiting both anterograde and retrograde amnesia, at the same time she now recognizes her name? It's not medically...usual."

"If she's telling the truth," Gerry said.

"Of course I'm telling the truth!" Alexa said, snuffling. "Who would make this up?"

"She's telling the truth." Dr. Steuben gave her brother a glance. "But this is just *not* what happens with a concussion or even the stress of having been mugged."

"I don't think I was mugged," Alexa said. "I don't have a bag, but I don't have my coat either." Her face brightened. "Something must have happened inside."

"Something you can't recall."

Dr. Steuben ran down a list of questions, with no luck: Alexa didn't drink to excess, never touched drugs, no history of mental or physical illness.

Agreeing to meet back at the apartment in an hour, the Steubens left to check Alexa's apartment for clues. Joel reluctantly agreed to keep Alexa until the Steubens returned; the incident with the guy on the sidewalk had left everyone shaken. Locking the door behind them, Joel couldn't stop thinking about what it must be like to be cut with a machete.

"I notice you didn't encourage them to call the cops," I said. "I also notice they're not even questioning our involvement."

Claudia pulled on her latex gloves as we returned to the site of the attack. She'd Changed halfway, the better to examine the corpse. We both hoped the street would stay empty; a bipedal, female herpet-American with fangs and purplish scales was no tourist attraction, even in Salem. "I didn't want the cops near them," Claudia said. "And yes, I gave them a little blast of suggestibility pheromone. This is *our* brand of weird, Gerry."

"Because it's magic?" I stared at the iron snowflakes, ranging in size from three to five feet tall. The detail in them was astonishing, more than man-made. Definitely not natural, definitely not an accident.

"No way. If Normal humans knew about the Fangborn, they'd think we're magic. We're not. Science just hasn't caught up with us yet. And Alexa didn't use magic, either."

I looked at the rebar, twisted into impossibly delicate, graceful shapes. "Science had better catch up quick. This is fucking weird. Almost, you know," I made booga-booga hands, "*magical.*"

Claudia hissed faintly, as she searched the body. "Gerry, it's only our ultra-conservative cousins who live in caves and cast bones who believe in magic. There ain't no such thing."

I crossed my arms. "And yet, a werewolf and a vampire stare at an instant modern art installation in the middle of the sidewalk. What's the deal?" I nodded to the wallet and other pocket detritus Claudia had collected from the corpse. It had been a difficult job; the body had been impaled about a hundred different ways from Sunday. When the cops finally arrived, they'd have a bad time with this.

"The name Ronnie Platt mean anything to you?"

I took a deep breath. "He works for Diego Cesar, a guy the Normals don't want to even think about."

Claudia showed me his cell phone: Hells. Ronnie had called in to his boss. But I was willing to bet he didn't actually know Joel or where he was staying, if he was after Alexa. There was no connection between the two I could see.

"Any reason Cesar or Platt would be slicing up people randomly?" she asked, as I pocketed the phone.

"Usually profit involved." I stared at the rebar. "I've heard Cesar has a strange kink about mystical stuff though. An unattractive habit of getting live goats and chickens from East Cambridge to...open up. To...examine. I can't make a case for him killing the missing persons though."

"Haruspicy—divination by the examination of sacrifices? That's an archaic kink." Claudia thought about it. "Assuming Alexa has never done this"—she nodded to the transformed rebar—"before, what's the time-line for the four other murders?"

"Nothing before last week."

"Something must have happened then, to trigger...whatever this is." She bit her lip. "Were any of the others in pairs?"

I started to shake my head, then stopped. "Not really together. But two were found in one neighborhood and the other two in another."

"Pairs—maybe they were trying to find each other?" She stared, thinking.

"What?"

"You didn't notice? When I was alone with Joel, he was the same as all our therapy sessions: passive, depressed affect. And when I was alone with Alexa—nothing. But when he was near Alexa and she was in danger...something happened. It felt like the call to Change, focused right in my brain stem. But like it was going to take over, not like I was in driving." She stared. "The two of them *fit* together somehow. Linked."

I considered. "You don't think they're like Fangborn oracles? Like the Triplets?"

"Oracles tell riddles about the future and sometimes they're lucky. And none of them have the telekinetic power to move anything bigger than a coffee stirrer." She nodded to the rebar. "You ever see an oracle do anything like that?"

"No."

"Right. Something else is going on here." She put the wallet back and pulled off the gloves. "Got a spare phone?"

I nodded and pulled it out a prepaid phone and tossed it to her. She called 911 to report the body. She'd ditch the phone later. "You go ahead to Alexa's apartment, it's not too far. Make sure no one's waiting for her. I'm going to do some research."

I nodded innocently and raised my eyebrows. "Maybe check in with the cousins who live in caves?"

She gave me a look that said, *bite me.* "If you have time,

you might see if there are any similar patterns occurring outside Salem.”

“But...we shouldn’t go to the Family with this?”

She paused before answering. “Let’s make sure we have something real before we involve the rest of the Family.”

I left thinking—or trying to not think—about how the body of Ronnie Platt was pinned down like a bug on a board.

An hour later, having done all the possible tidying up, Joel summoned his courage. “So. Any idea what you were trying to do? Up there on the chair?” *With no clothes on?*

“Nope,” Alexa said. “This is freaking me out as much as you. Maybe not; I don’t actually remember what I was doing.” She glanced around the bare room. The only decoration was an ornate ceramic vessel on the mantel. “So how do you know Claudia?”

He felt himself go red and she cut in. “I’m sorry—that’s personal.”

“No, it’s okay; I’ve been having trouble getting past my wife...leaving. That’s why my cousin let me stay here while she was on vacation. A change of scenery—”

There was a rattle, the sudden sound of many heavy feet, then a pounding at the back door and the alley stairs.

Alexa froze. “What’s that?”

“Someone’s trying to break in! Quick, downstairs.”

Joel pulled out his phone, but with all the jostling down the front stairs, he got the wrong screen. He hit another button and, when she answered, he said, “Dr. Steuben, get back here *quick!*”

They stumbled through the shop door, pulled it shut and locked it.

A massive hand landed heavily on Joel’s shoulder. He staggered under it and briefly saw a shaved head and piratical eyebrows. The hand righted him and slid under his chin, holding him in a headlock. He felt powerful muscles in the arm tightening under his chin and didn’t dare swallow.

“The entrails of my birds led me to the other magical pairs,” a deep voice behind Joel rumbled. Alexa froze in her tracks, staring at the giant of a man. "When they couldn't show me what powers they had, their human entrails led me to you. I could smell their power; I can almost *taste* yours."

"What the hell?" Joel gasped, struggling to twist, but he would have needed a crowbar and three men to move the arm from his neck.

"Whatever you want—the cash register?" Alexa stammered, backing away. "Just take it."

Cesar shoved Joel toward her, holding him like a kitten by the scruff of his neck. "You have power. Show me. When I understand yours, maybe I can access my own."

"Are you kidding me? I don't—" She halted, having backed into one of the shelves of beads. She reached back, groping for a way to escape, but her hands brushed only against partitioned shelves of beads. A few fell to the floor, bouncing and rolling.

"Either prove what you are or he'll die."

Joel felt the hand tighten and thought he heard bones start to grind in his neck. "Alexa!"

Her eyes went wide. "You're crazy—!"

"You crucified my man on the pavement," Cesar said, "a study in elegance and brutality. Show me how." He pulled an eight-inch knife—no machete, but big enough—and held it before Joel's eyes. "I need to know where this power is coming from."

A tiny red crystal bead rolled across the floor, bumping Joel's shoe.

Alexa was crying now. "I didn't do anything! I can't—"

Another bead, smaller than the first, flew across the room. It smacked into a window, making a tiny *ping* before it vanished.

Impatiently, Cesar jabbed the knife deep into Joel's side. Joel screamed. Blood spurted, poured down his leg and soaked into the rough, antique wood, swallowing up and obscuring the red bead.

Joel dropped to his knees and clutched his side, trying to hold the flood back. His hands were scarlet and slippery in an instant.

Alexa flung a hand out in front of her, as if to protect

herself from the sight. "Stop it!"

The sound of fighting and screams—howls, really—came from upstairs.

"Best to show me, my dear." Cesar hauled Joel up by the shirt and jabbed the knife again. "Your friend will die soon, otherwise."

Another squirt of blood. Joel whimpered.

Alexa's hands swung up, palms out. Her eyes rolled back.

A black-faceted bead flew across the room, bouncing off Cesar's nose.

He swatted in front of his face. "Please. How can I make this plain to you? You'll *both* die if you don't—"

Alexa moaned. A skittering across the floor and tens of thousands of beads converged, rolling up Cesar's legs, swarming over his body, their colors rippling and glowing.

Cesar was able to brush whole handfuls of the tiny assailants off, but they were quickly replaced. The more the beads moved, the more energy they summoned, and the more they multiplied.

The doorway heaved and splintered; Joel saw a wolfman in a flannel shirt and jeans and a purplish snake-lady with fangs break through. Joel was certain he was hallucinating from loss of blood because they both looked like they'd been in a fight. The snake lady looked like Dr. Steuben.

More than that, the beads were changing their original colors and shapes, forming a giant scarlet snake encircling Cesar. Beads rolled into his ears, piercing his eardrums, boring their way into his brain. As he tried to scream, a flood of animated glass rushed down his throat, their facets causing a thousand tiny scratches as they filled and distended his stomach. His eyes bulged under the pressure of vitreous fingers; he sank to his knees. The shimmering red snake continued to constrict round him, even as his lungs were so full they could no longer compress.

Filled with power and unable to control what she'd inadvertently summoned, Alexa directed it to the next threat: the vampire and the werewolf in the doorway. Waves of glass, crystal, wooden and plastic beads turned on them, lapping up the walls like flame.

The vampire hissed, "Joel, she'll listen to you!"

Joel hauled himself up, trying to ignore the patterns his blood now made, a living arabesque dancing across the floor.

He was going to die; that was clear. But he had to end this. "Alexa! Knock it off!" It sounded lame as soon as he said it, but the sound of his own voice helped him focus. "Alexa, you're gonna kill us all!" he screamed hoarsely.

The beads and blood continued their dervish dance and the apartment walls shuddered horrifically, as the nails trembled within them. The porcelain urn on the fireplace mantel shattered. The ashes flew into a whirlwind, hovered for a moment, then skipped across the floor.

A piece of bone emerged from the maelstrom. More fragments followed, mixing with the ash. A shape emerged from the swirling cloud, a woman's form, more and more cohesive with every second.

Lenore! Joel thought.

He struggled to get up and failed. He dragged himself toward the gray-veiled form of his dead wife. As Joel disturbed the patterns of blood still writhing across the floor, the droplets flew up, adding body to the shape of the woman.

Halfway to his goal, Joel collapsed. He'd lost too much blood. He raised a hand, gasping for breath.

"I'm sorry, Lenore! I can't." He sobbed. "I'm sorry—Lenore, I love you!"

The shadow reached out for him. With everything he had left, Joel reached for his wife's hand. A faint smile, benediction in the dusty whirlwind.

Joel collapsed.

Alexa looked up. She blinked, once, twice and the wildness left her eyes. The wind stopped. Ash and bone fell to the ground and a million beads scattered across the floor. Silence filled the room.

"What," Gerry said, gasping, "the skedley *fuck* was that?"

"Telekinesis, pattern sympathy, I don't know—heads up, Gerry!" Claudia shouted.

He turned in time to catch Alexa as she swayed and fell.

"Shit!" He set her down carefully, checked for a pulse. "She's alive."

Claudia crossed to Joel. "So's he, but not for long. Call 911!"

"Hey, Dr. Steuben? How was that for a cathartic event?" Joel smiled as his heart slowed, then stopped.

Joel woke up in a hospital room, he didn't know how much later. He had a scrubby beard that itched. The room itself was nice and it was private. He couldn't hear anything. Nothing beeping, no intercoms, nothing.

The silence worried him. Cesar's hideout? A hospital? One way or another, he didn't like the quiet.

He was giving serious thought to just leaving, in spite of the backless gown, the tubes running out of both arms and the unbelievable pain in his chest and gut, when Dr. Steuben opened the door. Joel's muscles relaxed and his panic subsided. She looked like the woman he knew: no fangs, no purple hair, no scales. Killer bod under a white lab coat. Her brother Gerry appeared behind her, blocking the sunlight streaming through the doorway.

Dr. Steuben looked at his chart and monitors and smiled. "You're healing up. No permanent damage, no infection. Good."

"Where's...how's Alexa?" he asked.

Gerry shut the door and pulled two plastic chairs to the bed. "She's why we're here."

"Oh, God, she's dead, isn't she?" Joel sagged. He'd had enough of death. "What the hell happened, back there?"

"No, Alexa's fine," Dr. Steuben said. "She's confused, of course. Asking for you."

"Oh. But something must be wrong, if you're both...staring at me like that."

A flicker of surprised before she concealed it; he'd never challenged her before. "Not wrong," Dr. Steuben said. "An opportunity, if you want it."

She paused; her brother said, "Give him just a little push."

"No, Gerry. No suggestion. This has to be done right." She took a deep breath, looked deep into Joel's eyes. He might have been turned on or terrified at other times, but now...he was just focused.

"Alexa is a telekinetic, at the very least. She appears to control objects when she's in danger. And then there was that thing with your wife's image...and, well, we're still working on identifying exactly what the range of her talents is."

Talents? This was nothing like playing the piano or twirling a baton, he thought, not knowing what to say.

"Thing is, me, my brother...we're Fangborn. Our people work in secret to fight evil, so we know about power, trust me. But Joel...we've never seen anything like Alexa. She claims not to know anything about the snake imagery she created, but we sure do."

Claudia handed him a notebook, filled with images of women holding snakes. He'd seen one of them on a show about excavations in Greece, a bare-breasted woman, wearing a headdress, holding two serpents. Another was a stone from Sweden, much more stylized, but similar. There were pages of them, from all over the world, throughout time.

"Um, good." He looked at the IV bag, feeling woozy; these were some quality painkillers they were giving him.

"But since we've separated you two, there's been no trace of Alexa's power. Nothing. We've talked to her about it and we've all agreed. It has to do with you."

"I can move stuff with my thoughts?"

"No, she needs you, for some reason, to access her power. You're her focus. Alexa wants to help us, so we need you to consider our proposal, too." She shook her head. "There may be others like Cesar out there, looking for their own telekinetics. Think about them opening up the prisons of the world and worse than that. And if it was true necromancy we saw Alexa perform...the idea of someone like *him* raising the dead, raiding hell for an army? We need *you* on our side."

Gerry got up, began to pace. "Look, man, it's like this. Either you want to join us werewolves and vampires and oracles and try to protect Normals using Alexa's freaky powers—shit we've never even *heard* of—or you go back to your old life and remember none of this. Claudia will wipe your memory."

He turned to Claudia. "You can do that?"

"Yes. No pain, no trauma. No memories."

He was about to ask whether they'd just kill him and go about their business, but somehow he knew Dr. Steuben wasn't like that. And her brother; apparently he'd taken on Cesar's men when they broke into the apartment. They seemed to be telling the truth, as weird as it was. "You think I can handle it?"

"I do. And I can tell you believe us."

"I know." He scratched at the bandage on his arm. "This is a lot to take in. Do I have to answer right away?"

"Yes."

Gerry held out his hands, fists closed. *"You take the blue pill—the story ends, you wake up in your bed... You take the red pill, you stay in Wonderland and I show you how deep the rabbit-hole goes."*

Dr. Steuben showed the first signs of temper. "Gerry, don't. This isn't the time for—"

Joel understood. "No, it's okay, I get it." He looked at Gerry. "It's that big? Like Morpheus says in *The Matrix*?"

Gerry nodded. "It's how we spend our lives. I figure, something pretty hellish is coming, for Alexa—and you—to show up *now*. Something activated you and her and we need to find out what that is. There may be more like you and probably, others like Cesar coming. How did he know to go looking for you, when we didn't? This is all new and we need to get up to speed on it, like, yesterday."

"You—and Alexa—really need me? This isn't the drugs?" He shook his head. "I can help."

"Yes."

Joel had been depressed, he knew, and less than useless. But he'd seen Lenore and he'd desperately needed that. He needed to repay Lenore for that last blessing.

"If you say no, well." Dr. Steuben nodded resolutely. "We'll see if there isn't someone else out there with whom Alexa can work."

He looked at them, remembering Dr. Steuben as a vampire, her brother the werewolf.

Anything would be better than feeling this sad. This...alone. Maybe I can do something. Lenore would like that.

He pulled himself upright, as best he could.

"Sign me up," he said. "Give me the red pill."

Slider
Reed Farrel Coleman

1

Red flags on black poles planted in the sand every few hundred feet along the length of Brighton Beach. Black poles barely sway. Red fabric limp in the stillness and fog. Red flags mean no lifeguards on duty. Venture into the Atlantic, you do so at your own peril.

2

Thousands of windows look out onto the fog-heavy boardwalk, the beige sand, gray stone jetties, the shoreline, the now invisible ocean beyond. Not one pair of eyes has taken notice of the body rocking in the cold, soulless arms of the surf at water's edge. It is sin enough for a body to molder in a shallow, leaf-covered grave in the middle of a forgotten woods. There is something achingly perverse about it bobbing up and down in the shallows with only swirling gulls and hungry crabs paying it any mind. Especially this body— bloated and blue—once so perfect.

3

This is some wicked fog, Stallion thinks, peering through the landed cloud at the strike zone chalked onto the brick wall of PS 209. The pitching rubber is a crack in the schoolyard cement forty-five feet away from the beige brick wall. He winds up and releases the Pensy Pinky with a sharp snap of his wrist and fingers. That's the trick of a good slider: the grip, the fingers, not just the wrist. Stallion imagines he can follow the trajectory of the tightly spinning ball as it cuts through the mist between the mound and the chalk box. He swears he can see a visible, transient memory in its wake: a smoke ring, a contrail, a stickball worm hole. Then gravity yanks at it. The rotation of the ball skews ever so slightly. The ball veers down and to the right.

4

Dina D'Agostino was the neighborhood wet dream. There wasn't a guy from Coney Island Avenue to Shell Road, from the boardwalk to Avenue X, except maybe Jerry "Fagberg" Feinberg, who didn't jerk off imagining what fifteen minutes with Dag might be like. *Ask not what Dina D'Agostino can do for you. Ask what you can do for Dina D'Agostino.* To this day, Pete McIlroy—Ish because he' s half Pol-ish and half Ir-ish—got hand happy thinking about the time the two of them walked all the way to Plumb Beach. That was the night Anthony Peritorre broke up with her. His mom called her a *freakin' hoo'wa* (Brooklynese for whore). Although Dag was crying so hard her body shuddered, she laid down on the sand with him, let him slip his hand under her halter, slip his tongue into her mouth, slip his fingers under her panties—her pubic hair was matted cashmere. Sometimes, even now, he imagined he could still smell the musk and feel her magic on his hand. Of all things that persisted from his childhood, his memory of Dag was strongest.

5

Through the fog a pair of Ukranian eyes sees a bruise on the water—driftwood perhaps, perhaps the carcass of a lost dolphin. He imagines its story. It is what this ancient man does, he sees things and creates a past for them. Everything, he thinks, must has a past. Everything needs a past for it to have value. He has no need to embellish or create one for himself. The cruel forces of history have molded a past for him, one he cannot escape. The bodies, all the bodies he carries with him, give him no warmth, no peace, but they remind him.

He remembers.

First in the woods outside Kiev, the bodies-in-waiting kneeling at the edge of the trench. Some cried. Some begged. Most silent. None prayed that he could hear. Then the pop, pop, pop, pop of the Lugers and Walthers. With each bullet came the metal metamorphosis of human beings into cascading lumps of meat. Then—

> the quicklime
> the dirt
> more bullets
> more meat
> more quicklime
> more dirt
> more
> and
> more
> and
> more ...

Layers and layers like a trifle.

But what of the dolphin?

The dolphin, he thinks, has used up its life. Old and sick, it has separated itself from its family. Lost in strange waters, too tired to go on, it has beached itself in this odd little world where creatures swim upright through a dry sea.

6

No matter how much he tries, Stallion can't focus. His heart races, but not from pitching, not from stickball. He watches the pitch, Ish recoiling to swing.

7

Ish swings, his eyes locked on the spot in the air where he calculates the spinning pink ball will begin to veer down, to the right, under his bat-handled fists, and kiss the inside corner of the chalk box. For thirty years, he has swung and missed or taken the pitch, watching the ball all the way to the wall, witnessing the puff of dust as the ball bites the chalk and flattens against the brick. For thirty years, since they were seven, Stallion's slider has for the most part eluded Ish's bat. It's not that Ish never hits it—he does, but late in the game, when:

1)   Stallion's arm is fucked.
2)   When some of the piss is out of the slider.
3)   When the spin loosens up.
4)   When it flattens out.
5)   When it comes in like a helicopter.

But even then, he hits it straight down off his shin. And this is the third inning and Stallion is just getting warm and his arm is still full of vineagar.

Time slows down.

Ish is a camera.

He sees the ball so clearly it hurts. He sees the bat connect with the ball a few inches out in front of him, the rubber bending around the wood of the skinny bat, the ball flying away, disappearing into the fog, landing over the fence to the basketball courts. Ish's joy is short-lived. He knows something is wrong.

The universe is disturbed.

8

Old and sick, removed from his family to die in a strange little world, he is the dolphin. Dolphins are intelligent creatures. They recognize themselves in mirrors, teach each other how to hunt, to play with rings of bubbles. Too intelligent, he thinks, to believe in God. In this way, he is also the dolphin. After the Kiev woods, he was arrested by the Soviets and forced to serve in one of Stalin's suicide units. No gulag during the Great Patriotic War. No, just bullet catchers to waste fascist ammunition. Coming close to the dolphin, he remembers his comrade commander's inspirational pep talk. "My dear comrades, if you retreat a single inch or do not press forward, we will shoot you in the back and make stew meat of your worthless carcasses."

He survives, but to what good end? To die in this place, alone? For his whole life he has been passed from one butcher to the next. He reaches water's edge, the gulls squawking at him. The crabs ignore him. Some claw and peck away, unwilling to relinquish their prize.
The old man is not a dolphin.
> The dolphin is not a dolphin,
>> but a blue and bloated mermaid spit out by the sea.

9

Stickball is Brooklyn Zen, a meditation born of spare parts: a broom handle, a rubber ball, chalk, a crack in the concrete, a wall, imagination. *Om.* But Stallion and Ish are done now, out of the trance, back to their lives.

10

Sick with worry, Anna-Marie D'Agostino dials the phone and listens to it ring. A woman picks up,
"Hello."
"Is Peter there?"
Peter? No one calls her husband Peter. It's Ish. Everyone, even his captain calls him Ish.
"Peter? Do you mean Ish?"
Anna-Marie is flustered. "Peter, the kid from Manhattan Court."
The wife puts her hand over the phone, turns, and screams, "Ish, it's for you."

11

The old man has told his story first to the policeman and now to the detective over and over.
1)   I'm an old man.
2)   I walk on the beach.
3)   I thought it was a dolphin.
4)   No, I didn't touch her.
5)   I didn't see anyone else.

6)   How did I know she was dead? I have seen dead bodies before.

     Really? (Detective lifts eyebrow.) How many?
1)   Many more than you will ever see.
     Where? (Dubious)
1)   The Ukraine.
2)   Poland.
3)   Germany.

     Okay, you can go. I have your name and number just in case.

     So that is that, the old man thinks. He is dismissed. As he walks back to the boardwalk, he writes the mermaid's history.

12

"She asked for Peter," the wife says, handing him the phone. "She says she's Dag's mom. Who's Dag?"

Ish doesn't answer. His eyes get big. He swallows hard. Into the phone, "This is Peter."

"Peter, the kid from Manhattan Court? You're a cop now, right?"

"Yeah, Mrs. D'Agostino, a detective. You're Dina's mom. Is something wrong?"

"Dag's missing, that's why I'm calling. I haven't heard from her in days."

"Days, huh? Is that a long time for her not to be in touch?"

"Calls me every day. Comes over all the time, checking on me because I got the diabetes."

"Have you called around … friends, other family, like that?"

"I called the cops."

"You called the police?"

"Yeah, but it was a waste of time. The cop said she was an adult and that she'd turn up."

"But she hasn't?"

"No."

"How did you get this number, Mrs. D'Agostino?"

"I'm calling to tell you my girl's missing and you're—"

"I'm gonna look into it. I promise, but you gotta tell me—"

"Dina keeps a book. Only one name I recognized from the old neighborhood. Yours."

Ish smiles in spite of himself, the feel of cashmere on his fingers.

13

The old man is done with history, with all but one last body, with life. He doesn't hesitate to kick the stool out from under his own feet. Swinging from side to side, he thinks, I should have done this sixty years ago.

So much less pain.

So much less pain.

So much less pain.

So much less pain.

So much less pain.

No pain at all.

Nothing.

14

The dolphin is Jane Doe for only a few hours, until the boy who once clumsily rubbed her nipples and pawed her breasts, the boy who only once lost his fingers in the soft down beneath her panties, looks at the sea water and crab-ravaged body on the stainless steel table.

Turns to the ME, "That's her, Dina D'Agostino. I'll call the mother."

15

Ish looks at the photos of his wet dream's body, how she looked when she washed up on Brighton Beach.

Detective Conrad watches him. The case is his, the memories are Ish's.

"Old girlfriend?"

41

"Not exactly. Once when we were kids ... How'd'ya know?"

"I'm a detective. I got a shield to prove it and everything."

"Funny man, Conrad, but seriously, how'd'ya know?"

"That look on your face. What's the word ... wistful? Tough to be wistful looking at that mess unless you were seeing something else in your head."

"I guess I was remembering her as a kid. God!"

"See how she's dressed." Conrad said. "Hope you don't got a Madonna thing for her memory. Mary, Mother of God, didn't exactly dress like that. That one shoe she's wearing there got a heel high enough to make *my* nose bleed."

"I see how she's dressed. No, I don't suppose she was going to a quilting bee or for happy hour at Ruby Tuesday. You got her address book? When her mom called me, she mentioned an address book."

"Your name's in it, McIlroy, you know that, right?"

"So what?"

"Lotsa mens names are in it. My guess, clients."

"Well, I wasn't one of 'em. If that's what you're—"

"I had to ask. You'd've asked. Here." Conrad slid the phone book across the table.

Ish thumbed through the pages, stopped breathing for a second. Hoped Conrad hadn't noticed.

"Recognize any names in there?"

Ish lied, "No."

Conrad didn't believe him. Conrad didn't believe anyone. Conrad didn't believe himself.

16

The name painted on the back of the boat was Slider III and Ish didn't take any special care approaching her. Him, his wife and kids, had been on board Slider II and Slider III more times than he could count. The original Slider was something else. She wasn't much. Maybe that's why Ish loved her most of all. Those were good days, party days, fishing days, days when Stallion and him could just go out into Jamaica Bay and drink or get high, watching the jets fly their glidepaths into JFK. Sometimes they brought girls onto the boat with them, but mostly it was just Stallion and him hanging out. Where had those days gone?

17

Stallion was bleaching the deck. He'd already taken care of the cabin. Had the sheets and the rest of the shit from the cabin bundled up into a black garbage bag. It was about time to take her out of the water anyway. He thinks, if he had done it a week ago, when he should have, maybe ...

        If, if, if...

        Maybe

        Maybe

        Maybe ...

        what a fuckin' waste of time.

Then he heard the footsteps on the dock coming his way.

He turns, mop in hand, "Hey, Ish."

18

"Hey, Stallion. Cleaning her up. Gonna take her out of the water soon?"

"Yeah, one last trip for the season and then I'll take her out of the water tomorrow. You wanna come?"

"Depends."

"On what?"

"On the truth."

"Funny, Ish, all the years I known you, you never talked in riddles before."

"Never felt like it before."

"So why tonight?"

"Grieving an old flame. You remember Dina D'Agostino?"

"Dag? Sure. Who wouldn't remember her? Didn't you fuck her once?"

"Nope. I guess I wished I had. I guess that one night I coulda. She woulda let me, I think, but she woulda let me do

43

anything to her that night."

"Too bad for you."

"That's strange, Stallion."

"Yeah, what?"

"You didn't ask me how she died."

"How'd she die?"

"Strangled, but she was also tortured. She was a real mess. Washed up on Brighton Beach. The crabs and gulls had gotten to her."

"Too bad. How'd you hear about it?"

"Her mom. She found a book Dag kept in her apartment. Mine was the only name she recognized in the book, so she called. Heard I was a cop and figured I could help."

"A book, huh?"

"Yeah. Like I said, Stallion, her mom only recognized one name in the book, but I recognized another name in the book: Joseph Stallone. I haven't thought of you as Joey Stallone since we were kids."

"I don't think of you as Pete. So what?"

"You sound a little stressed there, Stallion. Something wrong?"

"You hit a homer off me today."

"I hit homers off you before."

"Never off my slider. Never, not once in thirty years."

"I don't suppose you ever murdered anybody before, Stallion. Sure, it's easy when you're raging, but when you calm down ... Why'd ya have to beat her like that? You musta made a fuckin' mess. I could smell the bleach from the end of the dock."

"I didn't—"

Ish showed Stallion his Glock. "I'm gonna kill you soon, Stallion. You can tell me why you did it and get it off your chest or you can take it with you. All the same to me."

Stallion laughed. It was a nervous little laugh, weak, unconvincing. "Get the fuck outta here. You ain't gonna kill—"

The shot ripped through Stallion's liver and he crashed to the deck, his right arm hanging over the side of the boat.

"Wanna bet?" Ish said. "You got a few more minutes to

think it over, Stallion." Ish took out a .38 drop piece he'd kept in his garage for years, wrapped Stallion's fingers around it, and fired into the dock. "Last chance, Stallion."

"She … she … she …" Stallion was dead.

19

When the cops broke into the old man's apartment after the complaints about the foul odor, they found the rotted carcass of dolphin.

Undying Love
Hilary Davidson

When I came to, a big man with a white beard was leaning over me. "Don't worry, man. It's cool," he said. "You're dead."

I lifted my head. A knife was sticking out of my stomach.

"Is this a dream?" The knife had a big wooden handle, like a kitchen cleaver.

"Heh, heh. Not on your life." The man gave me a shy smile that made his round face look boyish. "Look, I get this all the time. *No, no, I can't be dead. I still have so much to do,*" he mimicked. "Next thing they're thinking how cool it is they can walk through walls. By the way, I'm Bart."

"You're insane." I sat up, wondering why nothing hurt. My blue shirt was trimmed with a broad bloodstain. I felt lightheaded, but calm. "If you want to be helpful, call the cops," I snapped.

"Cops, that's sweet," said Bart. "Who you gonna call? Ghostbusters!" As he chuckled, his beard swung from side to side like a curtain. "Sorry. I died in 1984 and that song stuck in my head."

As I stood, the room spun and something caught my foot. Looking down, I saw it was my own body. It was lying on the tile floor of my kitchen with my right foot stuck inside. Baffled, I wrenched my foot free and fell. That didn't hurt either, but I seemed to sink into the floor. Bart grabbed me and pulled me up until I was standing over my body again.

"Here, drink this." He unscrewed a silver thermos and held it out to me. I sniffed it and took a sip. The liquid was cool as water on my lips, but it burned on its way down my throat, like vodka, but oddly sweet. "Have some more," Bart said.

That was when I noticed the cops standing near my body. There were two of them, both in the uniform of the San Diego Police Department. There was a woman with them, a tall brunette with a muscular build. When she turned her head I saw it was Kendra, my wife's best friend. She lived down the street from us. Her lips were moving but her words were inaudible.

"Hey! Kendra! Over here!" I yelled.

"Bro, you're a ghost. It's not like they can hear you," said Bart.

I stared down at my body. Not that I was going to admit it to Bart, but I was beginning to panic. There I was, in my own kitchen, with its familiar cherry-wood cabinets and granite island and mosaic tile floor, now accented by a big pool of blood around my body. My eyes were fixed on the ceiling. I counted to 20, then 30, then 60 and those eyes didn't blink. "Did someone murder me?" I almost squeaked.

"The rules bind me. I cannot answer that question," Bart sounded strangely formal. "Sorry, man. Have some more Lethe water. It helps you forget."

"But I want to remember! I want to know why I'm dead. Where's my wife?"

Bart shook his head. "The rules bind me. I cannot answer..."

"Shelley, where are you?" I yelled.

"Don't do this, man."

I ignored him. "Shelley!" I yelled. The kitchen dissolved around me and I was yanked forward like a marionette. There was a sound like crystal breaking and everything went dark. The next thing I knew, I was crumpled on a white carpet, this time in a room with a big canopy bed. My wife's bedroom, I realized. There was our wedding photo, framed in silver on her dresser. The bed's white silk drapes were pushed back and my wife was sitting on the edge of the mattress. One paramedic was wrapping her left forearm with gauze while another dabbed at her neck. I could see where the blade of a big knife had sliced into her.

There was a cop standing in front of Shelley. His questions

were making her cry. She was sobbing into a crumpled fist of Kleenex. I couldn't hear her words or his either.

"Shelley, baby, can you see me?" No one in the room flicked an eyelash at me. I kicked the dresser and my foot passed through it. As I fell to the floor, I started to slide through it. "No, no, up, up!" I screamed, waving my arms frantically as if I were a fledgling. A meaty hand grabbed my arm.

"Man, you're going to get yourself in a pickle," said Bart, pulling me up again. "You need to tiptoe, man. Otherwise you'll sink through to China."

He didn't sound like he was joking. "Where did you come from?"

"I heard you yelling. Good thing, cause this is a *monster* house."

"There are monsters?" I whispered.

"No, man, I mean it's huge." Bart spread his arms out. "For two people? Come on?"

"My wife and I are very fond of this house. We built it together."

"That so?" asked Bart. "How long you two been married?"

"Twenty-five years, in June." Something about the memory made me blank out for a moment. "Why do I feel so lightheaded?"

"You're in a transitory phase," said Bart. "Means you're passing through. Seriously, man, you need to drink some Lethe water."

"Lethe? That was one of the pools in Hades, wasn't it? The one people drank from to make them forget their lives."

"Wow, dude. You must've really paid attention in ancient history class. The thing is, you *have* to drink it. Otherwise you can't go on."

"I'm not going anywhere! I want to find out who killed me and attacked my wife. I'm not going to leave her alone."

Another detective came into the room. He wore latex gloves and held the huge knife that had been in my gut. It was in a giant baggie and the blood was so fresh you could see red ribbons dribbling down the side and pooling at the bottom. A uniformed cop pointed at the wound on Shelley's neck and gestured at her gauze-covered forearm.

"Was she attacked with the same knife?" I asked Bart.

"You know what I'm gonna say, don't ya?" He lifted a shaggy eyebrow. "The rules bind me."

"Whose rules are these anyway?"

That earned a sigh. "Look, dude, I'm not the netherworld's information booth. I'm here to help you get from one plane of existence to another. You're not making it easy."

"I was just murdered. What do you expect?"

Bart sighed. A cop put a jacket around my wife's shoulders. She stood up and left the room with him. The medics started packing up. "Where are you taking her?" I shouted.

"Look, in case you missed this, you can't interact with them. They're alive, you're dead," Bart spoke slowly, as if I were stupid as well as deceased.

"I can follow them. See what's going on. Figure out who's guilty."

"Whoa." Bart planted his body in my path. "You sure you want to know? Think about it. You might remember more than you want to."

"Get out of my way. I need to follow Shelley."

"You can always reunite with her, dude." Bart clapped one hand over his mouth. "Oh no."

"What does that mean, I can always *reunite with her?*"

"It's not mentioned in the rules. But I'm still not supposed to tell you."

"You want to stand here forever? Cause I'm not budging till you spill it."

"Okay, okay," said Bart. "If you had a strong emotional connection to something in life, that doesn't die when you die. It's like a rubber band. It can go slack, but it can also pull you back together suddenly."

"That was what pulled me into Shelley's room?" Bart nodded silently. "So anyone I love, I can... follow them?"

"You're not supposed to, man. It's against the rules."

"To hell with the rules," I answered.

***

I didn't learn much at the police station. Shelley talked to the cops for two hours, but I couldn't hear a word. When I tried to lip read, my eyes lost focus. I settled for looking over the shoulder of the cop who was making notes.

SC home alone, he scrawled in tiny chicken scratches. SC? Shelley Cervale.

Spoke to husband. Went to bed. OTC sleeping pills. Heard noise downstairs. Oh, Shelley...

Husband said he "wanted to talk."

Uncontrollable rages. Legal separation—check date. Affair with stripper. Pawned SC's jewelry. Drugs—cocaine? What the hell? What was that about?

He was crazy—told her he would kill her. Must be talking about the guy who broke in.

Defensive wounds? Like Shelley was going to let anyone but her cosmetic surgeon get close to her throat with a knife.

The cop's notes were crap. How was he going to solve the case with that? My attention wandered to the file on his desk. The top page had a photograph of a mesh bangle bracelet that was studded with diamonds. *Stolen from the home of James and Shelley Cervale, date uncertain. Harry Winston bracelet, total diamond weight 40 karats. Platinum setting. Reported missing by Shelley Cervale, Oct. 8.* That was a month ago.

I'd bought that bracelet for Shelley on our tenth wedding anniversary. She'd already announced that she wanted to sleep in separate rooms. I remembered hoping the gift would persuade her to ignore my snoring, but she was adamant. I tried to lift the page to see what was underneath, but I couldn't. My fingers sank into the pile when I applied force. I tried blowing on the pages to scatter them, but that did nothing. Another cop came in with a German shepherd. It strained against its leash, barking and trying to get at me. Why could I hear it but not human voices? Great, I thought, mutts can see me. I'd always hated dogs.

After Shelley was done at the police station, a couple of

patrolmen drove her home. I sat in the backseat with her and I could tell she was badly shaken. She stared out the window and gnawed on a fingernail. "Shelley," I whispered. "It's me, James. I love you." But she didn't hear a word.

Bart was stretched out on my living room sofa, hands knitted behind his head, eyes closed. "So, you learn anything?" he asked.

"Not much, except that a bracelet I gave my wife was stolen in January." It was a distinctive piece. If some con tried to fence it, he'd be picked up by the cops immediately. No one took Harry Winston to a pawnshop.

"You need a drink." Bart held up the thermos again.

"No, I don't want to forget anything. I need to remember more. Bits and pieces are coming back to me." I watched Shelley pour herself a scotch and make a phone call. More than anything, I wished I could hear her voice.

"That's a bad sign, dude. Look, I don't want to get rough with you, but you can shrivel up and evaporate while you're between planes like this."

"Why can't I hear what people are saying, even though I can hear other noises?"

"Rules. You can't communicate with the living," Bart said.

"But how am I supposed to go on like this?"

Bart shook his head, making his bead sway across his chest. "You're not *supposed* to stay, just pass through."

"What are you doing here then?"

"It's my job, man. Not like I've got a choice."

"What is your job, exactly?" I asked him.

"I'm a ferryman."

"No way! Like Charon? Are you kidding?

"Wow, you know your Greek mythology," said Bart.

"So is there a river somewhere I'm supposed to cross?"

"You're standing in it, dude."

I didn't doubt him. "So what happens after this?" I asked, nervous.

"I'm not exactly a hundred percent sure," Bart admitted. "It's a one-way ride."

"So it could be oblivion waiting on the other side?"

"Look man, if it were oblivion, you'd be dead and that

would be that. You wouldn't need a ferryman to bring you over to it. Right?"

"But you don't know. I mean, you've got rules for this part, but you don't really know the rest."

Bart sighed. "I'm kind of going nuts with curiosity, man. But I've got to do my job. That means getting you over safely."

"If you'll help me find whoever attacked my wife and killed me, I'll cross over."

Bart stared up at the ceiling, as if it were giving him guidance. "Can't do it. Sorry, man."

"I know. Rules."

The doorbell rang and Shelley answered it. Her friend Kendra was there. She handed Shelley a gift bag and hugged her. Shelley seemed to be crying on her shoulder and Kendra stroked her hair. Shelley finally pulled herself together and Kendra went away. I looked inside the bag. There was a box of chocolates from Donnelly's—Shelley's favorite—and a bottle of champagne. Champagne? I'd always hated Kendra.

Shelley went upstairs and I followed, Bart in my wake. When she came out of the bathroom, she went to the dresser and turned our wedding photo face down. Whatever I had left of a heart skipped a beat. *Don't be angry with me,* I thought, afraid of what I'd done. She took off her dress and I barely resisted the urge to whistle.

"Wow. She's a hot chick," said Bart.

"Don't you dare look at my wife!"

"Sorry, man. No offense."

He was right though. Shelley was stunning. Possibly more beautiful than she had been when we'd married. I thought about the warm nape of her neck and how soft her skin was and I swooned again.

I watched her sleep for a long time, then backed out of the room and headed down the hallway. There was a closed door at the end. I touched the handle, but it didn't budge.

Taking a couple of steps back, I made a run at it. As I passed through, I felt its weight, like you would feel steam on your skin in a sauna. Then I was in.

Bart came through the door behind me at a leisurely pace.

"You don't have to barge through it, man. Relax." His eyes took in the mahogany furniture and the art, lingering on a painting of a woman undressing. "So this was your room, huh? Some taste you got."

I tried to open a dresser drawer, but it wouldn't give. Frustrated, I put my hand through the wood, but I couldn't grab anything inside. Finally, I stuck my head in. It was awfully dark in the drawer.

"How the hell am I supposed to do this?" I asked Bart.

"What are you looking for, dude?"

"A clue. There must be *something* here." My room looked clean, almost sterile. Had somebody scoured away the traces of me already? Suddenly, memory hit with a force that made me gasp. "I wasn't living here anymore. I was staying at a hotel." I closed my eyes to summon the name and had a vision of a pink hotel overlooking the Pacific Ocean. "La Valencia. La Jolla."

When I opened my eyes Bart had the thermos open and was holding it out. "Seriously, drink this."

"No," I pushed his burly arm back. "Don't you understand? I was staying in a hotel and I came back here to... to..."

Bart threw some Lethe water on me. A little splashed into my mouth. "What did you do that for? I was trying to remember!"

"Dude, that is *exactly* the thing you're not supposed to do. You're supposed to go on with your memory wiped clean, like a baby coming into the world. You can't hold onto your memories."

"You can't stop me!" I shouted. "La Valencia!" Nothing happened. "La Valencia Hotel in La Jolla!" Nothing. I glanced at Bart.

"That only works with things you truly love." He sounded weary. "You have to be really connected with someone or something to have that work."

"So how do I get to the hotel?" I asked. Bart shrugged. "Fine. I'll find it myself."

* * *

That was easier said than done. I remembered that the hotel was a 15-minute drive from my house, but I couldn't drive. I guess I could have walked, but walking for miles in Southern California would have been weirder than being dead. Instead, I hitched rides in cars. No one saw me get in and no one saw me hop out. But Bart was waiting for me in La Valencia's lobby.

"How did you do that?"

"The rules, bro. I can't tell."

I went to the front desk. There was a note on a sticky yellow pad. *Mr. James Cervale, 526. Police will call before noon. DO NOT CLEAN ROOM.* At the elevator, I waited for another passenger to push the right button and rode up to the fifth floor. The door to my room was closed and I walked through it.

Inside, a dark-haired woman was pawing through the clothing that hung in the closet. "What are you doing?" I called, forgetting she couldn't hear me. She didn't turn around. I watched her take a pair of gold cufflinks out of the pocket of one of my jackets and toss them in a big black bag that was sitting on the bed. I peered into it and saw cash, credit cards, even a gold pen. This thief was clearing me out.

When she turned, I realized that I knew her. She was tall and lean and tan, but with an inflated chest that suggested a career in adult entertainment. Her eyes were big and blue and her mouth was plump, but her face was haggard, as if she were seriously ill.

"Jenny?" I said. "Or Julie? Jessie? What the hell is your name?"

She took one more look around, then opened the door. I followed her out. She scurried past the front desk. Outside, her flip-flops fluttered on the pavement. I saw the tattoo of a star on her ankle and I remembered that there was a dolphin on her hip. How did I know that? Down the block she went into the parking lot of a fast-food joint and got into a beat-up Honda. I couldn't hear what the man at the wheel said to her. His head was shaved and there was a dragon tattoo on his neck. Veins bulged under it and his skin looked faintly green. He grabbed her bag and rifled through it. His face got red and contorted. He was shouting at her. I'd never noticed before how ugly people looked when they yelled.

I rode in the back of their car until they came to a ragged motel that was nowhere near the Pacific. Inside their room was even grimmer, with yellowed walls and a brown bedspread. The man continued to yell and then the two of them were screaming at each other. He poured the contents of the bag on the bed, pocketed the cash and set the other valuables aside. There was a bag of white powder he stared at with obvious lust.

The man sat on the bed and spilled some of the powder on the bedside table. The woman sat next to him and he shoved her, but when she came back he let her sit. He cut the drug into neat lines with a razor, then snorted two. He did the same for the woman, then a couple more for himself. When he grabbed her hair and pulled her on top of him, I left the room. I didn't want to see any more.

Bart found me walking by the side of the road. "What's up, dude?" he asked.

"Leave me alone."

"Aww, don't be like that. Are you depressed 'cause you're dead?"

I walked on silently. Maybe if I walked long enough I'd evaporate in sunlight.

"Come on, man. You can tell me."

I shook my head.

"You remembered something, didn't you?" Bart looked sad. "This is why you need to let go."

"I think I stole the bracelet I bought for Shelley and pawned it to give money to that woman." The words were hard to lodge out of my throat, but I remembered the cop's notes. There were tears in my eyes and I tried to keep Bart from seeing them. "I was cheating on my wife with that woman. The stripper."

"I know, man."

"Why didn't you tell me?"

"Like I said, bro, I'm the ferryman, not the information

booth. I'm not supposed to tell you anything. Rules, okay? You leave your memories with me."

"That's how I pay you," I realized aloud. "How you pay the ferryman."

Bart nodded.

"But why would I do it?" I asked him. "I mean, I know I can be stupid, but Shelley is so beautiful and that woman..." I shuddered. "She looks like she's ready to die."

"Death changes the way you see the world. Shelley looks beautiful to you because you love her. That woman looks repulsive to you because, deep down, you were disgusted by her." He held the thermos out. "Now will you drink it?"

"No. I have to protect Shelley." I focused my thoughts on her and heard shattering crystal again. Then I was back in our house, watching her as she wandered from room to room like another lost spirit.

"How long do you plan to stay here, man?" Bart asked me.

I tore my eyes away from Shelley. Kendra and a few of her other friends had come over to the house. They were getting drunk on chardonnay together. From the way their faces moved, I could tell there was a lot of laughter.

"What are you hoping to accomplish?" Bart's voice was low.

"What if the killer comes back?"

"Nothing you could do about it, bro. Let it go."

"There's got to be something I can do," I insisted.

Bart grunted. We sat in silence for a while. The women started to clear out around eleven. When they were finally gone, Shelley went upstairs and brushed her teeth. Then she put on an ice-blue negligee I'd never seen before. Wow. If I knew she was dressing like that for bed, I wouldn't have been in a room down the hall. Then I felt ashamed, remembering I'd been screwing around with a stripper.

Shelley sprayed on some perfume. The doorbell rang. Shelley rushed downstairs. Kendra, her best friend, was at the door again. She came into the living room and gave Shelley a small box. The two of them hugged for a minute. That was nice of her, comforting Shelley, I thought. Then Kendra went to the kitchen and I heard the sound of a champagne cork popping. Shelley opened the box and I was riveted by the sight of the missing Harry Winston bracelet. There was no mistaking it. Shelley held it up to the light and put it on her wrist. Kendra came out of the kitchen with two champagne flutes. They toasted, drank and kissed.

"No," I said, watching them in horror. "No, they can't be..."

"Do you remember everything now?" Bart asked.

It was all flooding back. Shelley calling me at my hotel, saying she wanted to talk. Me sending the stripper away, then coming over to the house. Shelley leading me back to the kitchen for a drink. Shelley saying she knew I'd stolen her bracelet and spent the money on that whore I was sleeping with. How was she supposed to forgive me for that, she asked. Then I remembered hearing footsteps. I'd barely caught sight of Kendra when she jabbed the knife into my stomach.

"Shelley planned the whole thing." I sank to the floor, the room swirling around me. "But if she killed me, why does she look so beautiful to me?"

"Because," Bart said, "you've already forgiven her. Besides, the two of you did a lot of terrible things to each other. You really did pawn the bracelet for the stripper, you know. Kendra found it and got it back." He held the thermos out to me again. "James, it's time you drank this."

He was right. I took the thermos from his hand and gulped it all down.

Nice Guy Type
Sean Doolittle

I spent a few days on my buddy Treynor's couch, as far from the Jeanie situation as I could get before I ran out of buddies with couches. Trey waited a day and said, "Not that it's any of my business, but when we say 'the Jeanie situation,' what are we talking about, nutshell?"

"Her husband went through her phone," I told him.

"Shit. Then what happened?"

"He used her phone to call my phone."

"Logical."

"And yet insane."

"What did he say?"

I'd been trying not to think about that. Jeanie's husband was a meat cutter by trade, built like a cage fighter and, according to Jeanie, devoted as a grown man to inflated doses of the same Ritalin he'd been prescribed as a teenager. "He said he was going to hack me up and feed the pieces to his snakes."

"Well, shit," Trey said. "He's probably not gonna do *that*."

"Not if he can't find me, he won't."

In the mornings, Trey went to his job at the batch plant for the small town where he'd been living. I spent the days laying around reading the paper and watching television. Nights he came home covered in fly ash, whipped and dragging his tail. We'd order pizza or Chinese or go to the Mexican place two blocks over. It was the least I could do to pick up the tabs.

After five days of this, Trey handed me a beer and said, "Guess you probably need to get back to the job pretty soon, huh?"

I confessed that there was no job at present; the company had reduced half my department two months ago and I'd been more or less playing around on my severance. Ten years bought me eight weeks.

"Jesus." He sighed, leaned over, clinked his bottle against mine. "Why the hell didn't you say so? What's the market like?"

"Haven't really been looking yet, to be honest," I said. "And I still have my share from the house sale, if it comes to that." I saw the way Trey was fiddling with the label on his bottle and added, "But you're right. Thanks for letting me crash, I owe you one."

"It's not like that," Trey said. "You'd do the same."

I almost pointed out that I'd already done the same: once after his own marriage had split up, another time when his construction business went under and he couldn't find work for a while. But we'd known each other a long time. And I didn't see Trey very often since he'd moved out of the city.

"What I'm saying is, why not hang here awhile?" He glanced at me across the scratched-up, second-hand kitchen table where we sat. I thought back to a time when Trey had four employees and a nice house in Oak Heights. Things had changed all around. "As long as there's no pressing business, I mean."

I met his eye briefly. "You looking for a roommate?"

"I don't mind the company." He shrugged and tipped his beer. "And no offense, buddy, but I think you could use a change of scenery yourself."

I made a plan to head back to my apartment that Saturday and pick up the things I'd need for a while. Trey claimed he wasn't busy and offered to tag along. It took a few more beers than I'd expected to work up my nerve and Trey ended up driving.

It was thirty miles through the country from his place to mine. His truck guzzled gas, so we took my car. On the way, Trey told me he'd been saving his pennies and in six months he'd be able to get serious about setting up his own shop again.

"There's basically four guys in town," he said. "Two are solid, one only does decks, the other's been busted twice on regs this year. I've been doing odd jobs around. Nothing big, but people are getting the idea I do good work and charge fair."

"Sure they are," I said.

"I'll need get up and go money," he said. "But there's a guy at the bank who said he'd work with me."

I watched the bare cornfields pass by my window, stubble bristling and blurring beyond the glass. "For a minute I thought you were telling me you were looking for investors."

"What I was thinking was maybe you might be looking for a job at some point."

I laughed. "Please. I can't tell a hammer from a chainsaw."

"That's the truth. But you can set up computers. Run a website. Figure out, like, marketing and shit." He shrugged. "Something to think about, that's all."

I tried to imagine a scenario like that as I watched a flock of wild turkeys peck for grain along a far tree line. After a few miles, I said, "You'd be my boss, huh?"

"Well, hey. You got cash burning a hole, I'd consider a partner." He glanced over, grinned a little, looked back at the road. "Junior partner, maybe."

He took the new spur, got off the Interstate at the expressway and joined in with street traffic in the gathering dusk. I told him where I'd been living; he headed north on 60th toward midtown.

Along the way I cracked my window, letting in the sounds of traffic and a stream of crisp autumn air. My buzz had mellowed and the ride had been nice. I'd only been gone a week, but I felt like I'd been through something. The time away had been centering, it was good to see Trey again and the whole thing with Jeanie was beginning to feel like a harmless comedy.

I was feeling pretty good until we reached my street. Then my heart started pounding. I grabbed the wheel as Trey began turning, wrenched it back the other way and said, "Keep going straight."

"Whoa," he said. "One driver at a time."

"Just keep going." I scrunched down in my seat like a low-rent crook. "Take the next block."

We took the next block all the way down to the cross street, then came back two blocks the way we'd come. Finally, we pulled to a curb within view of my building but not within view—I hoped—of the big, spotless red Dodge Ram pickup waiting out front.

"Lights," I said. "Kill the lights."

Trey set the brake and twisted off the ignition. We sat there in silence, listening to the engine tick.

"Okay, I'll ask," he said. "What are we doing?"

"Staying out of sight."

"I got that. Why?"

"That's him, that's why."

"Where?"

I nodded. "Truck."

Trey followed my gaze across the empty boulevard to the muscular rig brazenly illuminated in the streetlight outside my building. The truck sat high on wide knobby tires, with riveted fenders, a gleaming chrome roll bar and hooded KC lights. A pair of novelty rubber testicles hung low from the trailer hitch.

"Inconspicuous," Trey said.

My throat felt dry all of a sudden. "I told you he was nuts."

"How long you think he's been sitting there?"

"No idea" I said and shivered like the feeble coward I'd accepted myself to be. "But he's sitting there now."

Trey shook his head. "Let's just go in," he said. "Hell, there's two of us."

"I count one including you."

"Come on. Grow a pair."

"No time for that now."

Trey sighed. After a minute, he drummed his thumbs on the wheel and leaned back. "So, now what?"

Honestly, there wasn't anything I truly needed in the apartment. Now that we were here, I was having trouble remembering why I'd bothered in the first place. If we turned around, we'd be back to Trey's in forty-five minutes. We could drink beer and watch SportsCenter and talk about this business he had in mind.

"Let's see what he does," I said.

He didn't do anything but smoke cigarettes out his window for almost two hours. We sat there and watched a tattooed, muscle-bound arm flick butts into the street. He seemed to smoke a hell of a lot for a bodybuilder, though maybe not so much for a butcher. Not that I knew either way. After the first hour, Trey wanted to know what was so extra special about this Jeanie person.

I admitted that there wasn't anything extra special about her. She was a thirty-five-year-old Zumba instructor with a great body and problems at home; I met her at the gym one day a few weeks ago. She laughed at my jokes, I bought her a few drinks and we'd been screwing each other silly ever since. That was all.

"The latest in a series of bad decisions," I said.

Trey said, "I guess that's my point."

"Were you making a point?"

"Sport-bagging married ladies? I don't know, man." He shook his head. "It doesn't sound like you."

"I was married ten years," I said. "I'm single for the first time since college."

"So go after college girls."

"Where would I meet college girls?"

"Exactly."

"I don't know what that means."

"A player would know where to meet college girls. You?" He looked at me. "Many things, my friend. But you've never been a player."

He had me there. While I was married, I'd been relentlessly faithful, even after I learned that Laurel hadn't. And all I'd wanted was to be married, even after she admitted that she'd been bored stupid for half a decade. In high school, I'd had exactly one girlfriend and I moped for two years after she moved away to become one of those college girls I didn't date until Laurel. Trey had known me a long time.

"Maybe I'm a late bloomer," I said.

"Bullshit."

"How do you know?"

"Because I know you," he said. "And you're not a dick. You're the nice guy type."

"I hear nice guys finish last."

"They also get caught banging the wife of a guy who wears a rubber apron for a living, apparently."

Again, hard to argue. "I admit I didn't plan very well."

"Uh huh." Trey watched Jeanie's husband toss another cigarette out his window. "Maybe."

"I don't know what that means, either."

"Look. Laurel cheated on you, right?"

"Serially, yes."

"And you're you."

"That's what she reminded me. Thank you."

"What I'm saying is, you were too all-around reasonable to send that bitch packing like she deserved and if *she* hadn't ended it? Buddy, you'd still be there getting your guts trampled." Trey turned toward me a little, leaned an elbow on the wheel. "Did you ever stop and think that maybe now, on some level, you're working through all that by pretending to be a wife-chasing douchebag yourself?"

This was about as much as I'd ever heard Trey spit out at one time and I didn't know what to say in reply. I could have pointed out that I wasn't really pretending—that I was in fact a wife-chasing douchebag at this point, and a tactically poor one at that, which was how we'd come to be sitting here, watching my apartment building like a pair of nerds. But Trey wasn't finished.

"And that maybe," he continued, "just maybe, on some level, you walked yourself into this situation because deep down you're too nice a guy not to feel just the teensiest, tiniest bit shitty about it?"

I stared at him. "You think I *want* this psycho to turn me into snake food?"

"Your words, not mine." He seemed deeply pleased with his own insight.

"Wow," I said. "For a psychiatrist, you're a hell of a carpenter."

"Yeah, well. You're time's up." Trey dug in his jacket pocket and pulled out his cell phone. "This is officially lame."

"What are you doing?"

He held up a finger as he dialed a number, then put the phone to his ear. "Yes, hello," he said. "I need to report a suspicious vehicle at 548 California. Red Dodge Ram Big Horn, license plate GR4-296? The driver..." Pause. "No. But he's been sitting there for hours. I think he's watching my building." Pause. "Yes, okay. I will. Thank you."

Trey put the phone back in his pocket. "There," he said. "Easy."

I felt supremely weak and foolish. And relieved. I said, "Why didn't I think of that?"

Trey grinned. "I thought of it two hours ago. Just wanted to see if you'd nut up."

"At least that question's answered."

We waited fifteen minutes before a black-and-white police cruiser trolled slowly up the street. From our spot across the boulevard, we sat and watched the unit pull over to the curb facing the Ram. A cop got out the passenger side, sidled up to the truck and tapped on the glass with the butt of her flashlight. She shined the light in through the open window, stood there talking a minute, made a shooing motion in the air, then stepped back as the big truck growled to life. Seconds later, the Ram scratched its tires and lurched away down the street like a pouting bully, rubber nuts swinging.

Having cleared the street, the cop holstered her flashlight and got back in the cruiser. The cruiser sat in its spot for a minute or two, then pulled away. That appeared to be that.

Trey started the car. "Let's do this and go eat someplace. I'm starving."

"Maybe on some level you feel empty inside," I said. "And you're working through it by chasing food."

"Maybe you're a dick after all."

"Your words, not mine," I said.

* * *

Trey stayed in the car and kept a lookout while I went up and packed a bag. I pulled together enough clothes for a week between loads, threw in the books from my night table, rounded up a few toiletries. The apartment felt odd to me, stifled and foreign and as I packed, I realized that not only had I never truly settled into this place—my first solo apartment since my early twenties—but in my mind ("on some level," as Trey might have said) I'd left it behind me already.

I thought about the things he'd said: about me lashing out at the world through out-of-character bad behavior, about subconsciously creating situations in which to sort out my, admittedly many, unresolved feelings about Laurel. All by myself, here in this midtown apartment I'd never come to view as home, I wondered if the guy wasn't on to something.

I didn't feel like myself and I hadn't for awhile. I kept expecting this to pass with time, but enough time had passed by now that I was having trouble remembering what myself used to feel like. If I was honest, the Jeanie situation hadn't helped matters. It had been thrilling and reassuring and sort of awesome, but it hadn't helped.

At the very least, Trey was dead right about one thing: I did know how to run computers. And IP cameras as well.

While we were married, Laurel had been respectful enough to do most of her cheating away from our tidy home. But there were a few times—half a dozen or so—when she'd made exceptions and had somebody at the house while I was gone.

Though she'd never known it, these occasions had all been recorded and memorialized on DVD. I used to think that I'd be able to use them against her in some way, if necessity arose. Possibly during the divorce. Even better, to keep the divorce from happening at all. Hell, I didn't know—maybe I'd send a few to her parents or post them on the Internet. Something to humiliate her the way she'd humiliated me.

But, of course, Trey was right about that, too: in the end I simply didn't have it in me. I used to watch them late at night just to torture myself, but even I could see something unacceptably pathetic about that and I'd mostly given it up.

Still I kept them, unlabeled, on a shelf in my office closet. I went in there now and grabbed the oldest of the bunch, starring Laurel and Trey, back when Trey had been staying with us (both times). These were not isolated incidents—if you fast-forwarded through them in sequence you could actually see Trey's hair thinning—but if any of this had played a specific role in Trey's divorce, I didn't know about it.

It certainly hadn't played a role in mine. In fact, these with my oldest friend were the only encounters Laurel had never confessed to me in the end. I suppose that proved, if nothing else, that her contempt for our life together hadn't been total.

I tossed the disc in the bag with my laptop and thought about playing it for him later tonight. We could talk about wife-chasing douchebags and see what he thought of things then.

Or maybe we'd just talk about this construction business idea. I honestly didn't know what I wanted.

I was on my way downstairs with my jacket and bags when I heard a muffled squeal of tires outside the building, followed by a thunderous, ground-shaking crash. I leapt the bottom steps and raced out the front door with my things, heart hammering in my chest and what I saw stopped me in my tracks.

Jeanie's husband had returned. With extreme prejudice.

And if I'd thought—on some level—that his being murderously crazy was at least partly an internal exaggeration on my part, an excuse to feel—on some level—justified in running away from my life for awhile, I realized that I had been both wrong and right.

Jeanie's husband—what was his name? Brad? Brett? No, but something else with a B—had driven his big truck with the rubber testicles straight into the grill of my car with Trey stuck behind the wheel. The car was at least twenty feet back from the spot I remembered. Trey must have had it running because steam billowed from the crumpled hood. The windshield had shattered. Nuggets of broken glass twinkled in the street.

The truck looked no worse for the wear. Even as I stood there, frozen on the stoop, Jeanie's husband pulled Trey out of my mangled car, held him up by the throat and began punching him dead-center in the face. Over and over. The guy was a beast; a six-foot mass of tendons and muscle, decorated all over with tattoos, topped with a buzz-cut. Trey, who'd done manual labor all his life and was not wimpy himself, whom I'd seen come out on top of a number of bar fights in our younger days, had gone limp in Jeanie's husband's grip.

Brandon: that was it. His name, impossibly, was Brandon.

And he kept right on punching. Trey's face by now was painted in blood. His nose was a flat place, his mouth a toothless dark hole.

I thought again about what he'd said earlier, about subconsciously engineering this situation. It occurred to me that Trey might have construed all this as psychologically incriminating (on some level), further evidence in support of his theory. Wasn't it convenient that he happened to be sitting behind the wheel of the car Jeanie's husband knew to be mine?

But on that point, he was finally wrong. It was a conscious act when I'd called Jeanie's husband at home, earlier this afternoon, to let him know I'd be stopping by my apartment tonight if there was anything he wanted to say to me. The truth was, the two hours Trey had spent waiting for me to "nut up" in the car, I'd spent trying to decide whether I should back down.

The truth was, I'd been glad when he finally called the cops. We'd known each other a long time.

As for the cops, I was still standing like a statue when the cruiser rolled back up the street. From half a block the unit hit its roof lights, sped abruptly and screeched to a stop in front of the building.

Jeanie's husband Brandon had drug Trey to the curb like a ragdoll, positioned him face-down on the concrete bumper and raised his foot when the spotlight hit him. The cops piled out with their guns drawn, shouting. I was convinced that if they'd arrived ten seconds later, I'd have witnessed my oldest friend being stomped to death in front of me.

I may have been a late bloomer, but that wasn't what I'd wanted. As far as I knew.

Kross Kill
J.M. Edwards

Malcolm Lloyd strode across the twelfth floor of Lloyd's Department Store's flagship building, grabbed the handle of his nephew's office door and pushed his way in.

"Are you making a mockery of our family, boy?"

At the intrusion, the roomful of punks turned his way. Three whites, two blacks. All five pimped out, wearing too-loose clothing and layers of fat jewelry that jangled.

Malcolm lasered his attention on Jeffrey. Golden boy stood near the floor-to-ceiling windows. Just beyond him, Malcolm could see the company sign. Snowflakes drifted past "Malcolm Lloyd's" signature logo, looking like the opening titles from some warm-hearted Christmas movie.

Jeffrey stared across the room. "Uncle Mal. We were just talking about you." The voice was icily condescending. The gaze looked ready to crack.

"What the hell are you doing, bringing your...other business...into our home?"

One of the white guys swung his gym-shoed feet from atop Jeffrey's desk and eased himself to stand. He tipped his orange hat sideways and sauntered over. Jeffrey moved to intercept, but the fellow stopped him with a sideways glare. "Yo' homey?" he asked Malcolm, in exaggerated black-speak. "Shee-it. And I thought it was just a dee-partment sto'."

"Jeffrey," Malcolm said, over the punk's shoulder. "If you don't get these...gentlemen...out of here now, I'll call security."

The guy in front of Malcolm stared up, eyes blazing. "You dissin' me?" He twisted his head, spoke over his shoulder to Jeffrey. "J-bo, yo' uncle dissin' me?"

"No," Jeffrey said, with a forced laugh. He shot his uncle a look that warned him to back off.

But Malcolm would do no such thing. This was his store, his life, and yes, his home. Malcolm Lloyd's department store had been a New York landmark since his great-great grandfather, the first in the family to carry the name, had opened its doors in 1854.

"Uncle Mal," Jeffery said, "don't you know who this is?"

Malcolm glared down at the little hoodlum. "I know all about you, Mr. Kross. You've made quite a name for yourself." Tilting his head, he added, "But how could a man get to your position without learning that it's disrespectful to wear a hat indoors?"

The little guy's eyes narrowed—he worked his jaw. "You can call me Kenny-K. And I'm gonna keep my hat where it's at because respect is due to me," he said, splaying his hands across his slender chest.

"Why do you insist on talking like that?" Malcolm asked, furious and baffled. "I don't understand."

"Maybe you'll understand me now. For your information," Kenny's affected dialect had disappeared, "my entourage and I are here at your nephew's invitation. We're conducting a business meeting. So why don't you hobble back to your hole, Uncle, while we make management decisions regarding the future of this establishment."

Malcolm's head snapped up. "What is he talking about, Jeffrey?" Then, to Kenny-K, "You have no authority here."

Kenny-K's eyebrows lifted. "J-bo? Better school your uncle."

The little man ambled toward the sofa. The two others sitting there slid outward, making room for the small guy, who dropped between them to slouch in the leather cushions. The other two men came to stand at either end.

"Uncle Mal," Jeffrey began.

Malcolm kept his voice low. "Get them out of here, now. I've had enough of your shenanigans this year. If the press gets wind of this—"

"Kenny-K is an owner now."

Malcolm flinched. "What?"

"It was *my* inheritance."

"You sold your shares to this piece of scum?"

"I'm funding Kross Kill." Jeffrey fingered the collar of his t-shirt. "It's a state-of-the-art interactive gaming."

"I've seen that garbage."

"Uncle Mal, please."

Malcolm fought the acid rising up from his gut. "How much?"

"You know that I held forty percent."

"You gave him all of it?"

Jeffrey shrugged. "I *invested* it."

Kenny-K spoke up from the couch. "Looks like we're in bed together, Uncle. Maybe you better start treating me like family."

Malcolm ignored him. "Jeffrey, those shares were your father's. They were meant for your future. For your security. And you gave it up for...this?"

"Kross Kill is cutting-edge."

Malcolm fought the breathless fire that seared from his ulcer. "Cutting-edge repulsive, you mean. Those video games are the worst of the worst. The violence is sickening— revolting."

"That's what's happening now, Uncle," Kenny-K chimed in.

"Stop calling me uncle, you disgusting little crook." Clamping his hand into a fist, Malcolm shook at Jeffrey. "Your friends here make money on graphic violence. Their games have been implicated in dozens of lawsuits of crimes against women, children, elderly. How can you support the filth they stand for?"

Kenny's voice cleaved the air. "You've never heard of the First Amendment? We're exercising our freedom of speech."

Malcolm spun. "That isn't free speech. When your customers target real people for killing, when you encourage contests that reward murder, you tread all over the rights of Americans. You're setting innocent people up to get killed. It's illegal. It's immoral."

"We don't tell no one to go killing nobody," Kenny said.

Malcolm's fury raced up from his chest, pounding in his

ears. "But you do. The people who buy your videogames—"

Kenny raised a finger, "Not video, Uncle. Digital."

"—those fiends have proven themselves capable of the worst possible crime. You're being sued from every possible corner. Soon you'll be shut down for good."

Kenny's face split into a wide smile. "We got us the best lawyer money can buy, don't we, J-bo?"

Malcolm's head throbbed. "Just get out of here," he said, his voice weary, "all of you."

"Not till we finish our business," Kenny said. "J-bo, how's that situation with Laney looking?"

Malcolm twisted to face Kenny. Laney's was the top department store in Los Angeles. Laney's had tried to get into the New York market for years, but Malcolm Lloyd stock was family-owned. That was the only thing that had kept the behemoth at bay.

"What *about* Laney's?" Malcolm asked.

"Oh, so now you're interested in what I have to say."

"What about Laney's?" Malcolm turned to his nephew, who took that moment to face out the window again. Snow flurries had kicked up and now the sign was obscured.

Jeffrey's voice was low, but Malcolm heard every word perfectly. "They're buying us out."

"They can't," Malcolm said. "I own forty percent. And the remaining twenty belongs to family. They'll never sell."

Kenny stood, reached into one of his capacious pockets and withdrew a switchblade. He snapped it outward—then folded the blade back in, as though playing with a toy. "We can be very persuasive."

Jeffrey shrugged. "Laney's is offering a huge premium to acquire the necessary shares for a takeover."

"But," Malcolm began, "the family..." His voice deteriorated into a croak, "They'll never sell. Never."

"Twice the stock value is a hard offer to turn down, Uncle," Kenny said. He snapped the blade out, then snicked it back again. "Maybe you should think about making a killing with your shares, huh?" Dark eyes smoldered with insolence. "Get it? A killing. Just like Kross Kill does best."

Malcolm swallowed, his Adam's apple scratching against

his suddenly too-snug necktie. He needed to get out of this claustrophobic room, now. "I won't let you get away with this," he said. "The family is behind me."

Two hours later, with a satisfied smile, Malcolm Lloyd dropped the phone's receiver back into the cradle. He grabbed the CD player's remote control, turned the sound up and sat back to stare out the snow-covered window, with B. B. King's blues a comforting background.

Contented now, Malcolm let the familiar strains of his favorite CD keep him company. Blood did run thicker than water. He'd reached all three shareholders—old Aunt Norma Atherton, her daughter Margaret and Margaret's daughter, Missy, the youngest stock owner and the last, best, hope of the family, even if she didn't share their name. He'd caught Missy between classes at Columbia. Missy felt exactly as he did. Laney's would not take over Malcolm Lloyd's department store. Missy, in fact, summed it up best. "This isn't just any business, Uncle Mal," she'd said, in her ever-earnest voice. "The store really is part of the family."

If only Jeffrey understood that, he thought. Where had he gone wrong with the boy? Jeffrey had been only twelve when Mal had taken his brother's son as his own, yet there had always been a disconnect between them. A chasm that they'd never bridged.

But Mal never expected Jeffrey to stray this far away from what was good—what was right. On the cusp of his turning thirty, he'd fallen in with another bad crowd. Mal shook his head. No. This crowd was worse, much worse, than bad. They were evil.

He had one more task. He picked up the phone and dialed.

"Charlie!" he said, when Charles Corning answered his cell. "You have some time this afternoon?"

The attorney's reply was terse. "I'm in court today. On a break right now. Why what's up?"

"I need to make some changes. Succession issues."

Before Charlie could reply, voices in the background called his name. "I have to go," the lawyer said. "Have your assistant confer with my office and I'll fit you in as soon as I can."

Malcolm hung up the phone with a vague feeling of discontent. Physically, he felt just fine. Fit as a fiddle, except for that damn ulcer, still shooting bile fireworks in his gut. Right now his will named Jeffrey as primary beneficiary. But Jeffrey's poor choices would threaten Malcolm Lloyd's legacy. Mal couldn't let that happen. Missy, however, understood. He'd change it as soon as Charlie made some damn time for him. Make Missy the sole beneficiary.

As his pain subsided, Mal started to notice the beauty of icy patterns lacing up from the corners of the tall windows. Missy would do the right thing. Majoring in business, with a minor in ethics, she was the girl who would take Lloyd's into the future. And maybe she'd have children of her own someday. And she'd teach them about the importance of family. And Lloyd's would continue to be a fixture in New York for generations to come.

Kenny-K didn't like being interrupted, especially when in "the zone," as he and Webs were right now. Alone in the giant computer lab, the two were conjuring up plans for the next generation of Kross Kill games. Webs held fingertips tight against his temples, staring at the monitor's blinking cursor. "Yeah," he said, softly, like he was taking a breath. "I see what you're saying."

Seconds later, the fingers were flying over the keyboard, Webs bringing to life the ideas rolling out of Kenny-K's mouth.

"You got it," Kenny-K said next to Webster's ear. "Okay, okay, now maybe put in a couple—"

Jeffrey Lloyd called across the otherwise quiet room. "Kenny!"

Kenny whipped around, screaming expletives at the intrusion. When he saw Jeffrey, he stopped. Forced a smile. "J-bo," he said. "I didn't know you were here."

"Yeah, I thought I'd stop by, see if you had some time. Hey, Webster," Jeffrey said, as the other man nodded a greeting.

Kenny felt a prickle of unease. Jeffrey never just dropped in. "Time, bro? You know I always got time for you. Something on your mind?"

Jeffrey stared up at the ceiling for a long moment. "No. Uh, well. Maybe."

Kenny stifled a hiss of impatience as he made his way toward the other man. Pulling money out of this guy over was like talking your grandma into financing your crack habit. Kenny-K was no babysitter and he was tired of making nice with this virgin, especially now when they were so close to finalizing the deal. "What on your mind this time, brother?" He knew how much Jeffrey liked being one of his inner circle. Using the "bro" word worked like a charm getting the asshole to fork over the bucks.

Jeffrey shifted. "I've been thinking," he said, slowly. "Lloyd's...The department store. The shares, I mean. What if we can't get the rest of the family to sell?"

"Your uncle been talking to you?

"No, I just—"

Kenny-K spread his hands out, palms facing upward. "He's *old*, man. His life—it's over. It's your time, now, bro."

Jeffrey looked away again. "I've got some money. Not as much as we need, but it'll help. And if I talk to some of my contacts, I bet I can get other investors."

"J-bo," Kenny said, coming in close and snugging an arm around the back of Jeffrey's neck. "You can't back out on me now. Not when we're so close." Jeffrey tried to pull away, but Kenny held tight, his face close. "Understand?"

"I'm not backing out on you. I'm just thinking ahead, is all."

Kenny winched his arm tighter. He whispered into Jeffrey's ear. "What you trying to tell me?" He released him sharply, propelling him away so hard that Jeffrey almost lost his footing. "You in or you out?"

"I'm in," he said, shakily, "but it's not going to do us any good to sell if the rest of the family won't. And...my uncle is making sure..."

"Making sure what?"

Jeffrey blew out a breath. "He's changing his will." Talking fast, he held up both hands as if to stave off an attack. "I don't know what he has in mind. I just know that I was his primary beneficiary and I heard something..." Jeffrey looked up at the ceiling again. Kenny resisted an urge to slap the prick's face. "I think he's cutting me out."

Kenny-K's brain analyzed this information, double-time. "You saying that when the old man kicks off, you get everything?"

Jeffrey gave a rueful smile. "Yeah," he said. "Right *now*. But that's all might change in a day or two. Unless..."

"'Less what?"

"Unless I talk with him. If I promise that we'll drop the deal with Laney's, he'll come around. I know it."

Kenny shook his head, very slowly. "We got plans in place."

"I'll come up the funding. I'll do it quick."

Kenny-K stared up at Jeffrey. The rich boy didn't know jack about business. Kenny needed Jeffrey's cash, but once that was settled, this asshole was history. Working his jaw, Kenny puckered his lips as though deep in thought. "Tell you what. Go talk to your uncle. Tell him we ain't selling to Laney's."

"You're serious?"

"You sure you gonna get me other backers?"

"Yeah, absolutely."

"Okay then." Kenny scratched at his cheek, then added, "And just to show there ain't no hard feelings, I'm gonna have Webs here design a new game. Gonna call it 'J-bo's Gold.' And you get to be the first to play it."

Jeffrey's grin told Kenny the boy was sold.

"Now, get outta here," Kenny said.

"You got it. I'll be back with the bucks before you know it."

Kenny waited till the computer lab's door shut before starting to work with Webs again. "Kross Kill fans won't wait long," Kenny said, almost to himself. "We need those upgrades."

"We've given them a high like no game's given them

before," Web said. "They expect it all the time now."

Kenny leaned back against the desk again. "Shit." He pulled out his switchblade and began playing with the spring mechanism. His teeth clenched as he envisioned Jeffrey's stupid grin. Webs kept at his programming as Kenny stared across the silent room.

The boy had been born with maids to change the shit in his diaper. He never knew what it was like to work hard, to fight for respect. Tall asshole, he'd been given every opportunity since the day he could put one chubby little foot in front of the other one. Kenny had built Kross Kill with blood and guts. Who cared if sometimes the players got carried away and the blood got spilled? It was like Hollywood. And pretty soon Hollywood would be knocking on Kenny's door, wanting to make a movie about his story. He blinked, bringing himself back to the present. No way he'd let Jeffrey ice this deal. Not now.

"Webs," he said, "how many 'special' fans we got out there?"

Webs didn't take his eyes off the screen and his fingers didn't slow, but a grin pulled up one side of his mouth. "We got hundreds, boss. Maybe more."

"You got a way to contact them?"

Typing furiously, Webs nodded. For a long, time the only sound in the cavernous room was the tip-tapping of Webs' fingers on the keyboard. When he finally slowed, he turned to face Kenny.

"J-bo's Gold, huh?"

Kenny nodded. "We ready to move to the next level."

Webs eyebrows came together. "How soon?"

"Get it done in twenty-four."

Malcolm pulled his cashmere coat on over his pajamas and grabbed a hand-rolled cigar from the humidor. His slippered feet made shush-slapping noises that echoed as he made his across the hardwood floor to the back of his palatial home. Bright moonlight on the snow-dusted landscape gave a perfect postcard look to the yard.

Unlocking the French door, he disengaged the alarm and stepped out onto the high balcony. Years of habit pushed him outside. Patty used to nag him to take the smoking outdoors. He could still sometimes hear her chastisements, God rest her soul.

Cold outside. But the breeze was gentle, curling Malcolm's breath into soft clouds that dissipated into the dark night. Stairs led downward to the pool house. Hadn't been used much since Jeffrey had been a teenager and even then the boy didn't have many friends to bring home. Malcolm sighed.

He lit his cigar and pondered the fact that he couldn't sleep. Realized it was because of unfinished business. In his heart, he knew that changing his will was the right thing to do. To leave everything to Missy. And now, once the decision had been made, it killed him to have to wait to have the matter completed.

He held the cigar between thick fingers, leaning his forearms on the chilly balcony rail. Shivered.

"Yo, fat boy."

Startled, Malcolm dropped the cigar. It somersaulted lazily to the patio below as the owner of the voice rushed up the pool stairs. The breathless instant that it took for Malcolm to process what was happening slowed him down.

He bolted for the door, but a sturdy arm clotheslined him, knocking him backward, his seat hitting the balcony floor with a jarring thud.

"That's much better," the same voice said. Malcolm could see him now. Nineteen or twenty, the pale young man stood with his back to the kitchen doors, his features in shadow. Scuffling sounds drifted up from below. The intruder wasn't alone.

Hot bile worked its way up Malcolm's throat. "What do you want?"

The man looked down; a broad grin stretched across his face. He leaned low, pressing a .45 caliber Sig Sauer against Malcolm's forehead, whispering, close: "Not much. I just want to be famous."

Nearby, others laughed. Two more young thugs clambered up the stairs, taking no care to be quiet. The nearest neighbor was a hundred yards away. They could make all the noise in the world and no one would hear them.

The two laughed as they swarmed the balcony. The taller one carried a camcorder, its blinding light causing Malcolm to shield his eyes. He couldn't see either of their faces. "What the—"

The man in charge grinned. "You're on Kross Kill camera."

As though a giant hand had just clamped around his bowels, Malcolm doubled over in fear. The three men laughed rowdily. One spoke to him. "Say hello to your fans."

A boot shot out, kicking him in the face. His head snapped back and he pitched sideways, falling against the balcony floor. Cold cement against his cheek. He felt the warm wetness of his own blood as it seeped away from his face. "Take what you want," he rasped. "Just please, don't hurt me."

The fellow with the camera moved in closer. His partner crouched onto his haunches, then flicked cigarette cinders onto Malcolm's head. "Look," the kid said, glee catching his voice, "he's an ashtray!"

The first man stepped forward to smack the kid across the face. "Get your idiot ass out of the picture."

The kid covered his mouth with the back of his hand. "Hey," he said, his voice trying for bravado, failing.

"Keep the camera rolling," the man said to the taller guy, "get as much as you can of all this. They want lots of footage of this uncle dude."

Uncle.

Malcolm writhed, trying to sit himself up, but the kid who'd been chastised kicked him again, this time in the stomach. Expelling a *whoof*, Malcolm's body went limp.

They'd referred to him as "uncle."

Jeffrey had set this up.

The depth of his nephew's betrayal shot pain through Malcolm's gut, but he forced himself upward. He would fight. Not for himself, but for the family. If he died now, this moment, everything would fall into his nephew's foolish hands and then all that Malcolm Lloyd's stood for in New

York—would be gone.

"You will not prevail," he said. Lashing his foot out, he kicked the first man in the shin, causing him to stumble. Malcolm scrambled to his knees, whipping one hand out at the camera. Missed. The boy with the cigarette went wide-eyed with disbelief and jumped backwards.

Malcolm drove himself toward the French doors, his fist closing around the knob and turning it with slow-motion, Herculean effort.

Something slashed across his back—something hard and sharp. He arched backward and even though the cashmere coat took the brunt of it, the attack propelled him forward. He stumbled, only to be grabbed by the collar and hoisted to his feet. They held him an arm's length away, effortlessly preventing his escape. "You getting all this?" the guy asked, then admonished, "keep my face out of it."

The cameraman didn't answer, but he kept the lens pointed Malcolm's direction, the whiteness of the beam still blinding him. Malcolm's feet were numb from the cold and from fear. Weakened, his knees buckled as blood trickled down his face and spilled out his back.

"Dude," the guy in charge called, "get this sucker's coat off. We want to see the fat man trembling. Want to see him piss his pretty pajamas."

Dude obliged. With his fingers still clamped tight around the cigarette, he tugged at the dark cashmere until Malcolm was stripped down to his flannels. The cameraman didn't budge, and except for the occasional nervous laugh, Malcolm realized the fellow hadn't said a word. Malcolm hadn't seen his face.

Sick realization dawned. "Jeffrey? Is that you?" Malcolm reached out to the cameraman, his adrenaline rush so strong that he almost broke free. "Jeffrey, how could you do this to us?"

Raucous laughter closed in on him. Ulcer pain and blood loss shot sparkles of light before his eyes.

"You ready?" the guy in charge asked, still holding Malcolm by the collar.

When the cameraman finally spoke, his tone was comical,

amused. "You're a star, Uncle."

Not Jeffrey's voice. Malcolm looked around, as though expecting his nephew to emerge from the shadows. Not Jeffrey.

They shoved him to the ground and pressed the Sig against Malcolm's thigh. "We're gonna do this nice and slow," he said with a broad smile. "'Cause we only got one take."

Hands behind his back, Jeffrey stared out his uncle's office window, watching the Malcolm Lloyd's sign being removed from the side of the building. As days went, this was one for the record books. A sparkling January afternoon, sunny and almost warm. New Yorkers strolled the city, their jackets open in anticipation of an early spring.

Turning away from the window, Jeffrey drifted his gaze across the room, letting it rest here and there on some of the treasures his uncle had amassed during his lifetime. "New York Retailer of the Year" awards took up half of one bookcase. Milestone candids of Jeffrey and Missy took up the other half. Despite the fact this was now Jeffrey's office, he hadn't changed a thing. He still thought of it as Uncle Mal's.

He'd been dead for almost two months now. The police investigation stalled. Had Kenny-K had anything to do with it? Jeffrey often wondered, couldn't be sure. But Kenny swore he knew nothing about Uncle Mal's murder. Jeffrey stared outside now, seeing nothing. He'd been advised by his lawyer to give no statement, which he hadn't.

Down below, the crane operator must have jerked the controls too hard because the heavy green sign with the gold-script Malcolm Lloyd signature, lurched crazily. It wrenched away from the wall with a ripping sound that made Jeffrey blink. He sighed.

The intercom buzzed. Kenny-K had arrived.

"Hey, bro," Kenny said. He'd obviously adopted his "black persona" again, exaggerating his walk as he made his way to Jeffrey's desk. Jeffrey wondered how the black community regarded this guy anyway. But a big a star like Kenny probably didn't care.

Kenny smiled at the activity outside the window. "Today the big day."

"Yeah." Jeffrey dropped into the big leather chair behind the desk, suddenly rushed with the memory of climbing onto the seat as a small boy, his feet not reaching the floor. He cleared his throat. "What's up?"

"I want you to know how much Kross Kill appreciates your help."

Jeffrey stared out the window. The sign, freed from the side of the wall, swung in the sunlight like a hypnotist's gold watch. Jeffrey's fingers pressed into his brow. His stomach coiled up with each twist of the airborne logo. "You got the money you needed," he said. "I'm out."

"What do you mean, out?"

"I'm selling my shares of Kross Kill," he said, surprising himself with the pronouncement. "I'm out."

Kenny's face split into a wide grin. "That's exactly the plan." His gloved hand dug into one of his enormous pockets "And I even got you a going-away present." He pulled out a disk and smacked it down on Jeffrey's desk, keeping his fingers flat against it.

Jeffrey didn't have time for Kenny's antics today. He thrust his chin toward the disk. "What is it?"

"This here our 'pee-ace' de resistance."

Jeffrey leaned forward to pick it up, but Kenny's flattened hand didn't budge. "What is it?" Jeffrey asked again, annoyed. "I'm having a real bad day, okay?" he said. "I don't have time for games."

Kenny's smile stayed bright, but his eyes snuffed out—turning instantly hard, like dull flint. "You got time for this game, bro. Believe me."

Noises outside the office made Jeffrey glance up. Probably the press, again. Wanting more. Always wanting more. New Yorkers were irate over the name change. From the moment the word hit the street, there were boycotts planned, petitions signed and families picketing. Media hounds were always after him for an explanation as to why, after generations of Lloyd influence on the city, Jeffrey had decided to sell out.

For the first time since the contracts had been inked,

Jeffrey understood he'd made a terrible mistake. He hadn't realized what Uncle Mal had been trying to tell him all these years. He'd had to see it for himself to understand. And now it was too late.

The scuffling noises outside grew louder. "Kenny," Jeffrey began, but the smaller man interrupted him.

"J-bo's Gold," he said lifting the disk and handing it to Jeffrey. "All yours now."

Jeffrey slid the disk out from between the gloved fingers and turned the DVD-like disk in his hands, examining it. "What are you talking about?"

"Remember that new game we were gonna come up with? *Your* game?"

Jeffrey nodded.

"J-bo's Gold is our biggest seller," Kenny said. "Just got released today and it's playin' *everywhere*." He stood, a strange look on his face. "You are Mr. Popularity."

Just as Kenny turned to leave, the office door flung open. Missy tore across the expanse, her dark eyes flashing. If she noticed Kenny-K standing there, she gave no indication. "Did you kill Uncle Mal?" she screamed at Jeffrey. Her high-pitched hysteria echoed through the room. "How could you?...How could you?"

"I didn't—"

"It's everywhere. It's on the news." Missy grabbed for Jeffrey's remote control and pressed the power button. The built-in TV flashed alive. "It's everywhere," she repeated. "It started about an hour ago and it's been replaying ever since. How could you do this to us?"

Jeffrey's stomach churned. He sensed what was coming, even before the handsome anchorman gave his introductory spiel. The three of them watched the screen as Dirk Bentley smiled ruefully into the camera. "Again," he said, "authorities are not commenting on how soon charges will be filed against Jeffrey Lloyd, heir to the Malcolm Lloyd department store fortune. Our sister station, WASJ, has the story."

The scene shifted to a female reporter holding a microphone in the face of a teenage young man, whose blond hair whipped in the wind. "Can you tell us, Mr. Ryan, what made you turn in your Kross Kill game to police?"

Unfazed by the camera, the kid shrugged. "I worked at Malcolm Lloyd's during the summer and I met Mr. Lloyd lots of times. Felt bad when I heard he got killed." He shrugged again. "And then when I started playing 'J-bo's Gold,' the new Kross Kill game this morning, I recognized him as the victim dude." The blond fellow's face scrunched up. "Man, it was brutal."

As the female reporter launched into asking her quarry if this experience would affect his buying habits in the future, Jeffrey turned to Kenny-K. "You killed my Uncle Mal?"

Kenny lifted both shoulders, but his grin was from ear-to-ear. "Don't know what you're talkin' about."

Jeffrey stared down at the disk in his hand. "Dear God," he said. "This is it, isn't it? A recording of my uncle's murder." His gut shot a rocket of pain up his throat. Realization dawned in small, bitter waves. Suddenly startled, he looked at Missy. "But ...," he asked in a small voice, "why are they after me?"

Missy pointed to the television again. The reporter had finished her interview and the station now played a scene from the brand-new, just-released Kross Kill game, J-bo's Gold.

Uncle Mal's face took up almost the entire screen. Blood tracked down one cheek. He shivered, panting. Hot breaths poured out of him in quick roiling clouds. Jeffrey recognized the balcony of the house and his uncle's striped pajamas. Uncle Mal's face contorted. "Jeffrey? Is that you?" Malcolm's arm reached out toward the camera. "Jeffrey, how could you do this to us?"

Kenny-K's face took on a look of bland innocence as he faced Jeffrey. "Kross Kill already issued a statement saying we didn't know it was a gen-u-ine murder when you brought it to us. We're cooperating with the police."

Missy spun to face Kenny. "You asshole."

Kenny shrugged. "Bitch."

White-blind fury shot Jeffrey across the room. He tackled Kenny, throwing him to the ground. The smaller man's reflexes, or his anticipation of Jeffrey's move, gave him just enough time to yank the switchblade from his pocket and spring it into life. Jeffrey's left forearm jerked backward as the knife struck—but nothing could stop his blistering anger.

Jeffrey's driving rage and larger build gave him enough of an edge to pin Kenny to the floor and wrangle for the blade, even with his searing left arm. Kenny, however, was stronger than he looked, his wiry frame and street smarts kept him agile, capable, adept. In seconds, the blade was poised, ready to pierce.

Missy kicked Kenny's head. The small man shouted expletives, but never let go of the knife. Instead he drove it upward, slicing for Jeffrey's neck. The blade nicked him, but Jeffrey, so fueled by adrenaline, didn't slow.

Missy kicked Kenny again, harder and Jeffrey wrenched the knife from Kenny's hand. It clattered onto the teak floorboard.

Jeffrey grabbed it.

Still straddling the smaller man, Jeffrey stabbed Kenny's pale t-shirt, once, twice, three times. Five times. The little man went limp almost immediately, but the sound of metal cleaving meat gave Jeffrey a rush of power he'd never experienced before. He kept stabbing, despite Missy's screams, despite the sound of the door flinging open and people rushing in.

He heard a voice, coming from very far away, ordering him to stop, but his arm wouldn't obey. Lloyd's was gone. It was Laney's now. Uncle Mal had been right all along. He should have listened to the old man.

Tears streamed down Jeffrey's face. His arm muscles cried out from the strain as he pounded the knife again and again into the slender chest. Red paint, spilling everywhere. The more paint the better, he thought. Get this on film! Sell millions of copies!

Jeffrey's mind shouted, blocking out all other sound. Kross Kill? No, this time it's kill Kross!

From far away, Jeffrey heard the voice again; a male voice ordering him to stop.

"No!"

Missy screamed as she ran forward, tackling him. He went

down, his petite cousin on top of his chest. "Stop," she cried. "For God's sake, stop."

Only then did he see the police at the door, guns drawn. As he stopped struggling, Missy righted herself and the guns' muzzles lowered, pointing to the floor.

Jeffrey looked down. Blood poured down from his neck and chest and splattered from the mess that had been Kenny-K.

He tried to get up.

"Don't move," one of the officers shouted.

The knife dropped from his limp fingers. He looked up at Missy. "Please," he tried to say, "don't let them take Lloyd's away."

Paramedics rushed to surround Kenny-K.

"It's too late," she said quietly. "You destroyed everything our family stood for."

Jeffrey was hoisted to his feet, turned around and handcuffed as another cop read him his rights. Blood on the floor made it slippery and hard to stand. Just outside the floor-to-ceiling windows, he caught sight of a bright red "Laney's" sign being set into the place where "Malcolm Lloyd's" used to hang.

"Missy—" He turned to face his cousin.

Hatred scorched her eyes. "Go to hell."

He fought the cop who was tugging at his arm. "But then why—why did you save me?"

Missy shook her head. "You still don't understand, do you?"

As Jeffrey was led away, Uncle Mal's voice cried out from the television news: "Jeffrey, how could you do this to us?"

Loose Lips
Andrew Grant

The ambulances had left—slowly and with no need for their sirens—but three of the fire trucks were still lined up outside the terminal building, their hoses snaking through the open doors, when the colonel sent word that he wanted to talk to me.

Appropriate, I thought.

After all, talking was at the heart of this whole situation.

The trio of young sergeants he'd sent seemed surprised when I didn't object to following them and burned off the remains of their nervous energy by screaming wildly at the four separate airport security guards who tried to block our path as they ushered me along a succession of grey, featureless service corridors. Their pace increased the further we went and I was beginning to suspect they were lost when we turned a corner and stopped dead in front of a plain, unmarked door. Two of the sergeants grabbed my arms, sandwiching me between them as if they were worried I might change my mind about being so co-operative. The third paused for a moment, nervously straightened his tunic, then knocked.

The colonel was wearing the steel blue uniform of an Air Force officer—a reasonable choice, given our surroundings—but I knew he worked for Moroccan Military Intelligence. He knew that I knew—our paths had crossed a few years ago when a roadside IED had put an early end to a job I was doing just north of Rabat—so he quickly dispensed with the usual pleasantries.

"Commander Trevellyan," he said, sitting down and planting his immaculately shined shoes on the edge of the rickety desk that separated us. He didn't have much choice.

Aside from the two chairs, it was the only piece of furniture in the tiny room. "I've just read your statement."

I sat opposite him, but didn't reply. I was too busy thinking about how unusual the situation was. There I was, cooped up in a meeting, but with no inclination to speed the proceedings up.

"Forty-seven words," he said. "And that includes your name."

I fought back a smile. I could hardly tell him the brevity was deliberate. If I'd covered more of the angles on paper, how could I have been sure he'd have wanted to drag me half way across the airport to question me in person?

"So, forty-five words, really," he said. "I have a terminal building on fire. A jail cell destroyed. Four dead bodies to account for. A fire fight to explain away. You're the cause of all this. And you give me, what? Fewer words than I'd find on a pizza menu."

He had a point.

"First of all, allow me to apologise," I said. "When my government first approached yours to float the idea of this afternoon's operation, we had no idea things would turn out the way they did. I'm just glad that no innocent lives were lost."

"Do you expect me to believe any part of that?" he said.

I thought for a moment. The part about the innocent lives was true, but it wasn't really the time to split hairs.

"When we heard that Essam Ekramy was planning to pass through Casablanca, it was too good an opportunity to pass up," I said. "You know how infrequently he shows his face these days."

Essam Ekramy was a forty-four year-old Egyptian engineer. His specialty was desert irrigation, but it wasn't his unrivalled expertise in making water flow through hostile environments that had caught the attention of the western intelligence agencies. It was his unique ability to channel information. For seventeen years he'd worked for London and Washington. They'd kept him under deep cover throughout the Middle East, extracting a regular flow of secrets from the loose coalition of terrorist groups that infest the area and returning a stream of highly damaging misinformation. The trouble was it turned out that Ekramy's sympathies had gradually changed. During the final year of his employment he'd reversed the flow of his covert pipeline, selling out his former masters and doing all he could to aid the groups he'd formerly harmed. When his change of allegiance came to light he was forced underground, unable to trust anyone on either side.

"I know all about Essam Ekramy," the colonel said. "I met him, back when we were friends. We drank tea together, more than once. But you told us you were only planning to contrive an 'accidental' meeting as he was making his way through the terminal. That you wanted to talk to him for a minute. Sow the seeds of some toxic rumours. And then let him go on his way."

"That's right," I said.

I wasn't lying. That's exactly what we'd told Moroccan Intelligence.

"It was a simple enough plan," he said. "So. What went wrong?"

"Well," I said. "As you know, the opportunity for conversation turned out to be somewhat limited."

"Gunfire can have that effect," he said.

A set of steps had been wheeled up to greet Ekramy's plane and the moments after he appeared at the top of them were a little tense, it's true. Because I wasn't the only one waiting for him. Two of the groups he'd inflicted the most serious damage on over the previous decade had sent people to meet him, as well. One group had infiltrated a pair of operatives into the refueling crew. The other had placed a sniper on the roof of the terminal.

Ekramy didn't have a close protection detail and he wasn't wearing body armour, so my money would have been on the sniper—assuming he was any good. He would have had the best chance of escape, as well. Or he would have had, if it wasn't for the two agents I'd sent to shadow him. They'd neutralised him before he even had Ekramy in his cross hairs. The real fireworks kicked off on the runway though. The fuel truck pulled up in its usual spot and the terrorists did a credible job of pretending to work the pipes and pumps, but when Ekramy appeared they dropped the airport equipment and tore open the front of their overalls. One pulled out a short-stock AK47. The other produced an Uzi. But again, my agents—two who'd helped move the steps and two posing as baggage handlers—were a step ahead.

A net reduction of three terrorists is never a bad thing. The airport security chief obligingly took the credit for their deaths. And I didn't take my eyes off Ekramy until he'd been led away into 'protective custody' by the same six Moroccan Intelligence officers who'd insisted on sharing their lunch with me twenty minutes earlier.

"Gunfire can be a little distracting, indeed," I said. "It seems some other people must have heard about Ekramy's travel plans. People with a less enlightened attitude than either of us."

"It seems you're right," the colonel said. "I wonder how word happened to spread?"

"Someone must have talked."

"Perhaps," he said, pulling a suitably puzzled expression. "But who?"

"I was going to ask you the same thing."

The colonel swung his feet back round to the floor and leaned towards me, across the desk.

"You're not suggesting there's a loose tongue within His Majesty's Intelligence Service?" he said.

That's exactly what I was suggesting. But not because I believed it. The right hints had been dropped in the right places, but it had been done by my people, not the Moroccans. How else would we have known who to watch in the buildup to Ekramy's arrival? I only said it to rile the colonel and waste a little more time.

"The death of Ekramy is not in my country's interests," he said, when he realised I wasn't going to reply. "We had no grudge against him. We weren't the ones who mistook his loyalties. Our fingers did not get burned. And we certainly don't welcome casualties in our international airport. Perhaps you should look closer to home for a culprit?"

"If we'd wanted him to be killed as got off the plane, why

would we have brought extra people to help protect him?" I said. "He survived those attempts on his life. We helped ensure that. And he was perfectly fine when he was taken into your custody. In fact, here's an idea: Maybe you wanted him there all along, so you could deal him to our American friends?"

"Absolutely not," he said, leaning away from me again. "We never dreamed of such an outcome."

At least I wasn't the only one who was lying, now.

"Anyway, at this stage the point's moot," I said. "And that's probably just as well. You know how the Americans are. They wouldn't look kindly on you snatching him from under our noses, only to let him get blown up ten minutes later in one of your own holding cells."

"We didn't snatch him," the colonel said. "You handed him over. Willingly. Almost like you wanted him in that cell."

"We didn't want him in any cell. We wanted to talk to him."

"You could have talked to him in the cell."

"What would be point in that? We needed him to go free afterwards, to act on what we told him."

"Really? How could he have acted? Because I hear that Ekramy was pretty much a hermit, these days. *Persona non grata* on both sides. So, what was this vital snippet of information? This seed you were so desperate to plant? I'd love to know."

"It doesn't matter now. The opportunity's gone. But if you're suggesting some kind of subterfuge on our part, that's impossible. I'm told the explosion was very localised. If we were trying to get him thrown in jail so we could assassinate him there, how could we have known which cell he'd be put in?"

The colonel steepled his fingers, than laid his palms flat on the desk.

"While you were dawdling your way through your forty seven word report, earlier, do you know what I was doing?" he said.

I shrugged.

"Waiting to hear from the pair of officers I sent to the

houses of all the airport police," he said. "Here's something I learned years ago: Where there's greedy, there's stupid. And one of them had been stupid enough to keep the fat wad of notes that—*someone*, shall we say—had given him, right there in his home."

"You're assuming it was a bribe?" I said, cursing the greedy fool we'd paid off three days before. "Maybe he was saving for a rainy day. Isn't fiscal responsibility encouraged in your country any longer?"

"It is. But we both know it was a bribe. And here's another interesting fact. The bomb that killed Ekramy? It wasn't planted in his cell. It had been hidden in a suitcase."

"How did the suitcase find its way to his cell? Another bribe?"

"It didn't need to be in his cell. It was left in the lost luggage office. On a particular shelf. In an exact spot against the back wall."

"I don't follow."

"I think you do. Because the lost luggage office just happens to share a wall with the cell that Ekramy was killed in."

"Really? And how would I know such a thing?"

"What would you say if I told you someone saw you going into the lost luggage office yesterday afternoon?"

"I'd say you were bluffing."

There was no way anyone had seen me.

"Or that the lost luggage clerk called in sick today, too late for a replacement to be brought in?" he said. "And that a bundle of notes was found at her house, as well?"

"I'd say that I deplored the lack of moral standards in the world today," I said. "And that I don't see what any of this has to do with me."

"Have you ever been to Casablanca airport before, Commander? Have you, perhaps, ever lost any luggage here?"

"No. I've never lost any luggage anywhere."

That was true. But it wasn't to say I didn't know someone else who'd lost their luggage here. Someone who'd later been detained and figured out the relationship between the two parts of the building.

"Are you sure?" the colonel said.

"Positive," I said. "But if you're suggesting that I arranged for Ekramy to be attacked so he'd be detained in order for me to have him blown up, isn't that a little impractical? Wouldn't I just let one of the other terrorists shoot him instead?"

"I guess you could have done—if you'd known about the terrorists' ambush, which you swore you didn't."

"That's right. But once it was clear they'd turned up, wouldn't I have taken advantage? Wouldn't a bullet from close range have been a much surer thing than a bomb blast through a wall?"

The colonel hauled himself to his feet as if he wanted to pace up and down, but he was penned in so tightly by the furniture he could barely shuffle six inches in any direction.

"You're right," he said, folding himself back down onto the chair. "There are pieces which don't quite fall into place. Yet. But you're the key to making them fit. I can feel it. So do you know what? We're going to stay in this room. We're going to talk. And we're going to keep talking until this whole thing makes sense to me."

"That's fine," I said, with a smile. "I'm happy to stay as long you want me."

And this time I wasn't lying. Because as long as his attention was focused on the things I was saying in that cramped office, it was kept away from a dusty silver S Class Mercedes which was making its way slowly south towards Marrakesh. And more specifically, from the woman who lay bound and chloroformed in its trunk. Reima Zergaw. Essam Ekramy's protégée. The person he'd ventured out of hiding to meet. The person who'd been knocked unconscious and bundled out of the airport while all eyes were on the fire in the cell block.

The person *we* wanted to talk to.

The Name of the Dame
Ted Hertel, Jr.

Early on, Eddie Herbert learned the power of the name. Knowing a person's name, especially a woman's name, could give him amazing control over that person. He'd read about this in one of his classes. His teacher, Mr. Bailey, had referred to this as "a myth," but Eddie didn't believe that for a minute. Knowing someone's name meant to know her soul, whatever that was.

Eddie wasn't the most religious guy around, but this naming idea went all the way back to the Bible, the teacher said. After all, when God named the animals, he started to control them. Eddie considered reporting Mr. Bailey to the school principal since he knew they weren't supposed to teach religion in school. But the old teacher had only just mentioned it once and besides he'd given Eddie the whole name concept thing. From there Bailey had prattled on about folktales like Rumplestiltskin and some broad who had to guess his name. And bam! When she did, was she ever in charge. Eddie knew from that moment on that he was going to put this power to work for him.

His first conscious use of this ability came while he was still in high school. It was a large school, over three thousand students, most of them faceless blurs. It didn't help anything that Eddie was a geek. No one really wanted to get to know him and, as a result, he didn't know anyone, either.

Then one day, across the large cafeteria study hall, he saw her. The woman of his dreams. Or she would have been if he'd had any dreams to begin with. He didn't know who she was, of course. That was the whole problem. But if he could just find out, maybe he could make friends with her, change her life. Hell, change *his* life. So each day in that cafeteria, rife with the smells of half-eaten lunches discarded by the hundreds, he contrived to move closer to her, until one day he managed to snag a seat at the table directly in front of her.

After Eddie dropped his pencil on the floor for the fourth time, snaking his head around at each opportunity to see if he could look up her skirt and see her panties, she got up from her chair. Then she walked around the table and came up to him. *At last*, Eddie thought, *she's noticed me. I'll just introduce my—*

That's when her flat open hand hit him square in the face, knocking Eddie off his chair and sending his glasses skittering across the floor.

"Listen, creep, you drop that pencil on the floor one more time and I'm gonna shove it so far up your ass that it'll come out your nose."

One of the hoods who harassed him on a daily basis stepped over the prone Eddie and laughed. "Well, she got you good, asshole."

Groggy, it was all Eddie could do to mutter "Who? What?"

"Ellen Zingzheim, freak." The punk held out his hand to help Eddie up, which Eddie thought was a nice gesture until the guy punched Eddie hard on the shoulder, sending him staggering. But to Eddie that didn't matter because he'd what he wanted.

Ellen Zingzheim. Her name floated in his addled brain like cream on milk. Ellen Zingzheim. She'd talked to him. She'd actually said something to him. Sure, they weren't the words he'd hoped to hear, but it was a start. He knew her name. He'd never forget it.

It came to him now that what old man Bailey said fit right in here. It had sounded like a load of horseshit to Eddie at the time, but now that he knew Ellen Zingzheim's name, he suddenly understood. He understood what it meant to know a name. And he knew what he could do with it. Shakespeare had written, "What's in a name?" Hell of a lot *he* knew. Because there was a hell of lot in a name.

Ellen Zingzheim, he said it over and over to himself. And

Eddie felt his power grow.

The first thing he did that night when he got home was to look up the name in the telephone book. Thank God her name wasn't Smith. There were hundreds of those in the phonebook. Ah, but Zingzheim. There were only five of those, three of whom lived nowhere near the school. That left two likely candidates. The first call he placed was right on the mark. No, said the friendly sounding woman who answered the phone, Ellen wasn't home yet. Cheerleading practice. Could she tell her who called? Eddie left the name of the basketball captain, then hung up. He had her.

That weekend Eddie made sure to ride his bike past her house a dozen times, hoping just to catch a glimpse of her. That was another thing. His cheap parents wouldn't buy him a car. In fact they almost never let Eddie use their car, which was fifteen years old anyway and he wouldn't be caught dead in it driving past Ellen's house. The last time he biked past he saw her leave in a convertible with, who else, the captain of the basketball team. In some strange way this pleased Eddie, who thought he had done a fine job setting her up. But in another way, it pissed him off no end, since he wanted her for himself.

But with the control the power of her name gave him, he set out to make Ellen Zingzheim notice him. He started sending her unsigned cards, calling her and hanging up after he'd heard her voice, walking to her house and ringing the bell, then hiding behind the tree to see if she came to the door. When the cops finally caught him, he got a stern lecture from his parents. The second time they found him in the Zingzheim bushes, the cops told him enough was enough. The third time he got expelled from school and had to be bussed halfway across town to a worse school where, being a geek, he was beaten up on a daily basis. He never saw Ellen Zingzheim again.

But he didn't care because he had learned that if he knew a person's name, he could do anything he wanted to them. Well, at least as long as he was a bit more subtle about the whole thing. For example, that redheaded bitch in college who wouldn't give him the time of day. Once he found out that her name was Karen Geiger, easy enough to do with that picture book of the freshmen they handed out, he did everything he could to make her notice him. Even told her about old Bailey's "name myth," but pretended he'd thought the whole thing up himself. When she'd finally had enough of Eddie, she called him "Zitface" to his zittyface and that was it. Wonder how she liked all those pizzas that showed up that Saturday night? Or the busted dorm window in her room? Or the four flat tires on her car? Or the slashed clothes in her closet?

This time it was the woman who left the school, hysterical and in tears, as Eddie watched her parents drive her away in the middle of her first college semester. Well, the school wasn't all that good, anyway. Plenty more fish to name. So he cast his line out into the waters once again. But the results always remained the same. Lust turned to hate.

After Eddie graduated from college and moved to Chicago, he found that it was not all that easy to meet women and learn their names. There were dating services, but that always required the woman to actually want to date him. He couldn't learn a name until one of them would agree to go out with him first. That just never happened once they viewed his tape, which he thought was a pretty good one. The women he met in chatrooms always seemed to be too far away to do him any good. He hated the bar scene ever since he inadvertently wound up in a gay bar and had the crap beaten out of him, just like in high school. So he was stuck with women he could meet at work. But he wasn't interested in any of them. They were too short or too tall. Too fat or too thin. Too ugly or...well, there was no such thing as too pretty, of course.

Then, one day, he saw her. Thick shoulder-length blonde hair, she strode sensuously onto the elevator with him and a half-dozen others. Full red lips, blue eyes, long legs, familiar somehow and yet not. Like a movie star whose name he couldn't quite remember. She had the face and the figure of an angel. So he made up a name for her. Angela. How perfect for the perfect woman. He'd never done that before. Never actually given a woman a name. He glanced at her left hand, looking for a ring and found none. He was sure that she looked him over as she got on. He watched as she pushed the button for the twenty-eighth floor. His office was on the sixteenth, but at least he knew where to find her.

Eddie spent the rest of the day with his door shut devising a plan to discover Angela's real name. Because he remembered something else Mr. Bailey had said in that sociology class years earlier. The idea was that you had to know the "true" name of the person you wanted to control. Once he knew Angela's true name, then the power would be his again. *She* would be his. This time there'd be no mistake.

But Eddie hadn't changed. He was still a geek, shunned by all his office co-workers, never invited to anything after that disaster the first time he went out with them. That was the Friday night of the week he'd started working there. How was he to know that the secretary of the boss was also the mistress of the boss? No one had mentioned that little tidbit to him. He was lucky he wasn't fired, the boss told him, even as the secretary/mistress was slapping Eddie's face as he was taking his hand off her breast. And this had happened even though he knew her name. Not one of the other women in the office ever spoke to him again, so knowing their names didn't help him, either.

Angela, however, was a different matter, Eddie was sure. So the very next day he put his plan into action. He got to work at the exact time he had yesterday, hoping to catch her at the elevator. That didn't pan out, so the next day, he showed up a full hour ahead of schedule. When she hadn't arrived by the time Eddie had to be in his office or risk losing his job, Eddie decided he'd have to put Phase II of his plan to work.

Phase II was a masterstroke, Eddie was convinced. He'd simply go up to the twenty-eighth floor of the building and check it out. See what offices were there. Strike up a conversation or two with people he ran into. Maybe wander around long enough even to run into Angela herself.

That's where the genius of the whole Phase II plan existed. He'd pretend they'd met someplace, a party or something, fumble for her name, maybe snap his fingers once or twice like he was trying to remember and then she'd almost subconsciously blurt it out trying to help him. Then he'd have her and he could ask her out if the timing were right. Of course, if she turned him down, unlikely since his approach was so clever, well, at least he'd know who she was. He'd use that power to eventually win her over, he was sure. He had plenty of time.

Confident in himself, he told the male secretary the bastards had assigned to him that he had to see the man upstairs, an oblique reference to someone above him that would prevent the so-called secretary from finding Eddie for the next half hour or so. He confidently strode to the elevator and pressed the "up" button. The car whisked him to the twenty-eighth floor where he got off. So far, so good.

Of course, that's when the plan, like all of Eddie's plans, went straight to hell in a handbag, as his mother always said. "Handbasket," Eddie could still hear his father scream at her, "it's handbasket, not handbag, you stupid bitch." His father had always screamed about everything. The only time his father wasn't screaming was when he was drinking. The old man had screamed and drank so much that he'd finally blown out his own circulatory system when he'd died right there in front of Eddie.

Eddie observed immediately that this was a floor that had at least a half-dozen offices on it, not just one big office taking up the whole floor with people wandering around looking busy but probably doing very little actual work. This stumped him. There was no one in the hall. There were no open office doors. There were no windows facing the corridor that he could look in to see if she were there. Well, he couldn't just stand outside the women's restroom and wait for her to show up. Of course, if push came to shove, he'd have to do just that.

Then it hit him. What if she were just visiting someone up here that day? What if she didn't work here at all? What if she had noticed him staring, no, no, gazing approvingly at her and for some reason was offended? Hard to believe, he knew. What if she just pushed "28" when her real destination was any of the other forty-seven floors in the building above the sixteenth, just to throw him off her trail?

Dogged by "what ifs," Eddie walked the length of the deserted corridor hoping to run into someone, anyone, who could help him out. "Say, I was just looking for my friend, you know, the blonde with the really nice tits. Can you tell me where she works?" No, that didn't have quite the cachet to it that Eddie was hoping for. Not that he knew what a cachet was. Probably something to do with money. He'd just heard the term used on a few occasions was all. Time to come up with Phase III.

He turned to go back and that's when he saw her coming out of an office door just down the hall. She was heading toward the elevator and he was only about twenty feet behind her. As he passed the door she had come out of, he glanced at it. It was the entrance to a law firm and had a heavy brass plaque on it. There were no names on it other than the name of the firm. Was hers one of those three snooty-sounding last names?

No matter. This was still perfect, Eddie thought, *just perfect.* He hurried to catch up to her, trying to remember his carefully rehearsed speech. Because the 28th floor hadn't been laid out as he'd thought it would be, he'd been momentarily thrown off his game. But he couldn't believe his luck. He was back in stride. The world was his, if he could find out her name.

He arrived at the elevator just steps behind her. That had given him time to admire her backside, which was as lovely as her front side, both of which were in a nice tight white dress.

Okay, be smooth, he thought.

"Hi. Remember me? I'm Jimmy. Jimmy Carver." No point in handing out his true name, after all. Not at this stage of the proceedings. It wouldn't make any difference to her. "We met at that thing a couple weeks ago." Ah, the perfect opening.

"What thing?"

Oh, hell, she wasn't supposed to say that. She was supposed to say "Oh, sure, I'm" and then give her name. What thing? What thing?

"You know, that thing over there on, was it Wacker? Or State? That thing at that bar."

"Oh, that thing," she said, but sounded a bit unsure.

"Let's see, you're, um, um..." and here Eddie remembered to snap his fingers like he was trying to recall her name from the evening of that thing at that bar. Just then the elevator door dinged and opened. She got on. As Eddie stepped in with her, she looked at him a bit puzzled.

"You're going up, too?"

Eddie had to think fast, since he had no idea where she was going. But the easy answer was simply to say "yes." So he did, then added, "Have to see the man upstairs, you know," like he'd told what passed for his secretary.

"God?" she asked, but with a smile, as the doors slowly closed.

What in the hell is she talking about? Eddie's upbringing and near daily beatings from either his father or his classmates had left him without a sense of humor. But the smile tipped him off and he sort of laughed. "Yeah, God. Or at least his man in the building offices," which was the one thing Eddie knew was near the top of the building. "And you?"

"Goddess," she replied. He needed no encouragement to laugh at this. "No, really, Goddess Cosmetics, up on forty-one." This made Eddie realize he hadn't pushed a button and he did so, hoping he'd remembered correctly that the building management office was on fifty-five.

"So you work on twenty-eight but you're going up there..."

"Just to meet with my client." For the first time Eddie noticed a slender briefcase in her hand. "What's taking you up to the big guy?"

Fortunately, the elevator arrived on forty-one and Eddie was saved from answering this, since he didn't have the faintest idea what errand would require a man of his importance to visit the building office.

Angela stepped out of the elevator, then turned and put her hand on the door, keeping it from closing. "So, you want to have a drink with me tonight at that same bar where the thing was when we met a couple weeks ago?" She gave him a radiant smile that was impossible to refuse, not that he had any intention of doing so.

"Sure," he said.

"See you there at six?"

"Okay." She let go of the door and it slid shut.

Only then did it occur to Eddie that there were two problems. First, she had never given him her name. Major failure there. But there was always tonight. And that was the second problem. He, of course, didn't have the faintest idea where that bar was where the thing was held a couple weeks ago. Son of a bitch.

Eddie spent the rest of the day avoiding work since he had to come up with Phase III. Or was it Phase IV? No, it had to be III. He hadn't actually done III. If he hadn't run into Angela up there on twenty-eight when he did, he'd have had to come up with III. So this indeed was Phase III. Just a different Phase III was all. He discarded any number of ideas and finally settled on the simple one of just waiting for her in the lobby. He would pretend that he was shopping in the drugstore and watch the elevator doors from there. When she stepped out, so would he. The only flaw in this that he could see was that she might have left early to meet with another client or go to court or do whatever the hell lawyers did when they weren't in their offices.

But it was Eddie's lucky day. There she was, getting off the elevator just as he'd planned. He walked out of the lobby entrance of the drugstore and acted surprised when he saw her, heels clacking across the marble floor.

"Hey, funny meeting you here," Eddie said. "I was just on my way over to, well, you know."

"No, I really don't."

"But you said..."

"I know, Jimmy, but I figured you'd think of a way to run into me, since we both know that we've never met before."

"Then why...?"

"I was intrigued that you'd go to so much trouble just to see me. I thought it was sweet. Which is my name, by the way, since I doubt you know that, either."

In for a penny, Eddie thought. *Might as well go all the way.* "No, I'm sorry to say that I don't."

"Well, as I said, it's Sweet. Rose Sweet. As in "a rose by any other name...""

He had her.

That night after drinks, which led to a quiet Italian meal, they wound up at Eddie's apartment. He'd used her name often that evening and each time she seemed to warm more and more to it and to him. After years of seeing only the negative power in the names of women, he was finally getting some positive effects from his theory. Old man Bailey called it "a myth." Well, what would he think if he could see Eddie now? Eddie, who was about to get everything he'd ever wanted from the most beautiful woman he had ever seen. Eddie, a ladies' man at last, thanks to the power he possessed. Once again, Eddie felt that power grow and grow.

She led him into the bedroom and told him to get very comfortable while she spent a few minutes freshening up in the bathroom. Eddie's clothes were off almost before he knew it. He found a slightly used candle that he had bought once in case the electricity ever went out. Eddie lit it, then turned off the lamps. He flung the covers of the unmade bed onto the floor and jumped under the sheet. Rose came out wearing nothing but a black bra and panties, hands held demurely behind her back, allowing her breasts to be thrust out intoxicatingly. Slowly she walked over to the bed and then climbed on top of Eddie, straddling him with her legs, pinning his arms next to him under the sheet. Her long blonde hair hung down over him and he could barely contain himself.

"Oh, Eddie," she moaned.

"Oh, Rose, you're so..." In spite of the blood having in general left his head, he remembered that he had never told her his real name. She knew him only as "Jimmy," didn't she? Had she seen something with his name on it in the apartment? His name wasn't on the door.

"Yes, Eddie, I know who you are. I knew the minute I saw you on the elevator the other day. You're still the same geeky-looking guy you've always been. But running into you was totally serendipitous. I had no idea you lived in Chicago or that we actually worked in the same building. You still don't know me, do you? We went to college together. Oh, I had red hair at the time and there've been a number of other cosmetic changes, as well. So, recognize me now?"

Eddie had to think for a moment or two. After all, there had been so many in the past. But then the name came to him.

"Karen? Karen Geiger?"

"Yeah, I thought you might still remember me after all those horrible things you did. I know I never forgot you. The pizzas. The tire slashings. My clothes. You almost ruined my life. I was in therapy for years after that. And then there was that stupid name thing. That's the other thing I remember about you. Going on and on about that, like it was some brilliant idea of yours. Well, how do you like it that I know your name, that I've got that power you were so crazy about and that I'm sitting here on top of you and you're not going anywhere?"

At the moment, Eddie and his power liked it just fine.

But when she brought her arm around from behind her, the glint of the knife in it changed his mind.

Turns out names aren't all they're cracked up to be, power-wise, was Eddie's final thought.

The Great Plains
Chris F. Holm

It's ten after six when I pull in to the parking lot, sliding to a spot way out front of the IGA, ten spaces from the next nearest car. It's raining, or trying to at least. The pavement's wet and the occasional fat raindrop smacks my windshield at random intervals, either too early to the party or too late. Even chance the sky opens up at any moment, but it doesn't matter. I'm not here to shop. I don't plan to even go inside.

I've been coming here for two weeks now. Pulling in almost without volition on my way home from the plant. Something about wide open spaces that stills the mind. Something about my basement apartment that sets it reeling.

Garden apartment, my landlord calls it.

We don't call things what we mean anymore.

Like the plant. Conjures images of industry. Of making things with my own two hands. And time was, I did. We did. Then they promoted me to manager, and now instead of coveralls, I wear Dockers and a company button-down—a cheap short-sleeved poly-cotton blend with our logo on the breast—and instead of making things, I tear them down, one pink slip at a time.

Only pink slips aren't pink slips anymore. Now they're fat reams of cooling printer paper, all fine print and dotted lines, as if asking the recipients again and again for their consent in their own dismissal. It's so polite, it's sickening. A few years back, they'd get mad, at least. Now most can't even muster the indignation to make a stink. They just shrug as if to say it's not my fault. It's just the times we live in.

I liked it better when they got mad. They're owed that much, at least. And I'm owed at least that much less.

If you asked me what I'm doing here, I'm not sure I'd have an answer. Watching. Not watching. Thinking. Not thinking. Listening to the quiet.

I like the quiet. That's why I started coming here, to the Westfield Shopping Center, instead of the strip mall across the street. I'd started out parking there a couple months back, in the two-acre no-man's-land between the Walmart and the movie theater, where a Dairy Queen long since bulldozed once stood. But there was this guy a few years older than me—early fifties, I'd guess—who'd already staked the place out and every day, his Town Car would be a couple spaces closer to where I liked to park my Bonneville. At first, I thought nothing of it, but as the days wore on and he grew closer, it creeped me out. All the more so when I noticed he was watching me, glassy eyed and smiling—a vague smile, as though the punch line to a setup long forgotten just bubbled to the surface of his mind. Then one day, he climbed out of his car, ambled across the asphalt prairie toward me and asked me if I was looking. I thought he meant drugs. The only time I smoked pot in my life was in high school; I wound up dizzy and paranoid and vowed never to do it again and told him so. Then he offered to let me smoke something else entirely and I politely declined.

I haven't been back since.

Westfield, I like. Been some cars broken into here, I heard on the news, but only the ones left overnight. Guess the Walmart lot was spared on account of they were open twenty-four hours. Way the reporter talked, you'd think there was a death squad roaming the streets, instead of what was probably just some stupid kids looking for a jolt to knock their lives out of groove. By day, it's pretty quiet, but with enough foot traffic to keep the pervs away. My only company save customers is the odd delivery guy, hanging out and doing paperwork, clipboard propped up on the steering wheel.

Christ. Even FedEx guys got paperwork these days.

I watch the people come and go; the chaos not chaos at all if you sit there long enough—days, I mean. It's cyclical, an endless repeating pattern, every day the same, but not the same. As if their movements have some purpose. As if their subtle variations day-to-day are an improvement. A refining of the process.

As if one day they'll get it right.

It's an illusion, but a comforting one.

Plus, Westfield's got Jaime. Or Jamie, maybe, I don't know which. But I prefer J-A-I-M-E, so that's what she is inside my head.

Jaime waitresses at Applebee's or hosts or busses tables. I couldn't say for sure because I've never been inside. I only know her name because I heard the guy she leaves with call her that once as they were walking out. Separate cars—they're not together or anything. He seems an affable enough kid and by her body language she likes him fine, but he's three hundred pounds if he's an ounce and you can see his acne from a half a parking lot away. No way a girl like Jaime'd go for him.

Listen to me. As if I know her. As if I'd have a shot.

She's beautiful. Fair skinned and slight. Red hair; sad, knowing green eyes; a laugh that makes your heart skip on the rare occasion she employs it. She's better than this place. Better than the guy who's watching her. The guy who's old enough to be her father.

I wonder if anybody looks at my Sadie the way I look at Jaime. At fourteen, they goddamn well better not. But Jaime can't be more than twenty, so it's hard to find a brush so fine, I don't get painted with it, too. Maybe this parking lot's got pervs enough after all.

My iPhone buzzes. *Too nice a phone for a deadbeat like me.* That's what Melissa said when I last saw her. And she should know—she was the one who bought it for me. Back when I made manager. Back when she liked me better.

Speak of the devil. Or *to* him, Melissa'd likely tell you. Not that she has to. Her tone is harsh enough, the words aren't necessary.

"Where were you last night?" she says with no preamble.

"Hello to you too," I reply.

"I'm serious, Frank. Where were you?"

"I thought the papers you signed made it pretty clear you were done waiting on me coming home."

A long pause. "Frank, you missed Sadie's recital."

Shit, I think. "Shit," I say.

"*Shit?*" she parrots. "That's all you have to say for yourself? Do you have any idea how much this tore her up? Or how much it killed Connor when you showed up three quarters of the way into his game? Do you even care you didn't get to see him play? That every other dad gave their daughter flowers after?"

I should say I'm sorry. I should say she's right to be so pissed. That I'll try to be a better dad, a better man. Instead I say, "Don't talk to me like you're some kind of saint. Like I'm the only one to blame in all of this. 'Cause believe me, Mel, you're no fucking saint—and you're sure as hell not blameless."

More's said after that—by her, by me. But it's just variations on a theme. The same but not the same. We've been refining this process a while.

When she finally hangs up on me, I set the phone down and drop the seat back as close to horizontal as it will go. I stare a while at the dull gray fabric of the ceiling. Then I pinch the bridge of my nose and close my eyes and for a while I stare at nothing at all, willing the throbbing in my temples to cease.

I must doze off because when I next open my eyes, night has fallen. The storefront signs are dark and through the windows of the shops, I see the long shadows of security lights, just bright enough to deter a would-be prowler. A smattering of empty cars dot the vast, wet modern plain like the husks of dead things stuck in tar or perhaps frozen in the amber of the arc sodium lights.

The streetlight above my car is dark. Cracked. Broken. I'm at the center of a pool of liquid shadow. And suddenly, I realize what roused me.

I am not alone.

At first, it's nothing more than the soft patter of footfalls. A hushed conversation, like wind through trees. The words are lost, but the tone is mischievous, goading.

And then my passenger window explodes.

I jerk upright, now fully awake. My right knee slams into

my keys, still dangling from the ignition. The knee flares with sudden pain, the keys jingle like wind chimes. Tears well in the corner of my eyes.

A hand, reaching. Scrawny, delicate—almost feminine. Opens the door from the inside. Then a rangy kid with tight, curly hair and wide owl eyes ducks inside, freezing as his gaze meets mine. For a while, we're mirror images: he terrified of me; me terrified of him and of the tire iron in his right hand. Behind him, his buddies watch stunned, halfway between my Pontiac and their tricked-out Focus hatchback, as if wondering if it's time to flee. His eyes flit to my iPhone and my wallet, both resting on the center console.

"Take it," I say, my voice hoarse. "Take whatever you fucking want."

He blinks at me and drops the tire iron. Then he bolts for the Focus.

His buddies beat him there. It's rolling by the time he hops inside.

They peel out in a choking cloud of rubber, taking nothing—and who could blame them?

Nothing in my car is worth a damn.

Serenity
Brad Parks

On the sixth anniversary of his sobriety, Roger Clemens—
no, not that Roger Clemens—left the warehouse office of his
landscaping company at exactly 9:14 in the morning, praying
to God he could find an open bar.

The desire to drink had never really left through those six
years, making itself heard as everything from a dulcet whisper
to a rebel yell. It was the soundtrack of Roger's life, though he
had grown so accustomed to tuning it out, he never thought it
would be this all-consuming again.

Then came Billy Maundy. Billy Fucking Maundy, who had
managed perhaps four months of sobriety—combined—in his
miserable adult life. Billy Maundy, who was only there
because he didn't know which end of a weed whacker to use.
Billy Maundy, who had lost several of his teeth—thank you,
cocaine—but still smiled like the world's biggest jackass every
chance he got.

Billy Maundy, who might now ruin everything.

Roger locked the office door and crunched through the
parking lot, which he had recently covered in a fresh layer of
blue-gray gravel that came from a thirty-ton pile behind the
warehouse. The fleet of Ford F350's that carried his crews to
their jobs that Monday morning were already gone,
dispatched for the day, leaving just his personal truck, an
F150. Well, that and the employees' cars.

Crap. Maundy's car. Roger focused on it, that dusty,
dented, how-the-hell-does-this-thing-still-run Chevy Cavalier
so unbefitting of a tony town like Darien, Connecticut.
Maundy borrowed the car from his rehab program to get to
work. It had to be returned by 5 each day. What was Roger

going to do about that?

He thought about going back inside, grabbing the keys out of Maundy's pocket—assuming that's where he kept them—and driving it somewhere. But where? And how would he get back to the warehouse? It was another problem to deal with, another reason he needed that drink: To get his head straight, to be his old self just for a few hours, long enough to think his way out of this mess.

It's not like he had to worry about Billy going anywhere.

Every drunk has a story. And during six years of faithful AA attendance, Roger had heard hundreds of them.

Roger's was different, but not so different. He heard about other alcoholics who got their start sneaking hits out of their Dad's Maker's Mark bottles or convincing their older brothers to make beer runs for high school parties. Not Roger. He wasn't even at those parties. In college, he was a rower—a 6-foot-4, 230-pound heavyweight—so while his classmates descended into fraternity basements and enjoyed their flirtations with alcohol poisoning, Roger was hitting the water at six each morning. Even in business school, a veritable incubator for future alchies, Roger was the guy who held the same glass of wine all night.

Then, sometime in his early thirties, he discovered that a beer at night could taste pretty good and feel even better. Then he discovered vodka made the feeling come more quickly. Gin, tequila, scotch—it all worked.

Roger wasn't one of those guys who drank to wash away some inescapable pain. He didn't drink to forget the world or flee his marriage or soothe the ache of loss. He just liked it. In a strange way, he felt like it quieted his mind, stripping away the everyday muddle and allowing him to think clearly.

As such, cocktail time slowly came a little early each night. And maybe he could have a drink at lunch, as long as it was going to be a quiet afternoon in the office. He felt like he kept tabs on his drinking, but he got ever-so-slightly more permissive with himself each passing year. Problem drinking could be insidious that way.

Three weeks before his 50th birthday, after twenty-four years of service to one company, he got laid off. Corporate downsizing. In a place like Darien—a bedroom community for dozens of Fortune 500 companies—it felt like a virus that made the rounds. Had drinking played a role? Had people at his office noticed Roger slurring his words at late afternoon marketing meetings? Had that made him easier to terminate? Of course. Did Roger admit that to himself? Of course not.

Besides, it was a soft landing. They gave two years' salary—two years!—to walk away quietly. That, along with other savings, meant Roger felt no immediate compulsion to find a job. He told himself he had earned the right to relax for a while. And for Roger, relaxing and drinking had become conjoined.

Before long, he was in a perpetual drunk. His wife left the house early each morning so she never got to see the spectacle of him rolling over at ten, groping for the vodka bottle he kept under the bed and taking the long swig that started each day.

On more than one occasion, when he hadn't remembered to stash the vodka and couldn't get himself upright enough to walk downstairs to the liquor cabinet, he crawled to the bathroom and drank mouthwash instead.

Around the time Roger was descending into full stupor, Billy Maundy was finishing high school. Barely. In truth, the principal let him graduate just so she could be rid of him; and so neither she, nor anyone else in the school system, had to admit how thoroughly they had failed him.

Billy had been one of the most confounding students to ever move through Darien public schools—brilliant, charming and a total fuck up. From the time he was small, his standardized test scores evinced genius even when little else about him did. Many a school psychologist had shaken her head and doubted the scores because ... really? That Billy Maundy?

But, no, Billy was that smart. He was a classic example of how schools—legally required to have resources for special needs students—have virtually nothing in place for kids at the opposite end of the spectrum, the super-gifted ones who grew easily bored in classrooms where there were few challenges. He could have a ninety-eight average in one subject, and absolutely enchant his teacher with his ability to grasp concepts and make connections. And then in three other subjects—where he had deemed the teacher incompetent, the material worthless or the subject matter dull—he'd neglect to turn in routine homework assignments.

Teachers threw up their hands. School counselors were perplexed. Notes went home, but his single mother, overmatched by Billy and his three younger brothers, simply didn't have the energy or time to get too involved. She'd deliver a lecture or threaten to take away his computer—Billy loved his computer—but never carried through on it. She'd send him back the next day, not the least bit chastened.

He was a loner through most of elementary and middle schools—his peers bored him, too—then fell quite easily into that disaffected high school crowd, the kids who hung around the brick wall outside school, smoked cigarettes and moped about how much everything sucked. Billy had a quick tongue and a way of seeing through grown-ups' bullshit, such that a group of older kids happily adopted him. That was how he first tried marijuana. And ecstasy. And anything else that he could smoke, swallow or sniff.

Getting high was never boring. It became his life's ambition.

Of all the factors that could have finally pushed Roger to rock bottom—and there were several things in close competition—it was his liver that got there first. Roger started noticing blood in his urine and took himself to a doctor. A bilirubin test confirmed it: Unless he stopped drinking, Roger would be dead in six months, a year tops.

Of course, by that point, just about everything else in his life was broken, too. His money was gone and his over-leveraged house was teetering on the brink of foreclosure (Roger had taken to "investing" while drunk, with predictable results). His wife had left him, saddling him with alimony payments. His job prospects, after two years of unemployment, were dim. No one was looking for a 50-something white guy who had been laid off by the only company he ever worked for.

The only thing that kept him going was this dim sense of self-preservation, that he was too young to just pack it in and let himself die. So he quit drinking. Cold turkey. He went through a week of withdrawal that introduced him to an agony he never knew existed, then somehow came out of it. He started attending AA meetings at the First Congregational Church and got himself a good sponsor, a pillar-of-the-community type who encouraged Roger to rebuild his life and to start by getting a job.

And then it just came to him: lawn care. It was perfect. He had always been an avid gardener, even taken a turf management class on a lark one time. The local market was robust. Darien is one of those fancy towns where mowing one's own lawn was either considered an eccentricity or taken as a sign of financial distress by the neighbors.

Besides, Roger was tired of commuting to Westchester, tired of working in a glass tower—not that any of those places would have hired him anyway. He wanted to do something where he could be outside, get his hands dirty, feel the heat of the summer and the cold of the winter.

He cashed in his last T-bills—the ones he swore he'd never touch—leased some equipment, paid three months' rent on an office and blitzed the town with advertising. Roger was a marketing guy, after all. Figuring out how to sell stuff was the one thing he knew how to do.

That's how Roger Clemens' Quick Strike Landscaping was born. He festooned his ads with baseball references—his top-of-the-line package was called the Cy Young—and did all he could to trade on the famous name that was somehow his. Oh, there were some casual inquiries from lawyers representing the other Roger Clemens. But, fact was, landscaping Roger was born Roger David Clemens—and a full ten years before the other one, whose real name was actually William Roger Clemens.

The way landscaping Roger saw it, he had more right to the name Roger Clemens than the baseball player.

It didn't take long for Roger Clemens' Quick Strike Landscaping to burgeon. The competition didn't have the marketing wherewithal, but it also didn't have one other thing Roger did: white guys.

Oh, no one wanted to talk about this part. Not in Darien, which liked to consider itself so progressive and open-minded. But the fact is, every other landscaping company in town— even the ones owned by Caucasians—would send a swarm of little brown men to take care of your lawn. And while some folks were truly fine with that, others were ... well, they didn't want to talk about that part.

Roger? He hired white guys. Yeah, they were all in recovery—Roger had become known far and wide through the AA network as a guy who would employ dried-out drunks—but when you gave them a shave and a haircut and put them in crisp, clean uniforms, they didn't look like alcoholics anymore.

So between the marketing, the white guys and Roger Clemens' 300-Win Guarantee—that if your work wasn't done on time, as quoted, Roger would give your money back plus $300 in cash—the business took off. Roger was able to pay back his business loans, buy some more equipment and begin paying down enough of his back due loans that the bank stopped bothering him.

Then came the real coup. The town of Darien decided it could save money by eliminating part of its public works department and outsourcing those responsibilities, slicing it up into several different contracts and putting out requests for proposals. With some creative coaching from Darien's First Selectman—who happened to be Roger's AA sponsor, not that anyone knew it—Roger Clemens' Quick Strike Landscaping tossed its suspiciously Red Sox-like hat into the ring.

And, lo and behold, every single one of Roger's bids happened to be the lowest. The First Selectman's advice, while expensive, had been quite sage. And so the Darien Board of Selectmen rewarded Rogers Clemens Quick Strike Landscaping with several rich new contracts.

It was a stretch for Roger, who needed a large outlay of cash to lease the heavy equipment, buy the insurance and cover the variety of other new expenses he was now incurring. He also had to expand his workforce, which meant he could no longer rely on drunks alone.

So, through his contacts in the addiction treatment community, he started hiring recovering addicts, too. And Billy Maundy—back in Darien and trying to get himself straight after five lost years in New York City—was one of them.

Roger nearly fired Billy the first week. The kid was friendly enough and Roger liked him personally, but he was near worthless when it came to manual labor. He was small and weak and had a laziness about him that was bad for morale: The other guys resented his goldbricking. And then came Friday, when Roger handed Billy his first paycheck. It was handwritten, of course, because Roger did all his books longhand. That's how he learned to do it when he took his one accounting class, thirty-whatever years earlier. Sure, he had a computer, but he only really knew how to use it for email.

Billy went out in the parking lot, opened the check, then came back into the office cackling. Before Roger even knew what was happening, Billy went over to that little-used computer, downloaded some free accounting software and showed Roger how easy it would be to digitize his books. Or, rather, how easy it was for Billy. Roger marveled at how intuitive Billy was behind a keyboard. What would take Roger hours of burying his head in an instruction manual, Billy could accomplish in thirty seconds of trial-and-error fiddling.

That gave Roger the brainstorm: Billy could do his books. Ever since the business expanded, Roger had been feeling overwhelmed by it anyway. It was taking too much of his time, keeping him chained to the office more than he liked. He had been thinking about hiring an accountant, but he was loathe to add any additional expenses on his balance sheet. Having Billy do it for $10 an hour felt like it made a lot of sense. For Billy, futzing with a computer was a welcome alternative to blister-inducing labor. So it was decided. Billy became Roger's Guy Friday.

It took Billy a week to get everything up and running. It took him only slightly longer to figure out what was really going on.

With Roger gone much of the day, Billy had the office to himself. Roger didn't worry about it—everything of value was locked up in the safe—but Billy had free reign on the files, including the contracts Roger Clemens' Quick Strike Landscaping signed with the Town of Darien. Billy had such a quick mind for numbers—and was familiar enough with the company's cash flow—to see that all of the contracts had been underbid, which is how Roger had won them. But there was one contract that was different. It was for "landscaping consulting management," whatever that meant. It was, technically, a professional services contract, which meant the town wasn't required to select among the lowest bidders. And Roger was padding the bejesus out of it, billing for all kinds of mythical services rendered.

Exactly half of the money from that contract was missing. But it didn't take long for Billy, snooping through files, to figure out where it was going. The Town of Darien's First Selectman was getting himself a fat kickback.

For a few weeks, Billy sat on his new knowledge. He recognized its value, just wasn't sure the best way to monetize it. In the meantime, he went on his best behavior—he always could keep his shit together for short spurts. He even put together a client management database for the homeowner side of Roger's business, integrating it with a calendar so Roger wouldn't have to rely on the office dry erase board.

Then Roger, who was simply trying to show his gratitude, made his mistake. He gave Billy a bonus. Two hundred dollars. No big deal, just a little something extra.

But it was in cash. Billy had gained a variety of freedoms at his rehab, a residential program where the "guests" slowly earned privileges. Managing his own money wasn't yet one of them. He had to turn in his check to the program, which banked it for him. It was just one more way to keep temptation at bay.

And then, wham, Roger unthinkingly dumped two hundred bucks in Billy's pocket. On a Friday, no less. Billy had it converted into cocaine within the hour, but didn't use it. No, he sat on it all weekend—almost literally, since it was strapped to his inner thigh.

Then, on the way to work that Monday morning, he pulled over to the side of Boston Post Road, rolled up one of the few remaining dollar bills, and took his first hit in three months. Just two lines. Enough to give him the balls he needed for what would come next.

He got to the office late, after all the crews were gone. That was Roger's first clue something was amiss. Billy had always been punctual. As he got closer, Roger could see the young man was obviously strung out—twitchy, sniffling, animated. He was smiling and laughing and his eyes were darting all over. Roger asked what the hell was going on.

That's when Billy said he knew about the kickback.

This started a conversation, such as it was. Roger denied it, but Billy had him dead to rights. He even had the company books backed up on one of those cloud drives, so he could go anywhere—like a district attorney's office—and prove what was happening with just a few clicks and keystrokes.

Finally, they worked around to Billy's demand. Twenty grand. In cash. To shut up and walk away. Billy figured that would be enough to get him set up real nice somewhere far from Darien, somewhere he could get high and find a way to make enough money to keep getting high so no one could say shit about it. Billy knew Roger had the money and Roger knew Billy knew.

So Roger said fine. Billy had him by the short hairs. If the bribe was exposed, Rogers Clemens' Quick Strike Landscaping would be finished and Roger would be finished along with it. To say nothing of the illegality of his actions, and the fallout from that, he had signed long-term leases on the heavy equipment. Without the income from those town contracts, he'd be underwater in no time.

Roger had five grand in the safe. He'd get the rest from the bank. He told Billy to turn his back so he could dial the combination.

Then Roger grabbed the only thing he could find within reach—a long-handle shovel—and swung as hard as he could.

The shovel was new and sharp. And Roger was such a big man. Six years of landscaping had renewed all those long-dormant rowing muscles, adding to them if anything. Plus, there was the simple physics of swinging something that long with that much weight at the end of it. It generated a killing force and then some.

The blade connected with the soft part on the side of Billy's head, sinking in above the ear and staying there. He dropped heavily, awkwardly, like all the tension had left his body.

Billy never made a sound. It was Roger who groaned. He hadn't necessarily wanted to kill the kid. He didn't know what he had been trying to accomplish, truth be told. But there was no questioning what he had achieved. In one moment—one angry, unchecked, impetuous impulse—he had undone six years of good work. And all because of Billy Fucking Maundy.

He pulled the shovel out of Billy's head, needing to use his boot to get the proper leverage, and then laid it next to the body. There was no need to call for an ambulance, no point in checking for a pulse. The blood pouring from Billy's head was spreading quickly on the smooth concrete floor. Roger grabbed a canvas tarp, the kind that might be used for hauling away a pile of leaves, and tossed over Billy's upper half. At least that contained the puddle's spread.

And now what? Did Roger turn himself in? Take his cash and run? He didn't know where to start.

But he knew, suddenly and with total conviction, that he

needed a drink. It wasn't the booze he craved. It was the clarity—the way the alcohol had always stripped away all those extraneous thoughts and let him find the core of things. Sober he would stay muddled. Drunk, he could figure a way out of this jam.

So he pulled his keys out of his pocket, locked that front door and stalked toward his truck, trembling and sick and furious all at once. The part of him that was still wired to know where alcohol was at all times had already plotted a course. There was a bar just off the Merritt Parkway that catered to cops, shift workers and other people who worked strange hours. And drunks. It was a total dive, but it was open at pretty much any hour one could legally serve adult beverages in the state of Connecticut.

The thoughts were coming in a jumble now. Today. It had to be today, of all days. His sixth anniversary. He was supposed to receive a coin commemorating his big accomplishment at his AA meeting that night. They made a nice little ceremony out of the awarding of the coin with his sponsor—of all people—presenting it to him. Roger wondered what they'd do with the coin if he showed up shitfaced.

He reached his truck, pulled open the door and climbed in. As he jammed the key in the ignition, his eye caught the small, laminated card he kept dangling from his rearview mirror and it stopped him. Instantly. Even though he knew the words printed on it—knew them as well as he did anything in his life—he read them again: "God grant me the serenity to accept the things I cannot change; courage to change the things I can; and wisdom to know the difference."

He leaned back and read it again, especially the part about changing the things he could. Slowly, he removed the keys from the ignition, opened the door to the truck and started walking toward the backhoe that was sitting dormant behind the warehouse.

He had a hole to dig, something big enough for Billy and his beat-ass car. Then he had some gravel to move. Thirty tons of the stuff would make for a nice tomb.

Chatter
Gary Phillips

"I'm just walking out now. I parked on the street because I spotted an open meter, and since I was running late, it was faster to do that than go into the parking structure. Yeah, uh-huh. It went as good as it could I guess. You know whatshername from the mayor's office? Je-zus, what the fuck crawled up her ass? I've yet to be in a meeting with her on this and see the hint of a smile cross her face. Every fuckin' thing with this woman is like it's down to her and another broad on Survivor Island and she's gonna bite a chunk out of the other chick's throat to be the last ball cruncher standing.

"Huh? You're shitting me. Her and Morrell from the planning department? He's like what, 58, 60? And she's no more than 38, right? What the hell does she get out of doing him? I mean, God bless Cialis, but Morrell is a functionary at best. Yeah? That so? Huh.

"Hey. Shit. No, I'm all right. I was crossing the street and this asshole in an Escalade swooshed right in front of me. Naturally he had tinted windows and blasting some rap number. Probably juiced on his chronic. Ha. Come on, you know me, live and fuckin' let live, but goddamn, what ever happened to simple civility? See this is what I'm talking about in this matter, right? Wait, hold on. No, I just got to my car and fumbled my cell phone getting my keys out and working the latch.

"Anyway, we've got these do-right, moaning and groaning idealistic and unrealistic lefty organizations going on about oh what about the poor, the less fortunate, where are they going to live if the only concern is the bottom line? If you developers just build these upscale complexes without setting aside so many units for the low income...yeah, so their poor unfortunates can hog two spaces parking their Escalades after a hard day of selling dope.

"No, I'm not being racist. But it's true. We could have broken ground on this part of the project by now. We've complied with the Mello Act. We've built in the proper amount of set-asides for low- income units, but no, that's not enough. It's never enough with these people. Christ."

"Look, I know what the fuck I'm doing. The mark ain't on to me. I just wanted to scope him out, make sure I had the right gee, you know how I do. Plus it don't hurt to get the blood up, shit. Get the smell in the air, ya feel me? Hold up, hold up. I'm coming to this light and there's some po-pos. I gotta be cool. Don't want to fuck this up now. Yeah, I'm turning my sounds down. No, I'm straight. Ain't even got a throat lozenge on me let alone any weed. Yeah, I'm at the light. Yeah, naw, uh-huh. They're giving me their cop looks. I know these fools be running my plate.

"Hell naw, it's all good. We been over that, man. I'm going to use stolen plates for the job. Just like we're using burners too so it can't be traced to us. And I'm gonna be creepin' anyway. Ain't no way I'm getting' made. Told you, this is the shit, my nigga. Watching that black and white that night, with you know, the old dude, Colombo, playing Albert Anesthesia. What? Wait, light's changed. Cops be hanging back, letting me go first so they can try and gank me. Stupid motherfuckahs. Like I don't know what they're up to. Come on, you can't play a playah.

"Okay, they followed me for a couple of blocks then turned off. Come on, T, don't be paranoid. We got this tight. We taking that Murder Incorporated thing into the 21st century, dog. Them fools be trippin' using it for the name of a record label to show how hard they are. Shit. When this goes down, we gonna be set. Ain't nobody going to find out who we are. Everything handled by text messaging on throwaways. Man, we geniuses. I know, I know, you're right, don't get all bent. I got that. Yeah, Huh? What? I lost you for a second going under this overpass. Uh-huh, I can hear you now. Right. Right. Homeboy gets taken out of this world tonight on the dot and we make our bank and our rep. Man this is the shit."

"You cannot believe how bored I am. No, really. And the munchables, weak. Sautéed Portobellos, ahi with dill, that's so last year. And oh my God, Wood's speech. Snore time, I'm not shitting you. How the hell did this man make the money he's made, own a basketball team and none of that sophistication rub off on him? Mister one note. Here we are among the movers and shakers, where he has the chance to lay out his vision of downtown redevelopment—what? Yes, I know it's the choir, but that doesn't mean you half-ass the work. He has to inspire, not just reiterate the obvious. A goddamn chimp can do that. You've got to lead, inspire. Especially now when there's this scrutiny.

"Yes, of course I know that. I'm being hyper critical because this is about real consequences. Not only is there multi-millions on the line overall, but there can be a domino effect should any part of it derail. This means so much more than mere physical structures and the anchor businesses we attract for the mixed-use portion. This is about setting the standard for decades to follow. Yes, that's true. Why do you think I'm being so careful?

"Oh, hello, what's this? No, I'd stepped out to the patio and just spotted this bootylicious honey. I think she's cream and coffee if you catch my meaning. Ha, yeah, see, I'm down. Look, I'm going in. Let's synchronize watches 'cause it's poon tang time, brah. Okay, I'll call you later."

"Yeah, he was handsome, but he was way too full of himself. Going on about how he was the man, how he was at the center of this deal to end all deals that was going to revitalize downtown and what have you. Make us the rival of Manhattan we're destined to be. Girl he went on about all this with straight up seriousness. Can you imagine that? Like this project of his was the greatest thing like whenever. Really it's just fancy cracker boxes with a Target and a supermarket thrown in. One more big, ugly thing gobbling up more land till there's no green space whatsoever.

"No, I didn't give him my number, I lied telling him that I didn't currently have a working cell phone—which yes, I'm on right now of course. But I did give him my email and he of course gave me his card, writing his personal e-address on it. He's a VP with Wood's company. Then he gets a call on his cell phone and naturally he just had to take it being so important. You know, being all hushed and whispering into it like it was really vital.

"Huh? No, I didn't see a ring, but it could have been his wife or girlfriend. Then he said he had to run off to a meeting. Girl, don't I know that. What kind of meeting would he be going to at this time of night except a booty call? Shit.

"I don't know, maybe. It would at least be entertaining in a sociological way to go out with him I suppose. But then I'd have to sit through a lot of him talking about himself and me trying not to yawn or looked bored. I tell you though, it's a good thing—oh, sorry, excuse, me. Huh? Yeah, I just bumped into one of the servers from the party while I was stepping outside. He was like rushing off, struggling out of his jacket. Funny, the others are still here, starting to clean up.

"Wow, it's warm tonight. The air smells good after that rain we had this past weekend. So, what I was going to say was it's a good thing he didn't learn I'm temping for Dizaksun. No, I don't think this was some ploy. Girl, please, I surely don't think I'm all that, I'm not getting the swelled head. But yeah, it seemed genuine him coming over to talk to me and not about him getting some kind of inside dope. And if it was, why me? I'm going to be gone when the regular secretary returns once her ankle heals.

"Oh, so now I'm desperate for talking to him. Too late, dammit, you can't take it back. Of course I know Dizaksun is angling for a pretty big stake in this downtown stuff. But I think this guy, ah, Martin, Martin Conrad, was his name, wasn't that smooth or what have you. He wasn't trying to get anything from me other than what any man wants from a woman.

"Uh-huh, uh huh—ah, goodnight Mr. Browne—yeah, he's the one that invited me. Please. Girl your imagination is working overtime. Can I help it you couldn't get a babysitter tonight and couldn't come? I am not working anything. Browne and some of the other senior staff invited several of us.

"Okay, now you're just getting silly. You acting like I'm some kind of Sydney. What? You know, Jennifer whatshername married to Affleck on that show that used to be on, *Alias.* Yeah, like I'm some kind of spy or something. Listen, Mr. Browne is orthodox, understand? Very upright. Been married for eons to the same woman. He's short and he makes it a point to always look up into my face and not at my chest. The three weeks I've been at the firm he's never tried to put a hand on me unlike a couple of others there I could mention. Exactly, Jack Crane is out of control isn't he? I'm surprised he hasn't been slapped with a sexual harassment suit.

"I'm sure glad he wasn't here. Worry about him not this guy Martin. He's okay. Yeah, the more we talk about him the more I might just—ah, here. The valet just went to get my car. Huh, that's something. That server I told you about? He just drove past me going down the hill behind the wheel of one of those nasty SUVs. Nope, not sure what kind it was except it was shiny, black and big. How could he be blinging like that on his salary?

"I don't know. That doesn't sound right. Yeah, I guess this could be a second or third job, but what does that say about his priorities if he's working just to keep up with payments and gas in that thing? No, that's true. I'm going home and crawl under the covers. Might try to watch Tavis, but the Sandman is calling my name. You need to stop. I am hardly going to a motel to meet Mr. Browne for a quickie. You the one that needs it more than me. You realize that, don't you?

"Well, well, you can dish the dish but...oh, shit. I'm so busy yakking with you I damn near put a ding in this Porsche coming up while I drive down the hill from Wood's house. Look, I better let you go and use both hands to get off this narrow pass because I can't afford to have my insurance jump up after paying that kind of bill hitting a fancy car. Okay, right, see you in the morning. Let's try that new place for lunch. 'Night."

"Mom, how can you say that? Yes, I've got you on the head set, cognac on my nightstand and finishing up tweaking the report on my laptop. But I hear every word you're saying. Really. Cute, very cute. Well, let me tell you, when this deal goes down, they will have my picture next to multi-tasking in the dictionary. Yeah, uh-huh. Hold on. Just need to do this last calculation...yeah, this is the shit...sorry, mom, just getting carried away. But it's my passion for this project that's kept it on track despite, ah, never mind.

"What?

"Yes, I know you understand business, Mom. You ran the shop when Dad passed. And who was there each summer and winter break? Look, I'm not trying to be condescending. It's just I shouldn't be talking out of school, understand? No, it's fine, really. *Wall Street Journal* article? When was this? About a week ago? Hmmmm. No, you know that's just those jealous humps at Dizaksun trying to muddy the waters. That's an old trick competitors do to sully the winner. An unnamed source alleges there's accusations of us double-dealing, kickbacks, blah, blah, blah.

"Mom, think about it. I'm the VP of community relations. I'm the one that's smoothed this project through with all the pols hungry for headlines, the tree huggers and the bomb throwers. Bomb throwers? That means the so-called community leaders who stand around, not producing dick...ulp, sorry...and then they howl and moan supposedly in the name of their people when something positive comes along from the Man. But really it's just a way for them to get theirs too.

"No, I don't mean anything illegal. But a consultant fee here, a rec center there that employs some of their cronies. It's just how business is done. So there's nothing to worry about. Everything is fine. There's no investigation. Huh? What about next Tuesday for dinner. Sure, that Italian place. I love you too, Mom."

"Fifteen-Adam-eighty-three,   fifteen-Adam-eighty-three, report shots fired, one-four-nine Ocean Shore Drive, one-four-nine Ocean Shore Drive, Brentwood. Residence of Martin H. Conrad. Thirty-four, male, Cauc, brown hair, brown eyes. Five-eleven. Repeating information."

"What the fuck, dog? Naw, I got there. The side gate was unlocked and the alarm was off like we'd been told. I'm creeping up, Glock ready and shit. I go through the sliding glass door off the pool also like we wuz told and the mark, Conrad, had already been capped. One to the chest and one dead ass center in his forehead. He's still sitting in his bed, spilled glass of something in his limp hand. Motherfuckah never saw it coming. I could tell he had a laptop in there 'cause I saw the connection, but no computer.

"Hell, yeah, that's why I'm out of breath. Think I just watin' around there for Entertainment Tonight to fuckin' show up? I bounced out of there like my baby's mama was chasin' after me for Pampers' money. No, I didn't leave no prints. Like we planned, I wore rubber gloves.

"But straight up, my nigga, they trying to punk us. This is some shit that's for sure. Hey, you hear that? Ain't that a ghetto bird? Man, that's a chopper only I'm straining and I don't see nothin' over me.

"Aw fuck, it's you, dog, they at your crib you hard of hearing, motherfuckah. Run, goddamit, run."

"I don't know how else to tell you this, man. I had car trouble. I don't know why the fuck it stopped running, but it did. I went to that dude, that Conrad's house because that's where my car stopped. And the reason, like I've told you several times before, I was in that area was because I was coming back from this bar called the Shanty up there on Sunset. I know you checked that shit, Sergeant, 'cause I know you. And I can't tell you why nobody remembers me. That place was crowded. So if some nosey desperate housewife spotted my south of La Brea ass in her precious Brentwood neighborhood, that's why.

"And I ran because how crazy was it gonna sound that me, who's done time, for a beef you busted me for I might add, and here it was I just happened to stumble on a croaked bastard. Wait, I know what you're about to say. But I can't explain that gun in my apartment no more than I can explain geometry. That ain't my gun, ain't no prints on it. I know what your lab said, that was the gun that smoked homeboy. But look here, sarge, you been knowin' me since Eazy E cut his first record. The fuck would I be doin' sneaking around Brentwood. I got some kind of OJ fixation going on? I'm not crazy."

"Hi, honey. Yeah, I'm still at the station. I was just replaying the videoed interrogation of the suspect. Huh, I'm laughing because I first encountered this character, Choo-Choo, when I was in uniform and he was this snot-nosed look out for the slangers. Yeah...uh-huh. His real name is Antonio Stevens and I got him for receiving once. Right, and now it looks like I've got him for the Conrad murder, but I don't like the fit.

"Choo-Choo would never be mistaken for a mastermind, but even he's not stupid enough to leave the murder weapon in his crib. From what one of my CIs tell me, it seems Choo-Choo and his running buddy, Twin—huh? No, he's an only child. They call him Twin because he has a habit of always repeating himself. Anyway, it seems they were setting themselves up as hired killers.

"I know, pursuit of the American Dream. So these two numb chunks set out on this new venture, right? But you just can't advertise something like that on the radio. And they want high-end customers who can pay some real money. No rooty-poot shit for them, no sir. So, how do they get the word out. Guess. You'll never guess.

"They go to Pilates and yoga classes, trendy bars and what

have you in Beverly Hills and the Westside and leave cards on people's windshields. I'm serious. I've got a few as evidence. Check this out. It says, 'Got a serious problem? One that the normal methods can't fix? Need a permanent solution? Call and leave a text message at,' and they leave a number which leads to a disposable cell phone, a burner they're called.

"Actually, yes, that was kind of clever. Something like that old show, the *Equalizer*, right? Only it's reverse. Sweetheart, I'm not making this up. Twin's saving grace is his computer skills so he's like Mister Nerve Center in all this. And you've got to ask yourself, what moron would actually get in touch with someone who left this kind of notice?

"You know the more we talk about this, the more it might be that Choo-Choo would leave the incriminating weapon in his place. The Beretta was wiped clean and, except for that and what I got from the streets, that's all I have on him. A uniform found a bowtie and jacket like a waiter would wear in a trashcan a couple of blocks from Conrad's house. And the jacket is Choo-Choo's size, but what does that mean? A disguise of some kind?

"Conrad's alarm had been shorted and the lock on his gate had been jimmied. I guess, could be that Twin helped his boy do all that, but it just don't fit, honey. There's none of that kind of equipment at Twin's apartment or Choo-Choo's.

"Now you've got me believing what that chump said was true, he was set up. Oh I agree. He needs to be locked up. But more and more I'm feeling there's someone else behind all this. I mean, it's not that hard putting two clowns who would leave post cards advertising that they are killers-for-hire into a frame.

"Alright, I'm taking one more run at Mr. Twin who's so terrified he's given up Choo-Choo, Michael Jackson and Robert Blake. Want me to bring anything home? Sure. Okay, see you in about an hour, baby doll. Don't worry about that, I'm not that tired. Don't you know doing this detecting work the blood up? Yes, it does..."

* * *

"That's correct, it's me. I know what hour it is and I know it's your home. I dialed it, didn't I? Before you continue ranting, know that your clutch player, shall we say, has been checked. I find it insulting you didn't think I wouldn't make him. Driving that Porsche, shadowing me from the party. Like I'm going to get played like those two delusional homeboys I set up. When I came down the hill he tried to be clever, turning around and going the opposite way to make it seem he was just some westsider returning home.

"Don't cut me off when I'm talking, Mr. Wood, that's impolite. And you already have a price to pay for challenging me. Don't pretend to protest, you're not good at playing naïve, Mr. Wood. You now owe me double what we agreed to since you tried to break your contract with me, sir.

"What? I'm chuckling because you still insist on this bluster as if I'm one of thousands of ubiquitous real estate brokers or developers or what have you seeking your largess. We both know that you will gladly and promptly arrange to have the proper amount of cash, in non-sequential bills, ready to be delivered to me. In fact, *you* will deliver my funds. If you don't, that daughter of yours at that college on Long Island might trip down the steps and crack her skull open one sunny day on her way to biology.

"You see just as you have so arrogantly proclaimed on TV and magazines of doing your due diligence, I make it a priority to thoroughly know about my clients. Yes, well, now we're getting to an understanding, you and I. Very good, I knew you were a fast learner. Oh no, it will not be the place or time we previously discussed. Sad to say, I simply don't trust you. Get the cash together and you will hear from me where to make the drop, precise time and what have you."

"Our top story on Action News is that police are looking into the violent death of Douglas Wood, a key figure in a billion-dollar plus downtown redevelopment boom. It's been reported that strangely he was out walking underneath the Santa Monica pier after midnight. Why he was there, and at that hour, is part of the ongoing investigation. Action News is following a lead that there may be a witness. A marine just returned from Iraq had been out celebrating with his friends and reportedly was sleeping if off beneath the pier when he may have witnessed some sort of altercation with Wood and as of yet unidentified woman.

"And in what may be a related incident, the murder of Martin Conrad two days ago, a man who worked at Douglas Wood's company, is also under investigation. Action News is following up a report that the Securities and Exchange Commission had approached Conrad about possible irregularities in some of Wood's dealings. Particularly as it relates to monies involved in the Massive downtown redevelopment.

"But this is unconfirmed as of this broadcast and we will of course keep our viewers informed as we learn more."

Chemotherapy
A Greywalker Story
Kat Richardson

My would-be client started off by standing in the door, his face and front sticking out of its surface like a mortuary bas-relief. His puff of white hair looked like laundry lint arrested in its earthward-drift by something sticky on the door's inside panel. He wasn't quite looking at me. In fact, he was dead, which made getting information out of him a bit tricky.

I knew I didn't want the case—whatever it was—but it's often easier to say "yes" to the dead and inhuman than to say "no." They can make persistent pests of themselves, turning up at odd times, knocking on the walls and being general pains in my backside if I refuse. I'm the only PI in Seattle—possibly the only one anywhere—who can operate in their world as well as the normal one and they all seem to know it.

"They killed me. They killed me." His voice quavered with distress and indignation.

I nodded. "Okay. I get that. Why don't you take a seat, give me some details and I'll see what I can do for you?" I asked, but he just continued on the same complaint.

I rolled my eyes in disgust: a repeater. Ghosts come in a lot of varieties, from the ephemeral wisps and harmless unexplained cold spots in the hall, to revenants—conscious and alive in all but body. Repeaters have limited consciousness, looping through thoughts or events left over from their lives again and again. They're difficult clients; not very helpful if I can't knock them off their loop and they never pay.

I tried another tack. "Who are you?" I demanded. "What's

your name? Who killed you?" Questing ghosts usually respond to offers of help or requests for information, but not this one; he just kept blithering.

I heaved a sigh and got up to lock the door. I'd have to conduct this interview in the Grey if I were to get anything useful out of him and I'd need assured privacy to do that.

The Grey—the slippery overlap between the normal and the paranormal realms—is difficult and exhausting to work in for a naturalized citizen like me, though it's native country for ghosts and such. I didn't want anyone walking into the office while I was busy in it. My first Grey client said I "flicker." I don't know if that's the way anyone else sees it, but I don't want to freak out my normal clients if it's true.

I had to stick my hand into the ghost's left arm to reach the lock. A shock of cold electricity ripped up my forearm and plucked a profound chord on my ribs. I stifled the urge to gag and flicked the latch over, pulling my hand back as fast as I could. Greywalking had gotten easier with time, but it had never gotten much more pleasant.

The ghost jerked and stared down at his arm where I'd intersected it. Then the moment of volition ended and his gaze de-focused again.

I rubbed my now-aching elbow a moment, then took a deep breath and let go of my usual hold on the normal world.

The cold, unraveling feeling always starts in my chest, now. When all this began, there was a curtain between me and the Grey and I'd have to go through it. Now I have to filter it to keep it in check. Dropping that filter lets the Grey well up around me, but the feeling of the change starts in the knot of Grey-stuff that had been rammed into my chest way back at the beginning.

The Grey power grid snapped into view; bright, hot lines limning the world in neon. That was the easy part. The ghost in front of me was just a hazy mess afloat in a blazing wire-frame world. I'd forgotten to filter it to his level. I concentrated on it and the world became an overlap of misty images on images—time and place stacked on each other like overlapping film projections. Noisy with whisperings and clangings nothing to do with what was seen. And cold that stunk, suddenly, of disinfectant over persistent mold and old death.

I found myself face-to-face with a black man in his late sixties or so. He was very well-dressed in a suit he'd probably bought at Nordstrom and worn often to some office job—his residual concept of himself, complete with a memory of aftershave. He was a little stooped at the shoulder, but was still a tall guy.

"Hi," I started. "You wanted to see me?"

He blinked at me and looked me over as if I were the ethereal one. "They killed me..."

"So you said. How 'bout you come all the way in and sit down and you can tell me why I should give a damn?"

He didn't move. "You're certainly rude enough for the job, young woman."

At least he'd gotten off his loop though the tenor of the comment could have been nicer. I took half a step back before trudging across the misty floor to sit down in the gleaming shape of my desk chair. "I'm the only game in town, Mister. So, get to it or go away and leave me alone."

In the Grey overlap of the room's past and present, there were a couple of extra ghost chairs and desks standing around, some sticking out of the living fog of the walls. Most had been gone so long that only the memory of their shape remained. My potential client finally came in and seated himself in one of the missing chairs—a Scandinavian shadow from some late-80s incarnation of my office space. But then he stopped. At this rate, it was a miracle he'd gotten to me at all. I had to lean over the desk and poke him—literally—to get his attention again.

"They killed me..."

"Yes," I said. "Okay. What's your name?"

"Francis de Fayette Parker."

"And you believe you were murdered?"

"My family killed me like a dog in the pound."

I frowned. I can't count on ghosts to tell the truth or even to know what it is. Death does not impart wisdom. Or common sense. "Who in particular? Which of your dearly beloved did the dirty deed?"

"They killed me."

I gave in to the urge to sigh. "And what do you expect me to do about it?"

"Stop it!"

I leaned forward and braced my arms on the unseen surface of my desk. I was tired already. "Bit late, Mr. Parker: you're dead."

He glared through me. "They killed me! They killed me! Stop it!"

Damn, damn, damn. Looping again. The temptation was to hit him, but it's not so easy to smack someone who's only sort of there. I get lucky, sometimes, but it's not a sure thing and it's not pleasant for me to touch them. The dead press into me as much as I into them. It's a bit stomach-wrenching to be plunged into whatever emotions and physical turmoil they're still carrying around. Not to mention they're dead.

I'm not and I have that unfortunate level of sanity that abhors attempting to be both at once. This would not be inconvenient if every conscious dead and undead thing west of the Cascades didn't drift in and play hob with my life whenever the fancy took them. Plenty of not-so-conscious ones have a go, too.

I watched Francis Parker chant for a moment. As a ghost, he was a wreck. Short trigger radius. Short loop. He seemed to have retained his intelligence though, but only some on-again-off-again willpower. It had to be hell being him. Like a paralysis victim who could only blink, but was fine mentally.

That, I suppose, decided me.

"Parker!" I yelled at him. "Frank!"

He went on.

I braced myself and snatched at his wrist.

It felt as if he'd punched me in the gut. He flooded into me on a rip curl of chill, sucking my breath out and cracking me open. Gasping, airless, burning from the inside, ice-sheeted skin, crumble-boned in toxin-wracked flesh.

His eyes flared into incandescence and glared into me, breaking the loop. My body resonated with his voice.

Poison!

It burned into us, through the age and the illness and the

exhaustion...

I tore myself loose with the sensation of leaving skin behind on a hot stove. I swallowed convulsively and caught my breath, kept my distance.

Parker stared at me, his eyes as bright and alive as if he still wore flesh. And then the dulling started.

I couldn't let him go just yet. "When did you die?" I demanded. "I'll find out what happened, but give me a place to start."

"Feb'wa..." The left corner of his mouth turned up as he slipped into a seam in the mist.

I ripped my way out of the Grey and slumped at my desk, shivering and uneasy. There was something more than usually strange about Francis Parker.

Once I'd put myself back together, I headed up the hill to the County Records Office to dig up Parker's death certificate. I started in the current year, but finally found him in February about two years earlier. He'd died of complications related to cancer and his chemotherapy. He'd been seventy-two. This didn't look like a murder, but the corpse was convinced. Maybe he'd believed his pain pills or chemo were meant to kill him. I'd have to poke around a bit more if I was going to get him off my back. I wrote down some details to follow up, then made a phone call.

Detective Solis answered his own phone. He always says his name with the emphasis on the second syllable: "sol-EES." It strikes me as oddly appropriate, since "solace" doesn't seem like his gig.

"Hey, it's Harper Blaine. Can you answer a question for me?"

"Ask the question." The noises below his Columbian accent sounded like the Criminal Investigations office in the black-glass Justice Center a few blocks away. I imagined he was hunching the phone into his shoulder as he transcribed from one of his scribbled notepads, a frown creasing his round, pock-marked face.

"First, was there ever any kind of homicide investigation into the death of a man named Francis de Fayette Parker in February about two years ago?"

He paused before replying, "None I see here."

"And what would be required to open one?"

"On a two-year-old non-suspicious death? Evidence. Strong evidence. Maybe a confession, medical report, some physical evidence. Otherwise, we got enough to do here."

"What about an autopsy?"

"You have a suspicious report?"

"Nope. Death was while under doctor's care. No autopsy."

"Then you need an exhumation—if you got a body. If you got ashes, you're probably out of luck. But you need evidence to convince the M.E. to issue the exhumation order."

"That's nicely circular."

"Typical. But nine times outta ten on a cold homicide the perpetrator confesses as soon as we show the badge. Most people, they can't live with the guilt. You get a confession, you can get an exhumation to confirm it."

So I'd be working backward. I'd have to solve the case to prove that there was one. Or not. I did not bless Frank Parker for bringing his death to me.

Seattle has a reputation for cancer treatment, but there are still only a handful of hospitals doing long-term care. The doctor's name was on the death certificate, so it didn't take long to find out where he was working and make an appointment to see him. Parker's physician didn't remember him, particularly. He was in a hurry and aside from confirming the cause of death, he had nothing to say and refused to give me a copy of the medical record.

The long-term care ward Frank Parker had died in was just down the hall from his office and I discreetly headed that way. I had to steel myself against the brush of ghosts and streamers of emotional residue that hung the walls like rotting drapes. The area hummed with fear, pain and despair amid that strange odor of hospitals: chilled flowers, bland food and cleaning fluid.

I hunted around, just shy of making a pest of myself and being run off, until I found a nurse who'd been on the long-term oncology care ward when Parker was a patient. She also didn't remember him, but she was more willing to talk and to look into the files. She wasn't any less tired or harried than the doctor, so I suspected she was using me as an excuse to sit down for a little while. She paid no attention to the swirling fog of switched-off lives that flowed through the room as if it were a cul-de-sac in the stream of the afterlife.

"Looks like... two sons and a daughter-in-law came around a few times," she said, her aura a thin smog of exhaustion around her. She looked up from the file, creasing her face with thought, then smiled, a momentary blush passing through the dull color of her energy corona. "Oh, yeah... the couple had a toddler with them once or twice. Rambunctious little thing. Sad way to see grandpa though. Hmm. There's a note in here about one of the sons carrying in a gun once. We asked him not to come back, but we didn't enforce it."

"A gun?" I asked. "Why?"

She shrugged. "Who knows? Probably just a punk acting tough."

"Did anyone else visit Parker, volunteers, friends from church?"

The transitory color around her died. "No. We do have a few volunteers, but they don't come down here if they can avoid it. They call this Death Row, y'know. Every patient here's gonna leave in a bag. It's kinda depressing for the kids, so they bring us coffee and drop things off, but they find excuses to leave real fast. The older volunteers are better, but even they don't linger."

That was sad, but it didn't help me figure out what was driving Frank Parker out of his grave. "Were any of the family here when Parker died?" I inquired.

"Looks like they all were," she said. That didn't make it any easier for me, since it didn't narrow the field of suspects.

I tried a different approach. Maybe motive would be more enlightening. "What was Parker like; was he an easy patient?"

"I really don't remember," the nurse replied, shaking her head in an off-hand manner, little green spikes of dishonesty dashing away from her into the darkness that crept at the corners of the room. "This file indicates we had him on a morphine drip, so he must have been in pain most of the time.

Bad reactions to the chemo—the usual thing: nausea, pain, rash, vomiting, headaches, hair loss. He got a bit of a fever a few times, was too weak to move himself, needed a lot of help. The family seems to have pitched in a lot."

"Could his symptoms have been poisoning?"

She looked bemused. "Well sure. That's what chemotherapy is—calibrated doses of potentially toxic substances to kill off the cancer, but not enough to kill off too many healthy cells. All drugs are potential poisons and a lot of the drugs we use are heavy metals in the same broad family as arsenic and so on. Toxicity is all about the dosage. Chemo is low-dose. Poison is high-dose. But Parker must have been pretty bad or we wouldn't have given him the morphine. It does nothing but reduce the pain, so once we've got 'em on morphine, we're just waiting it out."

She made a face that hardened into a shell of professional distance, her aura going darker and colder before she went on, "Let's be real: this is the bargain basement of oncology. We're not going to work any miracles in a county hospital with no research funds and patients who are at the end of their insurance money. We do our best, but everyone knows this is the last stop and if we let every patient into our hearts, we'll go crazy. We can't let ourselves love them or become angels to the family. Some nurses do weird things when they think they'll be loved for this. The family can be just as bad. We can't let that happen, for all our sakes. It's bad enough knowing that some of these guys could go just a little easier, but we don't have the legal option to let patients opt out of life. If you think that makes me cruel... well we're the cruelest bunch of stone-hearted monsters you're ever going to meet."

She shoved the file back into a drawer as she colored under a sudden red flush of impotent anger, slammed it closed and stood up. "I have to get back to work."

"Just one more question," I said. "Do your patients ever... get a little help out of here from their families or friends?"

Her eyes narrowed to wary slits, colors flickering in her energy corona like suspicious satellites reflecting distant suns. "I wouldn't know."

"Afraid of cracking that stone heart of yours?"

With a snort, she turned her shoulder to me and began stalking down the hall, the colors around her form bleeding to the hue of a dark green sea. "I bleed gravel."

I shook my own head and left the hospital. I already knew about Parker's family from the death certificate and obit files: two sons, a daughter-in-law, a grandchild. If he'd been poisoned, it would have to have been one of them. The grandchild was out, being a mere toddler at the time and not likely to have slipped something clever into grandad's medication cup. I'd have to talk to the sons.

I put in another call to Solis. My mysterious leads had paid off for him in the past, so he reluctantly agreed to meet me at the address I provided. But he didn't like it and he said he'd be late. That was fine with me.

I used my cell phone to call ahead. Daniel Parker, Frank Parker's younger son, was just as reluctant to talk to me as the doctor, but he agreed, since I was nearly on his doorstep. He let me in when I arrived.

Daniel was about thirty and had the trim, quick wariness of a feral cat and a dark, old scar down the length of his left temple and cheek. He had a curious yellow-orange light around him as he ushered me in with a finger to his lips. "Tanika just fell asleep. Today's been rough, so can we keep this quick and quiet?" I guessed the color of his aura was anxiety over something that wasn't just me.

"Sure," I said, following him into a tiny home office lined with heavy tomes and stacks of discarded bar-review guides, files and scribbled yellow pads. "Is Tanika your daughter?"

"Niece," he said over his shoulder as he closed the door behind us. He took a seat near me. "She's been sick a while. Been a rough couple years for all of us, y'know, with dad and all. And what did you want to ask me about him anyway?"

"I wanted to ask you about what happened at the hospital."

He closed his eyes and shook his head. "Man, that was two years ago. Who'd make a big deal out of that now?"

I just kept my mouth shut and my eyes level on his face.

He dropped his gaze and rubbed one finger nervously over his scar. "Look, I was stupid, I ran with the wrong guys when

I was a kid. It was hard to get out. But some of those guys... they don't let go easy and they kept showing up. The gun— that was the only way I thought I could be safe then. I wasn't gonna shoot him. I just wanted to be left alone. If it came up now, I could be disbarred. But it was nothing. Nothing happened. Why ruin me over that?"

A thin scraping sound moved down the corridor outside.

"You didn't poison your father, then."

He jerked and stared at me. "What?! No! Dad died of cancer!" His professional demeanor and careful speech slipped back to his gangsta days. "Why you think anybody'd kill him? He was dyin' already!"

"There's a reason they call it 'mercy killing,' Mr. Parker."

He stared around the room as if trying to find an answer in the dim, book-filled corners of the tiny office. "God... they couldn't..." Something thumped into the door. Daniel's eyes widened and the muscles in his jaw bunched, making the scar writhe. He jumped to his feet. "The little mother—."

He yanked the door open and nearly stepped on the tiny child who tumbled into the room. He stooped and scooped her into his arms. She shivered and made a gagging sound against his chest.

She was the smallest five-year-old I'd ever seen and to my senses she flickered in and out of the Grey with the sighing of wind over dry grass, the flickering of someone who was dying. Skinny, with mahogany skin patched with rashes like ash smears and wispy dark hair that grew unevenly on her head. Something about her symptoms seemed horribly familiar.

Daniel Parker cuddled her close, in spite of the reek of vomit that clung to the child. "Baby, baby. How y'doin', girl?" he crooned to her, still kneeling on the rug, rocking, with his whole body wrapped around her.

I felt the pieces click together. "When did she get sick?" I asked.

"Year, year-and-a-half," he mumbled back. A couple of miserable tears squeezed from the corners of his eyes before he could bear to look at me again.

He started to say more, but a woman ran into the hall and

saw us. I guessed this was Janeece Parker, Daniel's sister-in-law. She was too thin, but beautiful in it, burning with an unpleasant inner glow that shone through from the Grey like shipwreck lights through Welsh fog, sending hungry green tendrils seeking in all directions. She stopped a moment, then darted forward, holding out her arms.

"Give her to me, Daniel." Command resonated in her voice and she gleamed brighter with unnatural avarice and twisted love. Her horrific aura thrummed and sent toxic creepers over Tanika, stroking and tightening with possessive pride. The sight made me ill.

Daniel's jaw bunched again and he started a retort, cut off by the doorbell.

I looked Frank Parker's daughter-in-law in the eye, almost feeling his presence against my back, like a bad spy. "That's probably the police. Answer the door. We'll take care of Tanika." No way I'd let her near the girl again; the ugly green threads of psychic avarice and sickness that tied her to the child told me she was responsible for Tanika's condition. I just needed some proof, which might be found in Frank Parker's remains.

Janeece flared her nostrils and glared at me, but she turned and went to the door to let Solis in. Daniel and I followed her into the living room.

Janeece jabbed an accusatory finger my direction. "That woman broke into our house! She's trying to steal my baby!"

Solis turned his impassive face to me. He looked at Daniel and Tanika. Then back at me.

"I believe she's been poisoning this child for more than a year," I explained. "My guess would be arsenic or another heavy metal." The rash and hair loss, the perverse pleasure her mother took in the girl's wasting illness, had all clicked into place with what the nurse had said and I knew what must have happened. I glanced at Daniel and lifted my eyebrow. Should I go on...? He gave a grim nod over Tanika's bowed head. "My guess is she poisoned her father-in-law, Francis de Fayette Parker, also. Exhumation should prove the link."

"What are you saying?"

We all looked around at the new player standing in the

open front doorway, clutching an attaché case. In thirty years, he'd be a dead ringer for his father.

"You're Frank Parker, Junior?" I asked.

"Yes. What's going on here?"

Solis fell back and to the side where he could see us all. He offered his ID to the newcomer. "Detective Solis, Seattle P.D. Homicide. I'm sorry. I'm here to arrest your wife for poisoning your daughter and your father."

Frank, Jr. stared at Solis in horror, then looked at his wife. "Dad wanted to go. But... not our little girl... Janeece? Why—?"

Daniel lost it. "You killed Dad?" he shouted. Still holding Tanika, he started toward his older brother, his scar dancing as hard feelings flickered across his face.

I could hear Solis muttering into his handheld for back-up.

I tapped Daniel on the shoulder. "Don't. You're all she's got."

He stopped moving, but quivered where he stood, clutching Tanika to his chest and staring at his brother and sister-in-law.

Four of Seattle's finest arrived a few minutes later and broke the party up, arresting both Frank and Janeece Parker. Family Services would come later for Tanika, but for now, she was still in her uncle's arms and, I thought, safe.

Solis just looked at me and shook his head as I slipped out in the press and confusion of cops.

I found my client lurking by the door. He wafted behind me for a block, then stopped. I opened my cell phone and pretended to make a call.

"They killed you because you asked them to, didn't they? 'Like a dog in the pound,' you said. An old, sick dog that any decent human being would put out of his misery. But the law says you can't do the same for a man."

"Frank is a good boy. Always does as he's told," he replied.

"And Janeece?"

"Janeece used to bring me custard every day—my favorite."

The oblique replies annoyed me, but there wasn't much I

could do. As a repeater, Parker's communication was limited, but he made do, just has he had in my office.

"You gave them up to save your granddaughter. But you know it's your fault, don't you? Janeece was a martyr to your illness—even while she killed you—and I'll bet she liked being admired for her apparent selflessness. The nurse on your ward warned me about that. Once you were gone, Janeece just replaced you with Tanika."

Parker looked past me. "She's the shining star of my life, that child."

"Yeah. Well. There's still a long road ahead for her and Daniel. You could have moved a little sooner, you rotten old corpse."

He finally looked right at me and I wished he hadn't. He grabbed my elbow, his phantom fingers sinking into my bones with a jolt of energy. I felt time reel and stumble. I wrenched myself away and looked at my phone. Six minutes had vanished in an instant. "Okay. Point taken. Are you satisfied? I stopped Janeece from killing Tanika the way she did you. When you said 'stop them' that's what you meant, isn't it? That's what you asked for. Are we done, now?"

The left corner of his mouth lifted into a smile, then he flashed into brilliance and faded away.

I would have to content myself with the thought that a young life was probably saved. The gods knew there was little else to prize in that situation. I rubbed my eyes and closed the phone.

The End is Never Pretty
Greg Rucka

Nessuno meets Barrett her first week in Monterey, her first class at the Defense Language Institute. He's half an inch taller and lean, wearing those half-frame wire-rims that try so hard to be fashionable, black hair and blue eyes. She pegs him for an analyst. They're in the Russian Refresher together, an intensive four hours every day with an instructor who is positively fascist about hitting the accent *right*. She learns his name through the roll, but that's all; the rote memorization is daunting, two hundred new words every week that don't leave time for much more than homework and headaches.

A month and a half later, now with Russia behind her, Nessuno switches to Uzbek. Barrett is there again. It's a much smaller class, the coursework moderately lighter. It's not until that first three-hour blast is over that they actually find themselves at the same coffee shop on Alvarado Street. She's drinking a double espresso, the sugar cube dissolving between her teeth, flash cards flicking past on her laptop monitor. She looks up to see him standing opposite her, the other side of the little table.

"My brain already hurts," he says and he grins.

"It'll get worse," Nessuno says.

"Brian Barrett." He offers a hand.

"Like the rifle." His grip is good, fingers long. "Petra Nessuno."

"Need a study partner, Petra Nessuno?"

Without hesitation, she says, "God yes, please."

***

Heath taught that there was no such thing as cover, which was to say that cover was the only truth that mattered. You cannot pretend to be the person you need to be to do what must be done, Heath would say. You are that person. The instant you doubt that, they'll smoke you out and tear you up. The instant you allow yourself to think that you are in any way lying, that is the moment the person you are doing it to will realize something is wrong. Maybe they won't know what; and maybe they won't know why; but they will feel that sense of off, the hairs rising on the back of their neck, hear that voice in the back of their mind begin to whisper and question, and that is the beginning of the end.

"And the end is never pretty. And it's always worse for women," Heath concluded.

Heath liked her "ands," used them with Peter Falk-ish enthusiasm, inevitably adding just one more thing. Petra imagined diagramming her lectures onto rolls of butcher paper that spilled out like an infinite hallway runner.

Heath handed her the files to prove the point. Some had photos. She was right.

It wasn't pretty.

Barrett, it turns out, isn't an analyst at all but a Special Agent for the FBI.

They never talk about why they need these languages they're studying so intently or how they'll use them. Nessuno guesses he's got to be on the CIS Organized Crime Taskforce, that Barrett targets those Eastern European bandits who literally sell anything and anyone they can get their hands on if there's a profit to be found in it. Maybe tasked to the nuke-hunters, the ones chasing fissionable material around the world. She approves of that, thinking that their operational theaters overlap, at least incidentally.

When they do trade war stories it's always in the past tense, the details omitted to protect the guilty. The time she was on a Cultural Support Team attached to an operator detachment and one of the black-clad women lead her into a hut with a half-dozen toddlers playing amidst the mix-and-match materiel of an IED factory. The time he was in a foot-race with a suspect in West Hollywood and got an unasked-for assist from the guy dressed as Superman outside of Grauman's Chinese Theatre. They share the personal details in brief: he's from Nebraska, mother still teaching primary school, father dead from cancer before he graduated college; she's born in Philly, but moved to Chicago when she was seven and her parents still run a restaurant at Six Corners. He's got three years on her, thirty, never married, no kids and when he asks her, she can answer the same, only younger.

First kiss is on Fisherman's Wharf. It's a Friday evening and early summer and cool on the water and the sea lions are a raucous audience, barking and snorting and snotting amidst the pylons below. It's a good one, the one they've both been waiting for and it leads to more, the curve running from tentative to passion steep and quick.

"Who knew language intensive could lead to this?" Barrett says when they break to catch their breath.

"It's all about mastering a new tongue," Nessuno tells him.

She takes his hand and leads him back to her apartment. They're indoors until Saturday night before finally venturing out for dinner and a stop by his place for a change of clothes. Then they're back to hers for more of the same, the sex touched with both urgency and the sense of the forbidden. It's not strictly an affair; neither is betraying another's trust. Rather, there's a peculiar sense of dalliance between two services, two different parts of the same world that could only happen here and now. When the time comes, they will each say goodbye and return to their duty. Each understands this without ever needing to say so aloud. What they have is for the moment alone and the knowledge of this inevitable end brings a melancholia that makes it all the better, makes them savor and relish one another all the more.

"This could be distracting," Barrett says Sunday afternoon.

"I should fucking well hope so."

He laughs. "Talk dirty to me in Uzbek."

She does.

* * *

It takes two months of placement post the additional briefing and training, by which time she's been Elisabetta Villanova long enough for her dreams to become Petra Nessuno's own. CWO-2 Petra Nessuno is ephemeral, ghostly, a manifestation that arises only when needs must, at dead-drops and brush-passes and counter-surveillance; emerging only long enough to make contact, to pass and receive intel before turning to vapor once again. It is not that Petra Nessuno is forgotten, not at all; she is ever-present, a mute observer who only breaks her silence to whisper orders, opinions and advice in Elisabetta Villanova's ear.

Initial target for entry is a man named Carlo Pallazzini, the meeting in Dubai, at Nad Al Sheba, the sheiks and the jockeys and their camels, a distracting amount of wealth on display. They've picked the same winner by coincidence. He likes what he sees enough to buy a celebratory bottle of Champagne to share. He is in "business." She's in "art." They exchange cards and a few very carefully-worded questions and then leave it at that.

Eleven days later, he runs into her—or believes he does—at a private party at the Galleria Borghese in Rome. They discuss their shared appreciation of Caravaggio. She knows it already, but when he tells her he collects, she's pleasantly surprised. He asks if Rome is home and she laughs and tells him only sometimes. He asks how long she's staying and she says until the day after tomorrow, at which point he asks to buy her dinner. They meet the next night at the Fortunato al Pantheon. He insists on paying.

She lets him kiss her good night and they exchange private numbers.

Sex, Heath said.

You have my complete attention, Nessuno said.

Are you queasy about killing the enemy? Heath asked.

No more than I should be.

Are you queasy about sleeping with the target?

She started to say no, was about to say no, but Heath didn't let her.

Get your head straight on that, Heath said. Your mission is to kill the enemy, you use a gun, you use a knife, you use a fucking stick if you have to or your bare damn hands and you don't hesitate. Your mission is to get close to your target, to learn what he or she knows and getting you on your back will help that, how is that different? How is that different than a stick or a knife or a gun? If you cannot get straight on that, if you're going to go all squeamish about spreading your legs if and when the time comes, there's the door, Chief.

Nessuno didn't move.

Heath paused, then sat down opposite. Spread her palms, raised her arms in a shrug before dropping them again.

Fucked up Puritan ancestry, that's what it is, Heath said. People want to muddy it up, but it's the same dispensation. You are your cover, there is no difference and that means your body is your cover, too. I'm not saying give it up first chance you get, because the promise is always better than the reality—or almost always at any rate—and hope and desire will keep them coming back for more. Up to a point and you know that, too. And yes, I am saying there are some out there who have no problem with you fucking killing a man, but they have a huge problem with you killing a man you're fucking.

And they're wrong. They'll get uncomfortable with it and maybe they'll call you a whore and you'll have to deal with that, too.

Nessuno grinned, trying to escape Heath's sudden intensity. Joking, asks, and you're going to teach me how to fuck like a pro, ma'am?

Let's just say that Elisabetta definitely knows what to do under the covers, Heath answered.

It never comes to that with Pallazzini. The promise is more than enough to keep him coming back another three times over the next six weeks.

Then he calls and asks when she'll next be in Moscow. She tells him what she's sure he already knows, what he's already learned from his own investigations into her. Her background and her finances and her relationships, all of them carefully constructed, monitored and maintained. Yes, she'll be in Moscow on Tuesday, as a matter of fact. He sets a meeting at the Baltschug Kempinski.

"Are you getting a room?" she asks.

"Business before pleasure," he says.

They meet in the Cafe Kranzler, off the lobby, Tuesday late in the afternoon. He's ordered caviar and Champagne and their conversation is in Italian.

"So, I have a problem," Pallazzini says. "A friend of mine, he's come into ownership of a piece and he wants to sell it, you know. These rich Russians, they buy up everything they can, don't know what to do with it, don't know what it's worth. This piece, he's looking for a private sale. I told him you could help him."

She turns her glass of Champagne between her fingers, smiles slightly. "Private."

"Yes. And I need to know, before I introduce you, is this something you can do? Is this something you can arrange?"

"It would depend on the piece." She hesitates, lets her smile show a little more. She knows what he's really asking. Is she willing to stray off the straight and narrow? Bend the law? Perhaps even break it? "And my commission."

"How much is the commission?"

"For something like this? I would want thirty percent, perhaps more. It would depend on the piece."

"We split the commission."

"We do? How very generous of you, Carlo."

"My finder's fee."

She shakes her head. "But I'll be doing all the work. That doesn't seem quite fair to me."

"You'll be doing no work at all if you don't get the introduction."

She shakes her head.

He takes a moment, butters his toast, eats his caviar, washes it down. Leans forward with a smile of his own, taking her hands in his. But there's no smile in his words.

"You think I don't know about you, Elisabetta?" His thumbs stroke the backs of her hands idly as he speaks, but she can feel his grip tighten. "You think I didn't look into you before bringing you this? You're not a virgin. I know what you make and I know what you're spending. I even know how much you're hurting right now. So you will ask for thirty percent and you will settle for twenty-five and that is what we will split."

He's looking into her eyes and she thinks to tell him that she knows all about him, as well. That she knows just how much he owes and to whom. That she knows about the weapons that have vanished from NATO stockpiles throughout Afghanistan, that she knows about the ones that most recently were stolen from Kunduz Airfield in the north. The ones that he tried to sell last week, but couldn't because someone had tipped the authorities off and the shipment was seized.

She looks at his hands holding hers. She smiles again, and says, "Well, when you put it like that."

It's a Molenaer, *The Cheaters*, stolen from the Netherlands last year and the man who reveals it to her says, in Russian, "The seller assured me its provenance was true and legally acquired. He even had the paperwork to assure the claim. You can imagine my surprise then, at learning it had been stolen and that I had been duped."

"I can, indeed," she murmurs, her attention entirely on the canvas that has been unrolled on the table between them. She bends to give the painting a closer examination, takes the small glass she carries from her purse, looking harder, checking the brushwork and the edges, even though she's already certain it's real. Government work brings government training and after DLI and Monterey there was art history, taught to her by a professor from Harvard, who despite himself was thrilled to be involved in something secret. She knows it's the real thing, but she takes her time so this Russian and his two off-the-shelf bodyguards, and even Pallazzini, can stare at her in this position, rather than at the painting. Pallazzini and the bodyguards do, but the other man does not, she notes.

Satisfied, she straightens, replaces the glass, says in Russian, "I would think it's authentic. You can assure yourself that the only lie you were told was about its origins."

"That matters to me," the man says. "I would not care to be betrayed a second time."

"It's in excellent condition. You could certainly have it returned, either through yourself or an intermediary, without much difficulty. I would be happy to help."

"Ah." His eyes do not leave her, gauging her. "That is not an option. I spent a lot of money buying the piece and even a finder's fee would not compensate for the loss. What I would much rather do is sell it, you see."

"There are men who would pay handsomely to own it," she agrees.

"That was my thinking. Carlo's, as well, I might add. Which is why I was so eager to meet you, Signora Villanova."

She smiles. The man is tall, slender, his hair long and straight, to his shoulders or just beneath. She puts him in his mid-thirties, the wire-rim glasses he's wearing along with the long hair giving him the appearance of a man perhaps younger than that. The suit is muted, but expensive and still he is watching her, appraising her the same way she appeared to appraise the Molenaer.

"This kind of piece can be difficult to sell," she says slowly. "You want the right buyer, of course, but also someone who can arrange things with the appropriate discretion. The piece is on INTERPOL's watch list, after all. Avoiding legal... let's call it 'confusion,' yes? That will require patience."

"That would be crucial."

"Anyone who arranged the sale would therefore expect appropriate compensation."

"I was thinking fifteen-percent?"

"It couldn't be done for less than fifty."

He smiles. "As much as I am in a hurry to see it sold, I am not in that much of a hurry. Twenty."

"Forty."

"Twenty-five."

She shakes her head slightly. "There is obvious risk, here."

"You're not a woman adverse to risk, Miss Villanova," he says. "If you were, you wouldn't be here."

"I am also not cheap."

His smile broadens. "How many languages do you speak?"

"Nine."

"Nine? Really? Fluently?"

"My Italian, English, Russian, Uzbek and German are fluent. Spanish and some dialects less so. I speak Farsi well enough to avoid embarrassment, as well."

An eyebrow raises. "Uzbek? Really?"

"My father is Uzbek," she says. "My mother Italian. I was born in Chicago."

"I am Uzbek," the man says. "You have a U.S. passport, then?"

"And Italian."

The man looks to Pallazzini for the first time. From the corner of her eye, she see them sharing a smile.

"Thirty percent," the Uzbek says, at length. "In the spirit of what, I hope, will be a profitable arrangement for all concerned."

He offers her his hand. She takes it, finds that his grip is insubstantial, like holding fog.

"I never got your name."

"No," he says. "You never did."

It takes the Molenaer plus two more pieces, a Picasso and a set of coins recovered from the looting of Baghdad, all brokered over the next four months, before she gets it, before she gets the name of the man she's been after all along.

The way she gets it is over drinks at Dukes in London. It's December, rainy and chill, and he asks to meet her at the hotel bar. The invitation takes her by surprise. Until now, all communication has been through Pallazzini. This time, the message comes in an envelope with her name typed upon it, awaiting her at the front desk of the Athenaeum, where she has been staying only a dozen blocks away from Dukes. The note inside is hand-written, inviting her for drinks and to toast their recent successes, signed "your Uzbek partner."

He's waiting for her when she arrives, in the far corner, a white-coated bartender and his drinks trolley standing beside the small table. The Uzbek rises when he sees her and his smile seems genuine as he looks her over head to toe. He takes her hand and kisses it lightly. Something has changed. For a moment she is aware of the lie she is living, banishes the thought with savage speed.

"Vosil," he says her, still bent, still holding her hand, gazing up at her. He's speaking English, barely accented. "Vosil Tohir."

"Thank you," she says. "I don't normally meet total strangers in bars, you know. Even ones as nice as this."

"Strangers no more, Elisabet." Vosil Tohir says, seating her before settling opposite. "Have you been here before? They say Ian Fleming drank here, that this is where he discovered the vodka martini. They make them true, so true, in fact, there's a limit of two."

"As I've had none, I'll have one to start," she says.

Vosil Tohir shows the man waiting patiently by his cart two fingers. Together they watch the drinks be prepared with efficient ceremony. Then the glasses are placed and they are alone at the table, though the bar itself is growing steadily more crowded.

"The money came through?" she asks after tasting her cocktail. She can already tell that there's a very good reason the limit is two.

"As of this morning. I must remember to thank Carlo for introducing us."

"One of the few good turns he's done me."

"Your relationship with him is not everything you wish?"

"My business hasn't suffered."

"That was not what I meant."

She swallows in time to keep from releasing a very inelegant shower of vodka martini, laughs against the back of her hand. "You think I'm sleeping with him?"

"He would have me believe it. From your reaction, I sense

another betrayal.”

“Carlo has a hint of desperation about him, I’m sure you’ve sensed it. I prefer my men more assured.”

She can feel his gaze on her, heavier. “Do you?”

The drink is threatening to muddle her thoughts and she picks her words with care. “I think you can tell.”

“I have taken a room here,” he says, after a moment’s thought.

“I’d hoped so,” she tells him.

These are hard motherfuckers, you understand that? Heath said. They’re hard and they’re ruthless but the worst of them are the smart ones. If they weren’t, we wouldn’t need to do this, we’d stick to fucking wet-work and drone strikes and that would be that. This guy or these guys or whoever the fuck they are, they’re smart enough we don’t even have names. And the smart ones, Chief, they’ll fuck you up in more ways than one.

Nessuno nodded, I understand.

Heath glared. No, you fucking don’t. Smart means careful and that means they’ll be up your ass with a microscope, they’ll be chasing every detail, they’ll check everything you say. And once they do that, they’ll check again and they’ll let you think you’ve crossed the bridge, that you’re in, but you’re not. There’s always one more thing, there’s always one last test, just to make sure. And then it’ll come, the favor or job or act that they’ll put before you and that is when you know and that is when the gates swing wide before you and you can see where you’ve been trying to get all along. But to cross over, oh, sweetheart, it’s made to hurt you, you hear me? It’s made to hurt you and to hold over you and to make you theirs.

Heath stopped abruptly, frowned, stared at the blank white wall.

To make your theirs forever.

The silence extended, drawn out until Nessuno could hear the muffled sounds of activity in the hall outside of their little classroom, until Nessuno wondered if Heath was still with her at all.

There are things I won't do, Nessuno said, finally.

Heath didn't turn from whatever it was she was seeing. Then that's you, Chief, she said. And maybe you'll even get to weigh your options and maybe you can even find some clever Hollywood-don't-know-shit screenwriter's way out and wouldn't that be precious? Maybe you can escape and they'll still trust you and maybe you can duck and even get out alive.

But maybe you won't

You didn't, Nessuno asked, knowing the answer, but needing to hear it.

There's a reason I'm an instructor and not an operator, Chief.

And?

And I get to live with that for the rest of my days, Heath said. However many more of them I can stomach.

Vosil Tohir has her using those passports and those languages. Mostly it's to carry messages to people she's never seen before and will never see again. Sometimes it's money, sometimes it's something else, but she has to be careful about when she looks because it's clear that Vosil Tohir was the target, but there's a new one now. Because Vosil Tohir gives the orders, but he also takes them and the question is from who?

Another six months more, and she sees him irregularly, Paris, London, St. Petersburg, Tashkent, Berlin. Sometimes he wants her beside him to translate and once he gives her a gun to carry concealed into a meeting, taking pleasure in showing her what she already knows about how to use it, where to hide it on her body. Twice he wants her to verify translations as they happen, and in Tripoli he asks her to entertain a friend of his.

He gives her new passports with new names to use, with instructions that they only ever be used the once, for this trip or that one and then burned. No phone calls, nothing written down and sometimes he shows up by surprise and sometimes she knows it's coming because she knew she was being followed.

But not always.

She knows he's making sure and she is Elisabetta Villanova so much now that CWO-2 Petra Nessuno is in danger of being left so far behind she'll be lost altogether. Some days she wakes up and it's an effort to remember the word of the day. Some days she wakes up and the fear crashes down and claws at her heart and clutches her gut and threatens to rise into panic. Some days she opens her eyes and he's been watching her sleep and she can tell he's gone through her clothes and her bag and her things.

Then he smiles and kisses her and tells her where she's going next, but not why.

It has been over eight months, the beginning of another winter, this time in Prague. They are tangled in sheets and catching their breath, and he kisses her brow, her nose, her lips, then suddenly slips away from her, out of the bed. She watches as he takes one robe and wraps himself, then tosses the other at her, on the bed.

"Come with me tonight," Vosil Tohir says. "I'll need my translator."

They drive for almost an hour in the darkness before pulling off to a side road, and it's another ten minutes before they reach the farmhouse. It's four in the morning and Nessuno has been whispering the whole time, warning that this cannot be anything good. Vosil Tohir has remained silent throughout their drive, occasionally humming to himself and she has known better than to ask.

But now they're parked and he kills the engine. She sees shapes of men coming out of the darkness and they're armed. They don't approach.

He turns in his seat to face her.

"We've made some good money together, love," he says. He's speaking in Uzbek. "We've had some good times, don't you think?"

She indicates the shapes in the darkness with her chin.

"Vosil. What's going on? Who are they?"

He touches her cheek, takes her chin in his hand, turning her eyes to his. "I'm very fond of you, Elisabet. You know that, yes?"

"You're scaring me," she says. It is the most honest thing she's said in years.

"Yes. Yes, I am." He studies her a moment longer, drops his hand and is getting out of the car. She turns to follow, finds one of the shapes is at the door, the weapon in one hand, the other ushering her out, now guiding her, not quite pushing, not quite holding. The other shape falls in with them, at her side. All three of them follow Vosil Tohir towards the farm house. Lamplight is leaking from between the boards, harsh and white.

A third man with a weapon is just inside and he speaks in Russian to Tohir as they enter.

"He protests his innocence, swears he's told no one a word."

"Do we believe him?"

The man shrugs. The farmhouse is large, musty with its years and all that its held. The memory of livestock and manure and urine float in the air. Dilapidated stables to one side, four stalls with their doors closed, their latches rusted and pitted with age. The man who spoke leads them to the second stall from the left.

She can hear whimpering from within. It sounds like a child nursing a broken bone.

Tohir adjusts his glasses with a sigh, then suddenly takes hold of her by the left wrist. She starts to speak, but then one of the men swings open the door and inside she sees Pallazzini lying on his side on old, moldy straw. His suit, like all of his suits ever, is expensive and well-tailored, but now it is spattered in blood, a crimson stain of it down the front of his shirt. His face is lesson in brutality, skin avulsed from his left cheek, a gash below his left eye. His right has swollen shut. His lips are torn, parted as he wheezes for air and she can see that his front teeth, the ones that remain, at least, are broken. Sweat, mucous, blood, all of it marks him and she remembers kissing that mouth and she cannot help but shudder and

Tohir, his hand still on her, feels it.

"Where we are now," Tohir whispers in her ear, "is beyond compromise. I want to trust you, Elisabet."

She forces herself to look at him and not Pallazzini. "Have I ever given you reason not to?"

His smile seems genuinely sad. "I don't need a reason, love."

She can think of nothing to say. There is no way to disguise her fear. He can surely feel it through her skin, she imagines he can hear the thrum of her heartbeat, sense the panic that is writhing, trying to break free of her control. The sensation is not unlike falling. She doesn't know who she is anymore. She doesn't know why she is here.

Tohir holds out a hand and the man who spoke gives him the pistol. Tohir now puts the gun into her hand, tenderly folding her fingers around its grip. She knows every eye is upon her, from Pallazzini still sobbing softly on the ground to the men with their guns around her.

"He knows you and he knows me." Behind the lenses of his glasses, his eyes are almost half-lidded, sleepy. "I want to trust you, Elisabet."

The scent of the barn has coated her mouth, caked in her throat. She swallows, tries to wet dry lips with her tongue, hears herself, hoarse, "Yes."

"Do you understand what I need from you?"

She nods because she is afraid to make a sound; not because of fear, because that fear has vanished, the panic stilled, but because the relief makes her want to sob, makes her want to cry with joy. His slender fingers still around hers around the pistol now in her hand. Pallazzini trying to speak, a mumble in Italian and the only word she can distinguish is one that translates from any language. No, no, please, no.

Tohir brushes his lips against her cheek, mouth hovering at her ear.

"There is so much I want you to be a part of, Elisabet, so much more we could do with you by my side. I need to trust you. My employer needs to trust you. Can we? Will you let us trust you?"

She turns her head and touches his mouth with her own.

"Yes," she says.

She shoots Pallazzini twice in the chest, using both hands, firing as if she's never fired a gun before. Pallazzini's body rocks on the ground, blood froths over his lips. His eyes glaze and then he does not move again.

She lowers the gun, feels herself trembling. Adrenaline has made every sense acute. Pallazzini voided his bowels, what was left in his bladder, and the scent is peculiarly rank, reminiscent of the battlefield. She struggles to regain herself, turns her head to see Tohir and he is watching her, still, but now with the barest of smiles. One of the men with guns has moved and she hears the complaint of rusted hinges, the sound of another stable door swinging open. She looks.

"That was for the past," Tohir says. "This is for the future."

It's Barrett.

He's been beaten as well, bound hands and feet. The damage he's taken has been more judiciously distributed. The missing fingers and the burnt skin, the filthy bandages, the signs of interrogation and torture. His right eye is shot with blood, damage around the orbit, but they've left him free to talk, to answer questions. In this fraction of time, in this moment of recognition, she is Petra Nessuno again. She remembers Monterey and Fisherman's Wharf and the taste and feel and delight of Brian Barrett. She can recall everything as if she is feeling it right then and right there. She sees his good eye widen, the rise of his chest drawing breath and she knows he remembers everything, too.

She remembers Heath.

She empties the pistol into Barrett's body before he can say her name.

His hands are on her hips the moment the door to the room is closed. She's felt his desire pulsing off him all the way back to Prague and now, unleashed, he's uncharacteristically clumsy, his urgency such that he can't be bothered undressing either of them beyond what needs to be freed for satisfaction. She stares at her hands where she's braced herself against the wall. She doesn't know who she is. She doesn't know why she's here. She feels like she's falling.

He finishes and leans against her back, kisses her neck, her shoulders. His hands run along her sides tenderly and then he withdraws and turns her to face him. Back to the wall, his arms trapping her at either side and he is kissing her once more, between her breasts, her throat, her mouth, before he stops and stares at her, smiling.

"You are dangerous," he whispers. "You are amazing. I could love you, Elisabet."

"Only could?" She smiles the way Elisabetta Villanova smiles at him. "What more do I need to do?"

He laughs, begins removing her shirt.

She talks dirty to him in Uzbek.

Gravity and Need
Marcus Sakey

Here's how Pamela introduced herself to me: "Candle wax washes out of sheets. Did you know that?"

People talk about love at first sight, but what they really mean is recognition. You look in someone's eyes, could be anyone, a childhood friend or a stranger waiting for the bus, and in an instant, things are different. Like they've pulled aside a curtain and let you look deeper than flesh.

What you see depends on who you are. Maybe it's peace and plenty. Maybe it's grandchildren bobbling on your knee.

In Pamela's eyes, what I saw was a reflection. And more than that, I saw her seeing her reflection in my eyes, the look bouncing back and forth like an endless loop of mirrors. Then she smiled, those lips turning up at only one corner, a hint of teeth and the next thing I knew we were going at it under the humming fluorescents of the stockroom, her legs wrapped around my back, her ass up on the packing crate of a forty-inch plasma screen.

In retrospect, everything that followed seems obvious.

It hadn't been easy getting the wheelchair up the hill and onto the embankment above the river.

Late sun spilled through the trees and set the steel tracks on fire. A hum of crickets rose loud and steady. The railroad bridge was lonely in the same way as the back side of strip mall. It's a part of civilization you aren't supposed to see; there's graffiti but no people.

"What are we doing here?" I watched the light rouge her cheeks, highlight her black hair. She looked away and I thought of the day we met.

The guy was ideal. Late twenties, outfit by Banana Republic, cheap shoes and a good haircut. Two years ago he probably had a goatee, and two years hence he'd have a BMW. Ideal.

"I need a new stereo," he'd said.

I shook my head. "You don't."

"Huh?"

"You don't need a new stereo. You need water. You need food and clothes and shelter." I held up my hands and smiled like we were buddies. "I'm not going all grammar Nazi. I'm just saying the things you need, they aren't any fun. They're just things you need. What's fun is the things you want. Right?"

He snorted. "Sure."

"Okay. So what kind of stereo do you want?"

The guy walked in thinking about a boombox. He walked out with a 5.1 surround sound system, a hundred-watt-per-channel receiver and a progressive scan DVD.

Understand—I didn't con him, and I didn't pressure him. Hell, I didn't even sell him. I just told him that it was okay to want something.

Everybody wants. Without that, what are you? Just an animal taking care of needs.

But I didn't waste a lot of time pondering it because all the time I was talking to him, I saw this beautiful girl staring at me, one side of her lips raised in a secret smile.

After you have sex with a total stranger on top of a three-thousand dollar television, what you're supposed to do is zip up, exchange fake numbers and never see each other again.

We went for Thai.

You know that moment on a first date when the conversation hits a lull? You'd been scoring points with the classics—the story about an old roommate's dog, the day you tried to quit your job, but were fired first, one about your wacky-but-beloved sister—when suddenly the rhythm is lost. You laugh a second longer than her joke is worth and fiddle with the chopsticks while the silence beats against your temples. It's unavoidable; after all, you don't know each other. The trick, though, is what comes next. Usually it's banal, a question about her job or yours, a reflection on the décor or the food.

What Pamela said was, "Do you think you could kill everybody in this restaurant if you needed to?"

I narrowed my eyes. Leaned back, looked around the room.

Her words spilled fast. "I'm not a psycho. I'm a writer. It's my job to think about things like that." She paused, brushed a lock of hair behind her ear, then looked down and bit the corner of her lip. After a moment, still staring at the table, she said, "Did I just blow it?"

A waiter came by and splashed water into our glasses, then sulked away.

"Well, it's like this." I scooped gomae, chewed slowly. The peanut sauce was delicious. "I think if I surprised the big guy at the end table with a chopstick in the ear, I could handle the rest of them with a chair. It'd be messy though."

When she looked up, it was with that smile and I felt something squeeze my chest.

Pamela's smile.

I used to babysit my little cousin when he was four or five. A good kid, but he got into stuff. One time, I found him in his parents room. He'd gotten hold of my aunt's lighter and was holding the lace curtains in one hand and the Bic in the other, the pale flame just inches away. He had a look of intense concentration, like he was doing math problems in his head.

I shouted, and he dropped the lighter and looked up, caught between the joy of his private world and the panic of the real one. He explained, without a hint of guilt, that he was trying to make more lace—he thought the intricate holes must be made by fire and he wanted to poke some more.

Pamela's smile is like that. Like she sees a secret the rest of us don't, a dangerous, wondrous secret. And every time she smiles, you think this time it might break free.

Only it never does.

The dying sun made the river sparkle like blood, warmed the metal of the wheelchair.

"Our place." Pamela turned to look at me. "Do you remember?"

Do I remember.

After the gomae, after the pad khee mao and the red curry, after the bottle of wine and the sweet Thai coffee, Pamela wanted ice cream.

"I know this shop," she said. "They have gelato, the real stuff like you get in Italy."

I raised my eyebrows and the collar of my jacket. "It's fifteen degrees out."

"Have you ever had real gelato?"

The place was out on Division, a twenty-minute ride. I kept glancing at her just in time to catch her glancing at me. The third time it happened, we both broke into laughter and then she reached over and took my hand, our fingers interlacing as though we'd done it a hundred times.

Gelato is smoother than ice cream and comes in more flavors. I had a scoop of white chocolate and one of pistachio. Pamela ordered espresso, sour cherry and pumpkin.

"You're kidding, right?"

"Why?"

"That's the weirdest mix I ever heard."

"I want them all. Why choose?" She worked her cone like a project, licking in small, steady strokes to maintain the shape, rolling it around her lips.

It was a little distracting, yes.

Afterwards, we went for a walk. A walk, in the middle of January, the streets buried in dirty sludge, the concrete icy, the wind cutting. We went for a walk and I put my arm around her and she fit her body into mine and neither of us shivered.

She told me about her writing, how she'd sold one book, a mystery novel, and had a second almost finished.

Told me about childhood, her parents splitting up when she was young. How that had never made sense to her, the idea that they changed their minds. If she ever got married, that was it, all or nothing, till death parted. She told me that she danced ballet when she was a teenager and that her favorite color was avocado, and that her first kiss was with a ten-year-old girlfriend and I held her and could have listened all night.

But it would have been better if I didn't.

My apartment was too small and hers was too far from my job, so we found a new place, a bungalow pulled back from the street, large and private, the ceilings at Wonderland angles. Pamela turned the second bedroom into a writing den, hanging photographs of crime scenes and a dry-erase board that traced the unhappy fate of her protagonists.

We played house. On the weekend, we built a nation of two and ruled it from the king-size bed. Dirty breakfast plates piled on the floor beside paperback thrillers and the New York Times. We'd watch the Spanish channel and make up our own stories. Once we spent all day pretending I was a pilot down behind enemy lines and she was the naughty interrogator trying to make me talk. She giggled while we shopped for shiny boots and leather gloves, but didn't break character after she put them on.

It was spring when we found the bridge and, by then, Pamela was all I wanted.

We were taking a walk. Funny, a lot of the milestones in our relationship involved walking. Sometimes irony is so neat you just want to shoot yourself.

The park was one of those pleasantly fake spots where the paths wander but the trees are well-disciplined. We must have been through it a hundred times. But that morning was the first we spotted the trail. Pamela took one look at it, smiled and then bet me I couldn't catch her.

It was a thin dirt track that wound under branches and

around bushes, the kind with something always snapping out to catch your face. She ran like a little girl, a doe, light on her feet and quick and it was all I could do to keep her in sight, much less catch her.

But every time I heard her laugh, I pushed a little faster through the tangle of woods.

Then, suddenly, sunlight. I slowed as I stepped from the line of trees. A ridge of gravel ballast crested in front of me, dull steel railroad tracks running along it. I shaded my eyes against the sudden brilliance.

Pamela stood on the very edge of the bridge, arms out, chest forward, blue horizon behind, nothing but the breeze and my prayers between her and a thirty-foot plummet to the brown river below.

Like she were cut from the sky.

"Of course I remember." My voice sounded harsher than I meant for it to. But lots of things don't turn out how we intend.

Pamela acted like she hadn't heard, her eyes locked on the river below. She squatted, then sat on the edge of the bridge, her legs dangling. "It was a beautiful day. Spring."

"I know." My hands shook, and I wasn't sure if it was due to effort or memory.

"It was like something from a myth." She reached in her pocket and took out her cigarettes. The smoking was new. I hated it, but under the circumstances, I couldn't begrudge her. With her right hand, she snapped a lighter, held it to her cupped palms.

Took a deep drag and then blew a stream of smoke. "We burst out of the forest to this place and it was like nothing else existed. Just you and me at the end of the world." She shook her head, took another inhale. "You came up behind and put your arms around me and pulled me away from the edge. We made love—" she looked around, pointed, "there, right on the tracks. Waiting to feel a train coming. You had gravel burns on your back for a week. And when we were done, you asked me to marry you. You remember what I said?"

I choked back battery acid. Looked down at my hands, folded in my lap, atop my ruined body. "I remember."

We'd been married for almost a year. The morning it happened, we had been screaming at each other. We didn't fight often, but when we did, you could have sold tickets.

It made sense. All we wanted was everything all the time.

I slammed the door as I left for work, but the battle kept raging in my head. I marshaled arguments to defend myself, launched the imaginary salvoes I thought most devastating. I was right in the middle of saying how tired I was of her divorce issues when the number seventy-two bus sheared off the back half of the Chrysler.

It's not like TV, with attractive doctors and snappy banter. In truth, I don't remember much. The rotting-flower stink of antiseptics. A bright light and a sense of motion around me, like a rock in the midst of rapids. Opening my eyes to see Pamela in a cracked orange chair at the foot of the bed. Her fingers squeezing my toes, eyes a million miles away. And then noticing that I couldn't feel her touch.

Funny thing is, I don't remember what we'd been fighting about.

I could still have a fulfilling life, the doctor told me. True, I would be in the wheelchair. I'd lost my spleen and one kidney, but my lungs, my heart, they were in fine shape. My dick didn't work and my legs never would. But I had the use of my arms, my mind. There were people worse off.

I said, aren't there always? Is there one poor, crippled, disease-ridden bastard out there that suffers worse than everybody and is allowed to be pissed about it? The doctor's lips went tight as he said that bitterness was a natural part of the healing process. Then he checked his watch, wished me luck and held the door for Pamela to wheel me out.

"We can make it, baby," she whispered. But I swore I could hear a question mark at the end of her sentence.

* * *

This is the bad part.

Before the accident, our world had a population of two. You know those disgusting couples that just draw into one another, that don't seem to even realize other people exist? We were them. And I'm not talking about the early flush of the first months. I'm talking about two solid years. More.

Funny thing about words. You always think you know what they mean, until life kicks the context out from underneath you. Same way every pop song turns into poetry when you're in the middle of a breakup—you see all that pain that you never connected to before.

Take the phrase, "I need you." There was a time those words might kick off a romp that could get us arrested in some states. We said "need" when we meant "want." Same as the kid looking for a new stereo.

It was only after the accident that I learned what "I need you" really means.

I need you to tie my shoes.
I need you to drive me to work.
No. Please no.
I need you to help me off the toilet.

Here's an ugly little home movie I'd rather not remember.

Establishing shot. A man sits in a wheelchair. His fingers clench nervously.

A door opens. A woman in a parody of a nurse's uniform struts in. A preposterously short white skirt reveals pale lace stockings. She closes the door with a theatrical flourish. "Good morning, Mr. Johnson."

His expression twists with desire.

She sways over and puts a hand against his forehead. Zoom in on her blouse, barely buttoned, breasts straining against the fabric. "Oh, Mr. Johnson. You're burning up!"

Makeup exaggerates her pout. "I need to cool you down

immediately."

Red fingernails unbutton his shirt. He touches her neck, traces the curves of her chest. Hoists himself up enough for her to tug off his pants.

"I should give you a sponge bath." Close-up of her nibbling on the tip of a finger.

"But I forgot my sponge. Whatever will I do?" She begins kissing her way down his torso. He can feel the light pressure of her lips, the warmth of her breath. So sweetly familiar. It's all he wants. He can feel it at his collarbone. At the hollow in his chest. At his navel.

And then he can't.

To her credit, she spends a long minute trying anyway.

When she looks up, he realizes he's not the only one crying. There's a terrible moment when they stare at each other, and then she covers her mouth with her hand, jerks to her feet and rushes for the door.

The camera pulls out slow on the man alone in his chair.

The blood-red in the sunset had given way to the pastel colors of those candy hearts you see around Valentine's Day.

"You said that if we were married, it was all or nothing." I took a deep breath. Afraid of what was coming. "That you didn't want to go the same way your parents had."

She nodded, still not looking at me. With a flick of her forefinger she sent the cigarette spinning bright into the shadows below.

The muscles of my chest tightened. All I'd wanted and I'd had it for so short a time.

"Has that changed?" I bit my lip, took a breath thick with fecund river smells. "Do you want a...a..." I couldn't say it. That word, it's like a home invader, a ski-masked freak in your living room. Once the possibility has been acknowledged, it never goes away. It becomes part of your reality and you wake up sweating at night sounds forever.

She spun. Her eyes flashed and I could see beads of sweat on her upper lip. "No. I don't want a divorce. You know better than that."

I let myself breathe. Our relationship had been forged of desire, a fantasy kingdom of want. But since the accident, we'd lived in a world of one-sided need. Selfish or not, there it was. "Look. This place...it hits a little too close to home."

She shook her head as if to clear it and moved behind me to take the handles of the chair. "Maybe it'd be better if I did want a divorce. Easier on both of us. But I'm," her voice caught, "I'm just not wired that way."

"Me either." Was I telling the truth? Would I stick with her if our roles were reversed? I really don't know. I just know I was relieved.

"Do you love me?"

"Of course." I struggled to turn around and touch her hands. The easiest way to see someone pushing your wheelchair is to tilt your head backwards, but there's no dignity in it. You're always staring up their nostrils. "Of course I do."

"I love you too, baby." Pamela smiled at me, that secret laced with darkness, the secret she never shared. Then she took a deep breath and shoved the chair towards the edge of the bridge.

On our wedding night, the bed rocked and shuddered halfway across the room.

When we were done, Pamela flopped on top of me, her dark hair draping my chest. I lay motionless, still inside her, feeling her every breath like it was me drawing air. Our skin pressed tight, our sweat ran together, our bodies connected and I literally couldn't tell where I ended and she began.

Gravel popped as my chair lurched forward. "Stop!"

The front edges of the wheels hung in open air. Vertigo squeezed my stomach.

Thirty feet below, the concrete base of the bridge struts loomed. Even if I missed them, the water was deep. I couldn't keep myself afloat, not with half my body waterlogged and useless.

Behind me, I heard her sob as she bent forward, braced herself and pushed.

The chair jumped four inches before my flailing hands found the tires. Hardened rubber burned my palms. Gravel slid over the side, hung in silence and then clattered against the concrete below.

"Stop!" My fingers locked like steel clamps. "Jesus!" The breeze seemed to tug at my dangling feet. My arms were strong from months of maneuvering the chair and I forced the wheels to reverse, but they skidded ineffectually in the loose ballast.

Fuck dignity. I looked backwards, staring at her upside down, trying to understand what was happening, hoping for some answer in her eyes, some hint this was a joke.

People talk about love at first sight, but what they really mean is recognition. You look in someone's eyes, could be anyone, a childhood friend or a stranger waiting for the bus and, in an instant, things are different. Like they've pulled aside a curtain and let you look deeper than flesh.

What you see depends on who—and where—you are.

When I saw what was in her eyes, I let go of the wheels.

In the sudden absence of resistance, we leapt forward, the chair cresting over the rim of the bridge and starting to fall, the river rushing upwards. Just as it went over, I thought, *Forgive me, baby,* and then I twisted my torso as hard as I could and flopped sideways out of the wheelchair, my body slapping against the bridge edge like meat.

Pamela's momentum propelled her. She let out a startled cry and, still clutching the handles of the wheelchair, hurtled off the bridge.

I scrabbled and fell, clawing at gravel that tore up in handfuls. My dead legs swung free. As my body slipped over the side, I made a desperate grab and caught the corrugated edge with both hands. The metal bit cruelly and my heart slammed against my ribs. I clenched my teeth and heaved, wriggling forward, rocks jamming into my ribs. When I finally felt the tug of gravity ease, I gasped for breath, muscles on fire, as I spun and wormed back to look over the edge.

She lay splayed on the concrete. Apart from the

disconcerting angle of her pelvis, she looked almost relaxed, like she were lounging in the shallows to battle the heat. Her left foot and arm bobbed with the current. Something sparkled just below the waterline.

Her ring. Sometimes irony is so neat you just want to shoot yourself.

Pamela's eyes were open, and locked on mine. An eternal moment passed. Then she coughed, and said, "I think I need you."

And through the blood, I finally shared the secret behind her smile.

It's a funny thing, needing someone. If it goes one way, it's a burden. If it goes both ways, it's a bond.

Our breakfast table is higher now and there are rails fastened beside the bed. Maybe we don't laugh as much as we used to, and everything comes a little harder. After all, not all secrets are pretty. But Saturdays are still our favorite. And though there are now two wheelchairs parked beside our bed, the man and woman in it are committed—all or nothing.

The Muskego Long Count
Tom Schreck & Nathan Banks

Here we go again.

It's not the first time this has happened. Some poor soul is getting scolded by that librarian bitch. She sits at her desk all day long, waiting for someone to overstep the building's policies.

As I turn the page of my Gun World Magazine, *I can't help but wonder what this poor soul is getting yelled at for today. Perhaps he sneezed too loud or the fan on his computer is creating a disturbance. Maybe he rolled his eyes at the late fee for his materials, which he actually turned in on time.*

Either way, it doesn't make a difference. I watch over the top of my reading material, as that snooty little lady stands up from her chair and starts her death march to her next victim. Her demeanor is appalling. As she nears the man at the computer, I swear I see a mischievous grin on her face. I can't hear what she's saying to this man because I'm just slightly out of range for her squeaky, brain-rattling voice. I can, however, see the man look at her in shock. He obviously can't believe that she's scolding him for what he's "done".

I can still remember when she scolded me for not following her unwritten personal policies. It all started with smoking too close to the building outside. It was raining that day and I shouldn't have to stand in the rain to smoke because I could get sick. Then she started watching me like a hawk searching for its prey, waiting for me to make a mistake. The final straw was when she came over and told me I couldn't be on the computer because I hadn't paid my fines. Those fines shouldn't exist because I returned those materials on time. I'll bet she checked them in late just so she'd have the opportunity to scold me.

I can still feel the humiliation. She's like all the other bitches, looking down on me, always waiting to put me in my place; always finding a way to make me feel small, always reminding me that I'm not good enough.

Her and her goddamn books; those books are more mine than hers. She will know soon.

She's headed back to her perch now, sitting there at that desk, waiting for the next violator. That next person won't be me however. Not yet at least. It's not the time for me to get revenge. That will have to wait until tomorrow, when it's her biggest library day of the year. Tomorrow is when I retaliate for her disrespecting me in the library. Tomorrow is the day everything will change.

My work here is done for the day. I've completed the research that I've needed. It's time to go home and make sure my device is ready for tomorrow, because tomorrow, I will be known as the man who blew up the local public library. I place my magazine back on the shelf and realize tomorrow's the day I crumple that bitch's empire.

Duffy

I couldn't freakin' believe it when they told me I wasn't getting paid after the fight. You had to love pro boxing. I get a call a week ago for a short notice fight in Milwaukee. They're willing to pay me a couple of thousand because they have no opponent for their main event fighter, but they can't afford to fly me. I don't have time to find a dog sitter so Al the basset hound makes the trip with me. He spent the night in the hotel room barking at the creaky air vent and I wound up with no sleep.

All that would be bad enough, but then I got ripped off with a hometown decision. I knocked down this big blond haired Wisconsin heavyweight with a body shot and he got the longest count since the Dempsey Tunney fight. The ref sounded like a record played on the wrong speed it took him so long to count to ten and, by the end of the fight, blonde's face looked like he stuck it in a blender. They gave him the win on points.

The usual boxing bullshit.

So when I go to find Richard the promoter, this tall lanky guy with a Brooklyn accent, they tell me he had to leave to get ready for the big library thing. Library thing? I don't know what alternative universe I had landed in, but I was sore, fed up and wanted to get started on my quaint little 16-hour ride home. Richard's friend, the scary looking guy with the Fu Manchu and the "Got Bullets?" t-shirt gave me directions to the Muskego Public Library.

The one redeeming factor about this trip was that I was in the home of Schlitz beer. They sold it out here in bottles and in the original formula. After the fight, I held a cold one to my head while I sat on the bed in the Red Roof Inn and consumed the other five watching an old episode of Pawn Stars. The last thing I remember was someone trying to sell Sammy Davis old home movies and the final beer leaving my forehead for my gullet. I lapsed off into semi-consciousness.

The creaky air vent continued to insult Al and he barked through the night. My body ached like it always did right after a fight and the Schlitz didn't promote REM. In the morning, I drank the free coffee in the lobby and ate two of the most disgusting pastries I had ever tasted. I got in the car and drove to Muskego.

It was Saturday morning around eleven and when I went to pull into the library parking lot it was almost full. This had to be one of the more literate cities in the world. When I entered the lobby, I noticed that there was a stage set up and about 300 people listening to group of six people discussing something. A sign in the lobby told me this was *"Murder and Mayhem in Muskego,"* an event featuring mystery authors.

What the hell?

* * *

I stepped out of the delivery van and ran my fingers over the embroidered brim of my cap that said "Joe's Coffee House." I slid the side door open, pulled out a cart and carefully loaded the two coffee bins. It's time to deliver the device.

As I push the cart through the front entrance to the library, I notice a librarian behind the circulation desk look up at me and I walk over to her.

"Coffee delivery for Murder and Mayhem, do you know where I'm supposed to take this?" I asked her.

I could practically hear the gears turning as she thought about the answer to my question. After what seemed like an eternity, she finally responded. "I'll show you to the back room."

I follow her back behind the desk and into the employee break room. It's a small room with a single table and a refrigerator.

"You can just set them up on the table there," the librarian said, as she motioned to the small table. With that, she left the room.

I place the first coffee dispenser on the table. The second one I open up and carefully remove my homemade bomb. It's fairly small, but it'll pack a helluva punch.

I fill the second dispenser 3/4 full with hot water from the sink and place a sign in front of it that says 'tea water'. Just before I place the lid on, I lay the metal tray in the top, which keeps the bomb out of the water. I admire the simplicity of the metal pipe and my crafty work of designing the explosive, then set the timer for 3 PM and secure the lid on the coffee urn. My work in the break room is done. As I'm walking out, I pass a man who has just walked into the library. He looks confused and out of place, as if he's not used to being in a library. He also looks like he hasn't slept well in the last few days.

I pass through the exit and head back to my van. After loading up the cart, I change into my second set of clothes. It's time to wait for 3 PM, which I'll do over last month's edition of Gun World.

Duffy

All right, I wanted to put an end to this bullshit. I wanted my check and I wanted to get on the road.

The librarians were in a flurry of activity taking care of these mystery authors who, by the way, seem to be just a tad on the odd side. Two of them just walked past me and I heard them say something about getting a beer behind the gas station. It wasn't noon yet and it was 22 degrees outside.

A coffee delivery guy was walking toward me and I figured he was as good as any to ask.

"Excuse me; do you know where Richard is?" I said.

He looked at me quickly and then looked away after muttering a quick "no."

All righty, a little on the squirrely side of normal. I had already established that I was in the wrong universe for the weekend.

A guy with curly hair and a black shirt had the mike and was talking about his TV show and how he doesn't write his books in a series because he doesn't want to be constrained. Next to him, a short guy with reddish hair and a pink shirt who said he was from Colorado agreed and went on about his own process and his way for developing characters.

Geez, talk about self-important assholes...

The MC stood off to the side and I noticed he was the only one wearing a tie and a jacket. When he chimed in you could tell he knew his stuff. The guy was really smart and handsome.

I spotted Richard. He was behind a set of shelves stocked with books. He didn't look any happier than he did the night before. He was about 6' 2" and looked like he just ate something rancid. Another guy whose nametag said "Dave" was with him and it looked like Richard had Dave doing all the work.

"Hey Richard, can I have my check?" I said. I had thought about warming up with an ice breaker, but my forehead had started to throb and I was losing patience.

He looked up at me without saying a word.

"Hey, Duffy, nice job last night; sorry about the decision and sorry about running out. This thing today is a big deal and I forgot," he said. He still didn't crack a smile.

"No sweat, but I'd like to get going."

"Sure, sure." He looked around. "Dave, where's the boxing checkbook?"

Dave looked up from under the table where he was stacking books. Dave was a short guy with glasses and he had sweat on his forehead.

"Richard, why would I bring the boxing checkbook here?" Dave said. I got the impression Richard annoyed Dave sometimes.

"Aw shit," Richard said. "Duffy, I'm really sorry. It'll just take a minute for me to send someone to get it. You mind hanging around?"

I just looked at him for a second. I took a deep breath and tried to keep my neck from twitching.

"No, that's all right, but I'm gonna have to get my dog out of the car. Is that okay?" If I left Al in there for more than fifteen minutes, the upholstery was in serious danger.

"I don't see why it would be a problem," Richard said.

* * *

Here I am again, looking over the cover of September's issue of Gun World, *observing the controlled chaos of the library's atmosphere. There's gotta be close to 300 people here between the event and the normal patrons. This is fantastic. 300 people and not a single one has a clue that just a few hours from now my bomb will explode.*

I go back to my magazine, continuing to read an editorial by Ted Nugent on how American's should have the ability to carry a firearm wherever they want. My glamorous reading is interrupted by that evil snooty little bitch again. It's 1 PM now and she's walking up to say a few words before the next panel begins. I can almost hear the clicking of her dagger length fingernails, as she drums them on the surface of the tabletop, waiting for the crowd to settle down and find their seats.

I've had it. I can't take it anymore. This librarian needs to go. Even as she stands behind that grey podium, addressing the attendees of her little event, I can see her scanning the crowd for policy infringers. Her capitalistic approach will end with one small, then very big bang! And the best thing about it is it's going to happen during the raffle drawing, which is only two hours from now. It looks like I'll have to start reading October's Issue of Gun World *before its boom time.*

Duffy

I got Al out of the Cadillac and headed back into the library. The wind had kicked up and the gray November sky was producing a small squall of snow. There was something much colder about Wisconsin than upstate New York. It chilled to the bone and I wondered for a moment if it was a physical temperature thing or if being away from home was more responsible for the intensity of the feeling.

We passed a group of smokers on the way back in. There was a great big guy with a beard and glasses', wearing one of those long dusters, next to him was an older thinner man with a white beard and the blond librarian was outside with them taking a break. Al paused on the way in and gave them all an approving look.

When we entered the library foyer Al caught sight of the cookie tray being placed on the registration table. He pulled fast and hard and the suddenness of his lunge enabled him to break free. I was a good step behind with no hope of catching him before he got to his prey. You might not picture Al as a jumper from his stature, but with the right motivation he was Michael freakin' Jordan.

A tray of cookies was motivation.

The poor librarian had just laid them down and was turning around when the bolt of black, white and gold shot across her peripheral vision. She let out a yelp which accompanied Al's percussive solo that included the sound of a crashing tray and two tipped over chairs.

I didn't bother to move. It wasn't that I lacked concern. I was still sore and under-caffeinated and I had also lived a life resigned to Al's antics. I used to follow him, fuss and apologize when he did this kind of shit, but I gave that up. Now, when citizens glared at me I shrugged my shoulders and said "Sorry." I tried to only say it once per episode.

Chocolate isn't good for Al and, after he had snarfed the row of oatmeal cookies, he went for the dark chocolate ones. I had no choice, but to intervene. I swooped in and grabbed as many as I could and, as Al went to bite the proverbial hand that feeds him, I hurled the treats behind me.

"Ouch—hey dude, watch it!" The now angry guy with the "Got Bullets?" shirt yelled. He was wiping the gooey chocolate filling off of his glasses.

I would've apologized for that, I really would have, but Al hadn't completely failed in his attempt to remove my hand from the rest of my arm. He got a good chomp in on my pinky.

"Mother fucker! Ouch! You son-of-a-bitch!" I yelled.

I'm not sure if the Muskego Public Library gets a lot of people yelling such things and most of the three hundred people turned their attention away from the mystery writer guy with the TV show who was still talking about his "process" to stare at me.

"Grrrrr...ruff, ruff, ruff aroooooo!" Al wasn't backing down and wouldn't any time soon.

"Fuck you, Al!" I yelled, oblivious to the crowd's attention. Blood flowed from the second knuckle.

The handsome, really smooth narrator guy was now at the microphone.

"Hey, shorty, keep it down!" I assumed he was talking to Al and it diffused a little of the awkwardness. Man, the guy was good.

I managed to get Al by the leash and hurried him through a door behind the circulation desk and got the hell out of there.

* * *

It's 2:50 now. In a matter of 10 minutes, this will all be over. That Witch is walking up to the front, ready to announce the raffle winners. Even from my safe spot across the main area of the library, I can see her grin, as her eyes dart back and forth in the crowd scanning like heat seeking missiles. Nine minutes from now her hold on the population in here is over. Nine minutes from now she ceases to exist. I anxiously wait for the clock to run out.

Six minutes left and time begins to slow. It's like when you're in that car, as it starts to slide out of control, and everything seems to slow to a crawl, like you're watching it in slow motion. That's what is happening right now—everything is slowing to a crawl with the anticipation of what is about to happen. In a matter of six minutes, this is all over. It's time for me to clear the premises of this doomed library. What good is revenge if you're not alive to enjoy it?

Duffy

Al and I snaked our way around the offices in the back of the library and found a conference room. A half dozen of the author types were gathered around the board table eating what looked like some outrageous homemade baked goods. Man, they catered to these people.

A tatted up, short blond woman was at the head of the table talking about the recent changes in the world of internet porn. I helped myself to one of the brownies and gave Al a look to let him know he was to behave. The tatted woman mentioned the term "anal prolapse" and I stopped chewing my double chocolate fudge brownie.

The librarian host of event scurried into the room with the "Got Bullets" guy and started moving the coffee urns and cookie trays.

"In five minutes, it's time for the raffle and the afternoon break," she announced to the writers in the room.

She began to wheel the cart with the two coffee urns out and the Bullets guy fell in behind her with the cookies along with the half dozen authors. Al and I were at the back of the line and I decided there was no reason to stop eating now. Besides, maybe I would win something in the raffle. Maybe they would auction off a boxer's eight round purse.

The congested office area slowed the line and Al found this unacceptable. He decided to wind his way through the legs of the various authors, stopping only for a short neck scratch from the tatted blond lady with the interesting vocational choice. The librarian and Bullets guy had made their way onto the library floor and walked to the back of the seating area to place the refreshments on some cabinet tops.

The line had spaced out and Al darted ahead to the Bullets guy who was walking straight ahead and talking to the librarian. Al went airborne toward Bullets with his eye on the pumpkin spice cookie tray and got about mid-thigh on the unsuspecting guy. Al let out a startling "Arooooo!" on the way down that startled Bullets. When Al landed in between the guy's legs he was in midstride and both he and Bullets went ass-over-tea-kettle.

"What the fuck—" the guy yelled hitting the carpet hard and getting covered in cookies. Al saw this as a triumph and began to eat the cookies off the guy's back. The librarian turned sharply at the commotion.

"Jon!" she yelped. Unfortunately, her sharp turn toppled over the coffee cart sending the two urns splashing to the ground.

"What the fuck!" the guy yelled. I couldn't tell if it was from the crash of the cart or if he wasn't accustomed to a basset hound nibbling pumpkin spice cookies off the top off his head.

He jumped to his feet, which sent all the cookies to the ground and provided exceptionally easy access for Al.

"What the fuck!" the guy yelled again. Clearly he was suffering from PBSD—post basset stress disorder. I had seen it a million times.

The rest of the room went silent while they looked at the carnage of coffee, cookies, sprawled out man and greedily chewing hound. The guy dusted himself off and, while he continued to decookie himself, he suddenly froze.

"What the hell is that?"

He pointed to the coffee urns. He wasn't yelling now which sent a chill through the room.

"What?" the librarian said.

In between the coffee urns in a dry spot on the carpet was an eight-inch piece of metal pipe. The cart doors were open and it had fallen to the floor in the crash. It had wires and a digital clock affixed to it.

"That's a fuckin' bomb!" the guy yelled. The clock on it was counting down from ten.

The room of 300 went dead silent. It was like they were too terrified to scream. I was frozen and along with everyone else I instinctively backed up. The room had formed a huge semi-circle around the device.

Nine.

The Bullets guy, the librarian and I exchanged looks. I got a sense that it was up to one of us.

Eight.

"Penny, what do you know about bombs?" the guy said.

"Only what I've read Jack Reacher does with them," she said.

"Me, too," he said.

Seven.

I had no time to ask who this guy Reacher was. Suddenly, I realized Al was next to the bomb working his way through the end of the pumpkin spice cookies.

Holy shit. He'd be blown to bits.

Six.

"Oh my God..." the librarian said

Five.

Al kept chewing.

Four.

"Fuck us." The Bullets guy said.

Three.

I froze.

Al stopped chewing. He walked toward the bomb and sniffed.

Two.

And he lifted his leg and peed all over it.

One.

There was a sizzling, electric sound followed by a small cloud of smoke. The digital clock went dark. The room was deathly quiet.

Then they erupted in hysterical cheers.

Al went back to eating.

The Bullets guy looked up at me. I looked at him, raised my eyebrows and shrugged my shoulders. The librarian lit a cigarette.

"That was pretty cool," Bullets said.

"Fuckin' A right," I said.

"That's a pretty fucking amazing dog," he said.

"I know," I said.

Al started on the next row of sugar cookies. I let him.

* * *

I stood outside the library, looking at my watch, dumbfounded. That damn bomb should have gone off by now... what's the hold up? Thinking maybe something was wrong with my watch; I looked around and saw a man leaving the library.

"Excuse me, do you have the time?" I asked.

"Why sure, it's 3:05 PM," the guy said.

"Thanks" I replied as I headed into the library. I had to see what had gone wrong. As I approached the magazine area, I started to see that something had definitely happened, but wasn't quite sure what. I stopped another patron who was walking towards the door on her cell phone.

"What happened in here?" I asked.

The lady stopped talking on her cell phone and began to answer me in a very fast paced reply.

"This guy's dog caused the coffee to spill and they found a bomb. Then just before it blew up, that dog peed on it and saved us all!" She said, going back to her phone call.

"What a wonderful dog!" I said, as I internally reminded myself this is why I didn't like dogs. They always seem to ruin everything! I looked around and, sure enough, safe and sound is that bitch and she's even smoking a cigarette—unbelievable. It looks like she gets one more year to live because next year I WILL succeed. With that, I spin on my heel and head out the door. I need to start building a better bomb—one that's doggy proof.

I will not let her demean me any longer. Next year, I will end her tyranny. I head to the parking lot.

I put the key in the driver's side door. I never wanted to leave a place more. But before I can hit the ignition, a voice rocks me out of raging reverie.

"Sir, sir!"

I can't believe it. It's her, the subject of my hatred.

"Sir, sir," She was walking right toward me. "Sir, stop."

I'm frozen. She has me and I am unprepared.

"Sir," she's now inches from my face. I've stopped breathing.

I wait.

"The magazines are not to be taken from the library," she says with that face. Her hand extends, palm up.

"Yes ma'am," I say and I hand over the copy of Gun World.

"Please follow all library regulations," she says before turning and heading back to the front doors.

Next year for sure.

Next year.

The Particular Talents of Lenny Bright
Zoë Sharp

Lenny Bright sat opposite the Holland and Seagrave Building Society in a gunmetal Honda Accord with the engine running. He hadn't taken his eyes off the front door for twenty minutes and right at that moment he would have sold his soul for a cigarette.

Lenny's cigarettes were in the inside pocket of his bomber jacket, but it was more than his life was worth to reach for them. He couldn't even chew his fingernails, on account of the string-back driving gloves he'd been told to wear.

"Come on," he muttered, flexing his skinny fingers around the rim of the steering wheel. "What's taking you so long? Just get the money and get out of there!"

As if on cue, the building society's door was thrust open. A figure emerged, carrying a large bag and hurried across the road towards him.

"At last!" Lenny said under his breath. The rear passenger door opened and the bag landed heavy on the cloth upholstery, followed by its owner. By the time the door slammed shut again, Lenny was already moving out into traffic.

"Not too quickly, Lenny dear," Mrs Esmé Wendover said from the back seat. "I should hate you to get a speeding ticket. My poor Harold never got one, you know, not in forty years."

"You'll miss your train if we don't hurry, Mrs Wendover," Lenny said. He flashed a cheeky grin in the rear-view mirror. "'Sides, it's your car, so you'd be the one getting the ticket."

"Quite so," she murmured, dragging her voluminous handbag towards her and burrowing through the contents. She paused long enough to favour him with a regal smile over her half-moon glasses. "All the more reason to go steady, then."

"Yes ma'am," Lenny said smartly, not altering his pace.

After nineteen years under the thumb of his domineering mother, Lenny was used to pretending to toe the line. Old Mrs Bright had a lightning tongue and the uncanny ability to hear the ring-pull being snapped open on an illicit can of shandy through two floors and a soap opera.

An academic make-weight, Lenny left school unscathed by the knowledge his teachers tried to impart. Then a despairing careers' officer dumped him into a youth training scheme at a local garage, where it was discovered, much to everyone's amazement, that when it came to anything mechanical Lenny Bright was a genius.

Of course, that didn't mean his new employers were prepared to pay more than minimum wage. Nowhere near enough for him to move out and get a place of his own.

His mother viewed his oil-stained profession with disgust. On his daily return, she made him strip and scrub down by the cold tap in the outhouse, in all weathers.

That winter was bitter and Lenny grew desperate. He was caught copying the keys to a customer's car and, although the garage didn't press charges, they gave Lenny his marching orders and put the word out. He couldn't get another mechanic's job for fifty miles in any direction.

Lenny told his mother he'd been made redundant. She berated him for his incompetence, kicking him out of the house during the day to wander the town centre. He spent his time daydreaming of his own space.

Two months later, Lenny trudged home to find the elderly Mrs Esmé Wendover sitting on his mother's sofa, drinking tea from best china. He was horrified. Mrs Wendover owned the car whose keys he'd copied.

"Since you stopped working on my Honda, it's just not the same," she'd said, making him sweat. "My Harold kept it running sweet as a nut." She'd sighed and fixed him with a fiercely intelligent eye. "All his tools are still in the garage. I'd like you to carry on servicing my car for me at home. I'm prepared to pay."

Lenny had gaped, right up to the point his mother stepped in and grimly assured Mrs Wendover that her boy would do the work for nothing. Mrs Wendover must have seen the urgent desperation in his eyes because she held up a peremptory hand.

"My Harold left me comfortable and I won't have charity," she said with a sweet smile. "Saturday at nine, Lenny? You know the address..."

So Lenny began looking after Mrs Wendover's Honda, driving her when she needed to go anywhere, like the garden centre, where his eye was caught by one of the assistants, Julie, who smiled at him with particular brightness.

That smile kept him warm when his mother sent him back, shivering, to the tap in the outhouse.

And then two things happened. By chance, he bumped into one of his old classmates, Daz, fresh out of prison for turning over a Post Office. Daz had seen Lenny running an errand in the Honda and had casually buttonholed him.

"Nice motor," Daz had said. "Fancy using it to earn yourself something extra? Decent bit of cash, no questions asked?"

"Doing what?" Lenny had said and then, before he had the chance to be tempted, admitted quickly, "Only, the car's not mine, see."

"Oh." He'd watched the respect die out of Daz's eyes. "Never mind, then, eh? See you around." And Lenny had watched him saunter away in an agony of indecision.

At the garden centre, he'd seen Julie poring over the classifieds. "They've done a conversion down near the canal," she told him. "Lovely places, but they want two months' rent up front." She'd eyed him with a certain gleam. "I've been thinking of taking in a lodger."

"I'll do it," Lenny blurted and went home dazed.

And the next time he saw Daz, Lenny listened.

* * *

They reached the station five minutes before the Southampton train. Lenny saw Mrs Wendover safely to her carriage, trying not to let his agitation show.

Half an hour later he picked up Daz and two heavyset mates outside a boarded-up pub in one of the sink estates. Daz handed him a pair of fake numberplates and a black balaclava.

"All right, Lenny mate?" he said. "Remember, you just sit outside with the motor running like a good lad and the money's yours."

"All right," Lenny had said gruffly, trying to swallow down the sudden lump in his throat.

He was already scared witless, even more so when they seemed to be heading for exactly the same branch of the Holland and Seagrave where he'd waited for Mrs Wendover that morning. He eyed the two heavies in his rear-view mirror and desperately searched for a way to tell Daz, but when they pulled up outside, he still hadn't found one.

Besides, Daz and his companions were already out of the car and charging across the pavement. Lenny debated on driving off, but the robbers were almost certain to get caught and he knew Daz wouldn't hesitate to name him if he betrayed them.

Instead, he waited, his nerves in tatters and dying for a cigarette, until the doors burst open and the three men emerged. Daz threw himself into the front seat.

"Go, go, go!" he yelled.

Lenny smoked the tyres halfway along the High Street, driving like a man possessed, drifting through corners and making wild turns to throw off any chance of pursuit. Eventually, he took them back to the pub by a very circuitous route, changing the numberplates back while Daz split the haul.

"There you go, Lenny," Daz said, putting a fat brown envelope into his hands. "You ever want more work, I can find you plenty."

"No thanks," Lenny said dazedly, staring at the crumpled edges of more money than he'd ever seen in his life before. There must have been hundreds! "I've got what I need."

Daz eyed him with speculation. "So, what're you doing with it then?"

Lenny looked up and smiled. "My getaway," he said.

Daz clapped him on the shoulder and laughed. "About time you moved out from under," he said. "You let me know if you change your mind though. You're a natural."

"Not me," said Lenny, shaking his head. *Never again*, he thought.

Several days later, Lenny was washing Mrs Wendover's car when the police turned up. Two large uniforms, reminding Lenny of the bank robbers and just as threatening. He thought of the money, still hidden under the mattress of the narrow bed he'd slept in from childhood and almost made a run for it there and then.

"Can you tell us your whereabouts on Thursday morning, sir?" one of the policemen demanded, pen poised over the page of his notebook.

Lenny's mouth dried.

"I, er—"

"What seems to be the trouble, officers?" inquired a voice behind them. All three turned to see Mrs Wendover had emerged from the house carrying a tray with two cups of tea and a plate of biscuits. "I do hope this isn't because Lenny was driving too quickly?" the old lady said anxiously. "We were rather late, you see."

"Er, no, ma'am," said one of the policemen, through a mouthful of garibaldi. He straightened importantly. "Actually, we're investigating a robbery—the Holland and Seagrave Building Society."

"Oh yes, I saw something about it on the news," Mrs Wendover said. "Dreadful business. And we were there only that morning, weren't we, Lenny dear?"

The policemen eyed Lenny with great suspicion. "Were you?"

He cleared his throat. "Er, yes," he said.

"I imagine that's what all this is about, isn't it?" Mrs Wendover said calmly. "Somebody saw my car and heard about the robbery and put two and two together and came up with five, hmm?"

One of the policeman shuffled his feet and mumbled an agreement. "A car matching the description of—"

"Lovely cars, Hondas, but there are *lots* of them about," Mrs Wendover interrupted. "Lenny's a good boy. He wouldn't get involved in something like that. And besides," she added to Lenny's astonishment, "by the time I'd finished conducting my business we discovered that I'd missed my train and he very kindly drove me all the way down to Southampton." She beamed at the policemen and held the tray out to take their empty cups. "So, you see, officers, it couldn't possibly have been him."

As they watched the police car disappearing down the drive, Mrs Wendover said breezily, "The first thing you should learn if you're going to break the law, Lenny dear, is to have a good alibi."

Lenny could only stammer, "How-how did you know?"

She smiled. "Because that particular branch of the Holland and Seagrave has the worst security in the area. It was only a matter of time before they got turned over," she said. "You've been looking incredibly guilty since last Thursday, dear. We'll have to do something about that conscience of yours."

"W-wh—?" Lenny stopped and started again. "Why?"

"Because you won't last very long as a getaway driver if you're going to stutter every time you're brought in for questioning. Those CID boys will make mincemeat out of you."

"There's not going to be a next time," Lenny said quickly. "I'm not doing it again."

"Don't be silly, Lenny dear," Mrs Wendover said. "I didn't stick my neck out for you, only for you to get cold feet now. As Daz no doubt told you, you're a natural. And I should know—my Harold was the best wheelman in the business. Forty years and never got caught. I knew if I offered you a big enough carrot you couldn't resist it. Why stop now?"

"Because..." Lenny began, then his voice trailed off. He'd

already counted out the money Julie needed for the deposit on the flat and there wasn't much left over. But supposing that wasn't the last of it? Lenny's mind was suddenly filled with thoughts of being able to take Julie out, buy her presents, of her clinging to his arm and laughing as they walked home by the canal. Maybe he could even buy a car!

"Of course," Mrs Wendover went on, "we can't afford for you to attract attention to yourself—no sudden changes in lifestyle, dear." She smiled at him, like butter wouldn't melt in her mouth. "So maybe it would be best if you stayed living with your mother..."

"The Particular Talents of Lenny Bright" originally appeared in Candis magazine (2007) as "The Getaway."

Last Call
Bryan VanMeter

When the Knicks missed the free throw, Charles Sawyer knew he was going to die. He had only made it this long because of his charisma and a particularly forgiving bookie that had gone to bat for him. Tonight was his last chance to make good on months of bad bets. Double or nothing on everything he owed. He was playing Russian roulette and the hammer just struck copper.

He sighed and kept wiping down the same bar he had owned and maintained for the past thirty years. Like a man with a terminal disease, he had come to grips with the possibility the risky cure might not work. There was no more bargaining, no more anger. Just acceptance that after tonight, Charles Sawyer would be no more. The bar he had bought with his own savings would be occupied by another or be left to rot like so many other buildings in the area. His regulars, people he had served every night for so many years, would move on to other bars and other understanding ears.

He looked up at the clock and saw it was eleven; time to begin his nightly routine. He counted the bottles of beer in the small fridge and went to replace the missing ones with cases from the back. He paused for a moment in the stock room, thinking he could just walk out now. He could go upstairs and grab the fake IDs beneath the floor in the living room. After about thirty minutes, the people in the bar might wonder where he'd gotten off to. In an hour, they might go looking for him. By one o'clock, they would call the cops, but he would already be on his way out of town.

He shook the idea off and grabbed another case of Miller Lite. If they were coming for him tonight, a couple of hours wouldn't matter. They'd find him and his end would be the same. His only hope was the bookie could buy him a day or two with the boss, giving him ample time to get away. If not, he'd be just as dead here as he would be a hundred miles away.

Besides, whether he'd be granted the time or not, this was his last night in his bar. His last night stocking the beer and wiping moisture off the well-polished oak. His last night hearing how Paulie once had a wild night with Gina Davis and she was a hellcat you better believe. Almost too much for old Paulie to handle. Almost.

It would be the last night he would hear John debate whether or not he would have just one more before he headed home. It was a decision that had only once ended in the negative when he passed out on the way to take a piss.

It was the last night he would pour Mike a brandy and coke. None of that E&J shit. Korbel. Only the best for Mike.

At midnight, the beer cooler was once again full. Unasked, he poured another bourbon for Jake. His latest girlfriend had thrown him out "'cause she was on the rag" according to him. To the best of his recollection, this was Jake's third failed relationship this year. As he poured, he silently hoped he would find the right one. He was kind of a train wreck, but beneath that rough exterior, he was a good guy.

As he tipped the bottle back up, he heard the door cry out as it was forced open. As it groaned closed, he realized he had no chance to make it to the morning alive. Walking up to the bar was Peter D'Agosta. He had served Peter his first beer what seemed days ago, but probably amounted to nearly a decade. Looking at the man framed in the doorway, the years peeled back in a flash to their first encounter.

"I'd like a beer, sir," the teenager said, setting his ID on the bar, eyes darting around the room.

"Is that so, Mr....," he said looking at the fake ID, "Mr. Thompson? What kind would you like?"

"Budweiser," the kid said more confidently.

He sat the beer in front of the kid, allowing himself a small smirk.

The kid scrambled for a crumpled five. "And, uh, keep the

change."

"Why, thank you, sir," he said making a show of putting the money in his apron. "It's a true gentleman who tips his bartender well."

The kid nodded and turned his attention to the TV, trying to look nonchalant. He drank his beer, occasionally looking around the bar with the same look a cat has when it leaves a "gift" in its owner's shoe. Charles helped the others around the bar, always keeping half an eye on the kid. He greedily drained the last of the beer and reached into his wallet for another five.

"Mr. D'Agosta," Charles whispered leaning over to the kid, "allow me to offer some sage advice. Always quit when you're ahead."

The delusions of cleverness drained from the kid's face and he bolted out of the bar. However, he returned many other nights over the years. Every time, they went through the same routine. Charles checked the fake ID, the kid gave him a five for his Budweiser, he drank it without incident and went home.

On his twenty-first birthday, the kid came in grinning like it was his wedding night, slapped his legit license on the bar and ordered his beer. Charles, instead, brought him a Manhattan and told the kid, now a man, to keep his money. Charles was going to buy his first drink and it would be a damn sight better than a Budweiser. The newly minted man grimaced with his first sip, but was in love by the last. Since then, Charles had never seen him drink anything else.

Now, he sat the drink in front of the man without any prompting.

As Peter reached for the cocktail, Charles could see the butt of his gun peeking from its hiding place beneath Peter's suit coat. Peter saw him staring at the weapon, but made no attempt to hide it. Instead, he raised a silent toast to the bartender, took a sip and surveyed the room.

By the time the clock reached one, Charles had made two more for Peter, several more drinks for the other patrons and had been regaled for the final time with Paulie's story. He washed the glassware in the small basin sink, checking each glass for any chips or small cracks, discarding those that had defects. There were no cut lips or cracked glasses in his place. Only two pint glasses had gotten chipped over the course of the night. He thought he would have to buy another case before he realized he'd never buy a glass for this place again.

He began consolidating the liquor bottles in the trough. There were always a couple of the most common bottles open down the length of the bar, so he wouldn't have to go up and back every time someone wanted a Jack and coke. As he poured the last third of a bottle of Korbel into one that was half full, he noticed the shotgun he kept under the bar. His eyes widened for a second, then darted up to Peter, whose attention had been diverted by Sports Center for the moment. He hadn't noticed.

He could shoot Peter right now. Haul up the gun and fill Peter's lungs with lead pellets, a look of shock etched on his face as he collapsed to the floor. With his face twisted in a grimace, Charles would lean over the bar and put the rest of the buck shot in Peter's head. Some of his customers would scream, some run out the door and some simply stare at him in disbelief. After that, he'd have to talk to the cops. They'd haul him in for questioning, probably set him free on self-defense. Then he'd be shot dead on the steps of the station by another of the boss' men or hauled away to be tortured for killing one of their own.

Suddenly, another thought crossed his mind. If he could hold out until two thirty, he might have a chance. Ten years ago, he got tired of turning off every light at bar close. He had bought an automatic timer to cut the lights at two thirty AM and back on at four in the afternoon. His nightly ritual was so finely tuned that he was usually on the top step reaching for the upstairs light switch as he heard the bang of the circuit being cut. Tonight, if he was quick enough, he might be reaching to save his own life.

Peter had no idea about the lights. They'd go off. Peter would be surprised by the sudden darkness and he'd reach for his gun, but it would already be too late. Charles would have the shotgun leveled on him. As Peter died, so would Charles. A few hours later and a hundred miles away, another man would board a bus bound for some small Florida sinkhole he could disappear into for the rest of his life. By the time the body was discovered, the bartender named Charles Sawyer would be nothing, but another story to tell over the third beer of the night.

He consolidated bottles, opened others, wiped down taps and cleaned up the small spills on the bar. When the clock turned to one fifty, he didn't have to tell anyone it was last call. They all knew the drill. They sidled up and ordered their last. The last drinks he would ever serve them. He told each of them it was on the house tonight. They all thanked him for his generosity, some asking why and receiving nothing but a small shrug and a smirk from him. He wondered if they would tell the reporters about it tomorrow night, remarking how ordinary last night was and how he had all bought them a round at the end.

At two, they started handing Charles empty glasses, thanking him for his service and wishing him a good night. He thanked each one of them for the last time. In his mind, he thanked them for all the years, all the memories. Shared stories, spilled glasses, meaningless arguments. All that had been his for the past thirty years. All of that he funneled into a simple "G'night," as he washed their glasses and put them in back their place behind the bar.

"Want another?" Charles asked, as the last of the regulars exited, leaving the door to groan back to its resting place.

"Thought it was illegal to serve after two," Peter said with a small grin gesturing to the clock that now read two fifteen.

"Surprisingly, I'm not concerned." He reached for the Maker's Mark and then hesitated. "How about a Budweiser? On the house."

He grinned. Charles saw a flash of the kid in the man on the barstool. "Sure. Like old times."

He poured a pint and set it in front of Peter. He then grabbed a bottle hidden in a dark corner of the bar, reserved for special occasions. He poured a small amount of the ancient scotch allowing the smell of peat and smoke to fill him. He drank deeply, feeling the years distilled in the glass of liquid amber spread through his body.

He poured another and held up a toast to Peter. "To old times."

"Old times," he said tapping his glass against Charles'. "So I gotta ask something. The first time I came in here, cocky as a king, you had never seen me before, but you had me pegged the moment I walked in the door. How?"

Charles smiled. "I suppose it doesn't hurt to put all my cards on the table at this point. You're the spitting image of your father. When you walked in and asked for a Budweiser, it might as well have been your father, fuming because your hormone addled mother had called him an asshole and threw him out while you were wriggling in her belly."

The kid smiled again. "Yeah, they fought like hell, but I've never seen two people more in love." The man frowned suddenly. "It was hard on her when he went. So quick. One day he was here and then he was gone."

Charles refilled the man's beer and leaned against the back bar. "He was a good man. It was sad to see him go."

The kid shook off the man and grinned a little. "I don't think I've ever had two beers here. You would only let me have the one."

"If you didn't have it here, you'd be off with your idiot buddies, drinking yourselves stupid and driving into telephone poles. Better to let you have the one than see teenagers in coffins."

"You gave me some real good advice back then," Peter said taking a drink of his Bud.

"Life lessons and booze. It's what I've been doing for three decades. If only I'd listened to more of it, you might just be drinking here right now instead of working." There was no regret in his voice, simply an acknowledgement of his situation. Regret was for people with lives ahead of them. One way or another, Charles Sawyer only had two minutes left.

"Well," the kid said, "since you gave me such good advice then, allow me to return the favor. Patrons know everything about the bartenders they go to regularly. I know you were married and it ended badly. I know that you always wanted to be a teacher, but college didn't fit after you came home in uniform. And I know for the last hour, you have been contemplating your moment to grab that shot gun sitting under the bar and kill me."

Both the kid and the man vanished, leaving only the killer to stare at Charles. "Let me tell ya, Charlie, that would be bad. I am faster than you. You know that. You might think it's more honorable to go out with your boots on, but if you try to kill me with that rusty hunk of shit under the bar, I might get mad and it might get real ugly for you. Real ugly."

Charles' breath caught in his throat for a moment, staring at his killer's face. He forced air back into his body and said, "You could just walk away, Peter. Tell them that I wasn't here."

"You know I'm not going to."

Charles drained the last of the scotch from his glass and set it on the back bar. He stared into the cold lifeless eyes of the killer. He saw no remorse or hesitation staring back at him. There was no determination or anger. There was no recognition of their history or even that Charles was even a human being. There was just blank, indifferent fate locked on to his eyes like the pavement rushing to meet a jumper.

His whole body tensed. The clock turned to two thirty. Charles lunged for the gun. Peter's hand leapt to his pistol, pulling back the hammer as he drew it from its home. Charles loosened the gun from the clamps that had embraced it beneath the bar for so many years. He swung it up toward the killer. Peter extended his arm, increasing the tension on the trigger as he aimed. Charles heard the click of the shotgun as the trigger released the hammer. He saw the trigger of the pistol meet the grip. Both guns belched fire and the lights went out with a bang for the last time.

A few hours later, Lucas Black boarded a bus as the sun crept over the horizon. After seeing him struggle, a kid from across the aisle helped him with his small bag. He thanked the kid and settled into his seat. He reached under his jacket feeling the bulge of the bandages over his shoulder, but no blood seeping through. He popped a couple of pills into his mouth to ease the pain and flipped through the sports section. Silently, he wondered if he could find someone to take a bet on the Celtics game. He had a good feeling that today was his lucky day.

Universal Donor
Jeri Westerson

Once again on the vinyl lounge chair, I inhale a whiff of antiseptic. There are others in their own chairs, blissful as they watch the frenetic images flash across the television screen hanging above us; images of people shooting other people in the Middle East and celebrating, burning American flags. Brown children cry for the cameras, their mouths grimacing as blood oozes down their faces from a bomb blast.

I look at the others in their own lounge chairs staring at these flickering images, their faces passive, blank. Already they have tubes shooting down from their arms like strands of bright red licorice dipping into plastic bags, filling. You almost can't tell if it's coming or going, not by looking at it.

Latex covered hands come at me. The nurse grabs my arm searching for a vein, probing with off-white fingers and ticking her head—as they always do—that she can't find it. But it's the same: Rubber tubing tied tight around my arm, needle piercing the flesh. Then at last the red, like an oil field's gusher, surges upward through the clear tube. A perfect candy red.

I can't watch that part of the process, of course. It's not natural. Blood is supposed to stay inside a body. Perhaps that's what makes the body rebel and why, after I lay there trying to think of anything but the fact of my life's blood seeping out—no, not seeping, but *rushing*, as if it's got a better place to go—that a cold sweat bubbles up all over my skin. I tell myself it doesn't bother me, psyche myself. But then the clamminess intensifies and the tunnel vision starts, darkening the edges of my sight like a lens on a silent movie camera—fade to black—and my hearing grows hollow, sounds tinny as if recorded on a very bad microphone. I don't know what I look like, but I am told that my skin becomes very pale and my lips colorless. I try to act nonchalant, but it must be obvious because a nurse looks over at me as if I had begun to mutate into something slimy and green and she calls the alarm. Tubes are ripped out and blankets flung over my helpless body and it's over. Again.

The nurse leans over and says, "You'll be all right in a minute. Are you okay?"

"Yes," I answer wearily. "It happens every time I do this. Did you get enough this time?"

"It happens *every* time? Then you shouldn't be here!" She leans closer, making certain I hear her. I am definitely close enough because I can see the light glowing behind the skin of her nose, up into the nostrils where it is red and bristly with hairs. "Don't come back," she says harshly, giving me a final look that seems to say "why are you wasting our time?"

"But I'm a universal donor," I whimper. "O Negative."

Doesn't matter. She's already gone. They tell me to lie there a while. Later they give me juice and cookies. They didn't get enough blood and must throw away what little I gave. They never get enough.

That's the problem with being a universal donor. There's a sense of responsibility. Even as I walk the streets, the warm pavement flat beneath my shoes, I feel the combination of dread and purpose pulling at my thoughts, a Chinese finger puzzle. I get little work done. I do sit in an office and I push papers and acknowledge coworkers and say "yes" to my boss and "no" to the office flirt whose skirts are too short for proper office etiquette and continue with my day. Life gets done. But I also think of this responsibility, this walking around each day with blood that others can have and use. I think it's a little selfish, just me and this blood. Except that I can't seem to give it up.

For me, the day is broken up into shards of time, one of which owns a brown bag with my lunch in it. I know I could purchase one of those little coolers or those soft brightly colored nylon bags I see on many desks come lunch time, but I like the simplicity of the brown bag, its strange dusty scent that reminds me of school lunches and blacktop and cold plastic benches. By the time lunch comes around, my brown bag is as wrinkled and worn as my suit, which I admit looks very much like a brown bag. It's an old suit. The tie is older. I don't consider myself very old, though the media would have you believe forty is old. Maybe it is.

It is an ordinary life with ordinary dreams fitting into an ordinary routine. I don't think I offer much in this little office with its politics and divorces and gossip and occasional work getting done. But even beyond the bologna sandwiches on Wonder Bread and the single navel orange and bag of potato chips that I eat almost every day, beyond my wrinkled suits and scuffed brown shoes, beyond my apathy for a sunrise or even the pigeons to whom I throw the crusts of my sandwich and the crumbs from the bottom of my bag of chips, I know there is something special about me. My blood type. I am O Negative. I'm a universal donor. I looked it up. It means my blood could be given to anyone, even someone of a different blood type. That means I—an ordinarily uninteresting man— can save a life. I remember sitting and reading that in a magazine. I was in my doctor's office, crossing and recrossing my legs. I had a bladder infection. But it struck me even then, the notion. Right away. *I could give my blood*, I thought, *and it could go to anyone. Anyone at all.*

It isn't so easy. The doctors call it the fight or flight complex. Some people are inclined to stand up and fight. Somewhere back in their primeval collective thought processes they were the ones who could stand up to a mastodon and kill it for dinner. Then there were others who took one look at that same mastodon and their skin would get clammy and tunnel vision closed up their sight and before they fainted outright, they would get the hell out of there. That was me. Not the one standing up to a metaphorical mastodon. I'd be the one running like hell.

Except I'd rather face a mastodon than a needle.

Each week I try again. It's amazing how many different places have blood banks. I've been to churches, soup kitchens, doctor's offices, malls and even a farmer's market. It's all the same. I fill out all the forms. I even tell the volunteer interviewing me how I have this tendency to feel as if I'll faint, but they always smile indulgently as I tell them. They squeeze my arm with mock affection, and say, "You'll be all right."

But I'm never all right. Sometimes I'm certain I'm going to fill that bag. I have earbuds on with loud music pulsing in my ears or one of those audio books, anything to keep my mind from the bloodletting. Always it comes back to the notion that a piece of steel is imbedded in my skin and into my vein, slicing through the membranes and layers and sucking out my blood and it starts all over again.

"Weren't you here last week?" a male nurse accuses. "Jeez, you think you'd've learned."

"I thought I could do it this time," I tell him sheepishly, but he isn't listening. He's actually snorting in disgust. I thought that was just an expression but he was doing it. Snorting in disgust. I have wasted his time, even though I am a universal donor.

Nightfall in the city is not like nightfall anywhere else. Dusk is uncertain. It is the time just before streetlights quiver to life, when neon signs perched above storefronts haven't decided whether it's dark enough yet to make a showy appearance. Shadows from skyscrapers fall on the streets and alleys with all the grace of a stray newspaper page laying gently on the pavement in its own silent death.

I like the anonymity of it, how faces change by shadows and neon. Lights appear in the high rises making false stars on a man-made horizon.

That works for me. I can understand it better than standing beneath the countless stars of the heavens. There's something frightening about being that vulnerable, like being underwater in the ocean and looking up all that way to the surface.

There's a scent to the city at night. It's different from the city in the daytime. During the day, it has the cheerful exuberance of wieners roasting on a street vender's cart; of the salty pungency of pretzel stands; the smell of cotton T-shirts for sale, hanging like medieval banners from a storefront, flapping and their fresh starchy perfume like mother's laundry room.

But it's different at night. Once the sun sets there is the unmistakable gathering of aromas from Italian food billowing on the breeze. It's as if it waits for night to fall before it barrages the neighborhood with berry flavors of cheap Chianti and the earthiness of oregano and marinara sauce. Patent leather and furs even have an aroma, oil and dusty musk. The exhaust from a taxi smells different when it stops off at a fine hotel, but only at night. It doesn't smell that urgent, acerbic scent during the day. Only at night.

I like to walk and take it in. When I do, I see much more than when I whiz by in a bus or descend into the oily darkness of the subway. Walking makes you a part of the city and at night, sounds and sights are especially acute. I peer at shopfronts and inside where people are a part of something rhythmic and visceral. They interact amid their artificial lighting like fish in an aquarium, while safe outside in a pool of a street lamp I am apart from them.

It's also how I find the blood banks.

Today it's a bookstore. Some sort of promotion about vampire books. Already I rub my arm where the needle stick will inevitably go and I feel the faint queasiness in my gut that always accompanies these excursions. But I go in anyway.

There are posters of the vampire books hanging from the ceiling and hardcover copies stacked on a table nearest the window. Those chairs, too. They aren't the lounge type, but the hard backs with swing-out arms.

There's a girl in Goth make-up with a pierced eyebrow sitting at the reception table where you fill out the forms. When I sit in front of her I can barely stand to look at her face with that ring piercing her brow where jewelry surely should not be. Once more I explain my queasiness, but even she reaches out with black-polished fingernails and says, "You'll be okay."

A very young man with a soul patch on his chin and pimples on his forehead who keeps calling me "dude" directs me to one of the chairs. In my head I start my chant, *you can do it you can do it you can do it...* When I sit in the chair, I slump a little, thinking that it might put me in a more relaxed position. I swivel and rock my head on my neck. He asks me to take off my suit jacket and when I roll up my sleeve he asks about the red dots that look like needle marks.

"They are needle marks," I tell him nonchalantly. "I gave blood last week at another blood bank."

"Oh," he says without more conversation and hefts my arm against his hip, tying tight the rubber tubing around my upper arm. He puts a rubber ball in my palm and tells me to squeeze. Dutifully I comply and he begins the usual. "Jeez it's hard to find a vein. Come on baby come on baby. There's the little sucker. Wait. There it goes. Hold on, let me get this. Squeeze it for me. Don't give up—ah, it's gone again." He slaps my arm, raising a welt. "I'm gonna find it. I'm gonna get you, you little blue vein. I'm gonna get you with my needle. Ah!"

I feel it. Some are better at this than others. He is rough though and I don't know whether I am going to make it even past the initial stage. I take a deep breath and stare up at the poster. It's the cover of the vampire book, but there's no blood on it, only a watercolor of a woman in some diaphanous gown. Then I start to think how you never see the word "diaphanous" unless it's associated with "gown" and whether I even know how to spell "diaphanous," not that I ever would. I wonder if it would spice up my sales report if I put in the word "diaphanous," but don't know how I would slip it in when talking about office supplies. They would think I lost my mind.

This musing helps me get over the first hump. The bag is dangling from the chair and I don't look at it. The young man who did the deed is standing not too far away and because there is no one in the store, I ask him what the vampire book is about and is it any good.

"I don't know. I haven't read it. But I like the chick who writes it. I read her stuff sometimes."

"Is it a series of books?" I ask. I am coming into my chatty stage, trying to keep my mind from the needle and the tube and the blood, but I can feel that it's probably not going to work.

"Yeah. That's all the shit she writes. Now take Stephen King. At least he goes into other shit sometimes. I mean, get a life!"

He is a witty conversationalist and I am enthralled. At least that is what is going through my head. But it's not working. I feel it's not working.

"Hey, dude. Are you all right?"

It's not working. It's really not working. The nurse comes over, looks me in the face and says, "Get that stuff out of him! Now!"

Humiliated again, I am forced to sit for ten minutes while the young man regales me on how horrible I looked "like I was about to faint."

"I'm a universal donor," I say weakly.

"No kidding," he says, but another customer comes in and he is on him like a vampire.

The vampire book reminded me of my ex-girlfriend. Actually, she really wasn't my girlfriend though she should have been. We went on a date two months ago, though I guess it wasn't really a date. I helped her move some furniture.

I knew her from work. She worked in the same office, but didn't stay long. Then she got a job in the same building and we got to talking one day in the lobby next to the newsstand.

She remembered me and wondered if I would help her move some furniture. Her old roommate was getting married and sold her a sofa. Could I come to her apartment on Saturday? Sure, I said because I thought she was kind of cute and she must be a little interested in me, else why would she ask? There were plenty of guys in the office.

So I go to her apartment and it's one of those old brownstones with a very narrow staircase and there is a wide, army green sofa sitting on the sidewalk. There is also a brass floor lamp, two boxes of books, one box of dishes and two large pictures in heavy frames. Nothing looks like it weighs less than forty pounds.

"So just us, huh?" I say, looking at the objects on the sidewalk. It's like a Moroccan bazaar.

"Yeah," she says. Her black rimmed glasses are perched on the bridge of her nose. Her brown hair is pulled back in a floppy pony tail. I like how it makes her angular face look.

She says, "Let's get to it," and she picks up the lamp. I grab a picture, but it is heavier than it looks. I think I picked it up wrong because now my back gets a shock of pain. Doesn't matter. I am following her up the stairs and get a good view of her round bottom in tight jeans. Each cheek jostles up and down with each step. I almost want her apartment to be on the top floor, but I change my mind as it winds higher and I get a little out of breath.

"Here it is," she says, but doesn't have to because she is walking over the threshold.

Small apartment with painted wood floors and a nifty bay window that looks out onto the full branches of a sycamore. Or maybe an elm. I don't really know my trees.

She puts the lamp in the corner of the bay, re-arranges it a little and glances over her shoulder at me. Her pony tail sweeps aside. Her nose twitches when she looks at me. I think it's cute.

"Just put that anywhere," she says to me.

I lean the picture against the wall and straighten my back. It doesn't help that shooting pain, but I smile and clap my hands together as if I am anxious to continue.

But she doesn't look at me and she is already making her way down the stairs.

We bring up the other items, saving the sofa for last.

She gets on one end and I take the bottom wondering if it would be more gallant if I took the front. Which was heavier? But she doesn't let me decide and we are going up the staircase.

I don't think it's going to fit. We have to turn a corner at the landing and it gets stuck. I'm holding the low end because I'm afraid it will cut loose and come crashing down at me like an army-green avalanche.

"Let's just push it," she says.

"It'll scrape the wall," I say.

She doesn't say anything, but makes an exaggerated grunt that may not be all that exaggerated and she heaves it up while I push.

A long, green stripe appears on the wall when we get it through and she makes a face, her eyes wide, her mouth grimacing downward like a tragedy mask and then her expression just as quickly disappears.

We finally get it in the room and move the sofa into different locations. Once she is satisfied, she slides over one of the arms and sits on the cushion with a loud sigh. Her feet are in the air slanted up against the sofa arm.

"Well, I certainly couldn't have done it without you." She smiles at me. "Want some wine?"

I nod and sit. I'm still winded and can't talk.

She gets a half-empty bottle of white wine out of the fridge and pours it in two balloon glasses. She steps out of her shoes and pads across the floor with her face in one of the glasses and her arm extended to hand me the other.

I taste it. It's chilled, but already stale.

When she sits again she is next to me. She smells like sweat and coconut.

"So. You really saved my life today."

I nod. "No problem. Just glad to help."

"Can I get you something to eat? I think I have some chips."

"Actually." I adjust myself to face her. "I was thinking of taking you out to dinner."

Her face falls. Her eyes change when they gaze at me. Before they were light blue, like the sky near the horizon. But now they are more like the blue in the back of an aquarium. Not quite real, but functional.

"Oh. You know, it's been a hard day. Tonight wouldn't do."

"How about tomorrow then?"

Both her hands roll the bowl of the glass. The stem's base sits on her thighs. "You know, all the rest of this week is no good either. Maybe some other time."

I nod and look at the ceiling. "You know, it's funny you

should say about 'saving your life.' You see, I'm a universal donor."

She squints. "A 'universal donor'? What does *that* mean?"

"Oh, you know. When you give blood. Some people are AB or B Negative. Only certain people can accept their blood. They have to match. But a universal donor's blood can go to anybody."

She shakes her head. A vague smile touches the edge of her mouth and she raises the glass to her lips again. "I didn't know that."

"Oh, sure. I'm O Negative."

"Then I guess you've saved a lot of lives."

"Well, I've never actually been able to donate blood."

"What? Then what are you talking about?"

"Just making conversation." I edge closer and touch the ponytail. She shivers and sidles away. "I really like you," I say.

"Well you're a nice guy, too," she says and stands. She clutches the wine glass.

I stand too and put the glass on the floor next to the sofa. There is no table to put it on. I touch her shoulder and lean in to kiss her. My lips graze hers and she yanks away, shaking her head like a dog shakes out a rat.

"Don't!"

"Hey," I say. My hands open. My shoulders rise. "Hey—"

"I think you should go now." She hugs herself, getting small within her own embrace.

"Okay. So tonight's no good. I'll call you."

I head toward the door and she is right behind me. There is something in the way she says, "Yeah. Do that," that doesn't ring true, but I can't put my finger on it.

"I'll call you," I say. The door closes and I hear the locks turn.

I inhale deeply, still smelling coconut. I like her. She's nice. And in a way I did save her life. She said so.

I often think it would have been nice if it ended that way. I like to think that it did. Sometimes when I think about it, she is sitting on the sofa and we are laughing over slices of pizza. Sometimes I imagine she gives me a kiss by the door.

It would have been better if it *had* ended that way.

But when she looked at me with such distaste—and there's really no other way to put it—I just didn't think I could, I *had* to take it anymore.

The lamp was close, but the wine bottle was easiest.

It broke, a million little shards it seemed, when the first blow fell. She didn't say anything either because it slashed right across her mouth. Maybe bits of teeth flew with the shards of glass. Hard to tell. Blood. Lots of it. Especially when I beat her head into the rug. For some reason, the blood didn't bother me. Maybe it's just my own blood that made me queasy. Funny.

By the time the sirens and red and blue lights raked across the buildings, I'm on the sidewalk on the other side of the street standing with the other gawkers, watching the ambulance driver and the coroner bringing back a black-bagged something on a gurney.

Her body, I guess. I had looked at her broken body a long time once I was done. The neck of the bottle was still in my hand (it was in my pocket now). I remember wondering what her blood type was. I should have asked her. But that was two months ago. Sometimes when I think about that day, I do ask her. But I never imagine it's something rare. It's only regular blood. Not O Negative.

Sometimes I wonder if I get drunk whether that will help me through the donation thing or not, but I realize they would probably notice and wouldn't let me even try.

I feel badly enough about the blood bank at the bookstore that I almost buy that vampire book. But I don't. Instead, I walk out the door and wander slowly up the street. It is eight o'clock by now and I feel a little hungry. There is a Chinese place not too far from here that I always wanted to try, but never seemed to have the time. I would have taken her to this restaurant, but I guess it's too late now. I wonder what she would have ordered.

I walk there and begin thinking about Chinese food and how those places all close on the same day and I can't remember what day that is. The same day as museums, right? Is that Monday? Is Monday a holy day or something? I guess everybody needs a day off.

The night temperature suddenly dips. It's something you notice only when you do a lot of walking. There is a specific time of the night where the temperature dives, as if you are walking out into a lake and the shore suddenly falls away at a specific point. The night does it, too, with its temperature and you notice that it drops. I think it's the night's way of saying "we're in a different time zone now. Button up your coat," and then I do because it is significantly colder, but this I like, too, about the city. It takes charge of things, winnows out the unnecessary. The city decides that it will be colder now and those who can't take it go inside or hover in doorways, stamping their feet, their hands thrust deeply into their coat pockets and their shoulders way up to their ears. I see them all the time. Dark silhouettes against the bare bulbs of porches. What are they waiting for? It's not going to get warmer until the sunrise. I don't suppose they stand there all night.

The Chinese place is around the corner and down an alley. One of those places that have been in the city for at least fifty years or even longer. Cities have places like that, places that are really old, where gangsters used to eat, guys with names like Vinnie and Guido bent over tables crunching egg rolls in their flat Sicilian faces and cracking open fortune cookies with their big sausage fingers to read the little slips of paper. That must have been something.

I turn the corner and start down the alley, listening absently to my footsteps echo. The alley is not particularly narrow and not particularly dark, but I wonder for a moment why my footsteps echo out of cadence with my feet.

When the knife unexpectedly slices upwards into my back, I suddenly think *that's why*, and slump to the ground. I feel that hard, steel blade go where it is never supposed to go. A hot pain, that's what it is. Hot. Slicing through all the layers of skin and into the muscle, nicking the kidney. Then all over my back I feel the rush of liquid that could be lots of things, like water and bile, but mostly, I know, it is blood. All that O Negative gushes out enough to fill several of those bags, but there is no one but the greasy pavement and gutter to receive it. I think maybe it's her old boyfriend getting revenge. It's an interesting thought. But I know no one can connect me with the murder. No one has. I guess you *can* get away with murder, except I'm not doing much getting away lying in the gutter. Funny.

The man rummages into my coat and finally finds my wallet. He wrestles with my unresisting wrist and squeezes my watch from my arm, but the joke's on him. It isn't even a Timex. He doesn't say anything as I lay there and when he leaves I am completely alone. It hurts, that hole in my back, and I remember thinking, *but I'm a universal donor. Someone really could use this blood. They really could.*

And the funny thing is, this time, I don't get queasy at all.

Acknowledgments
Jon & Ruth Jordan

Murder and Mayhem in Muskego is our favorite event of the year. It's filled with friends and family and people who love to read. Helping to put it together each year is a labor of love. The thing that really makes it work are the people who come to it. All the authors who give up a weekend, all the Friends of the Library who work to make it roll right, the staff at the Muskego Public Library working away as hundreds of crime fiction fans invade for the day and take over the place. And the fans and readers, without them the best panels and interviews in the world don't mean a thing. So if you've ever been to even one Murder and Mayhem in Muskego or if you've been to them all, THANK YOU.

This anthology was possible because of the wonderful authors in it. They have all attended Muskego at least once and, if that wasn't enough, they donated a piece of fiction for this book to help raise some money to keep the event going. We told them our plan to try and raise money and they stepped up.

And a real big thank you to Down & Out Books and Eric Campbell for publishing this at cost and taking NO PROFIT from it. He's donating every penny of profit to the Library to use so they can continue doing this event.

And if you are reading this, thank you for buying this and helping out. We love every story in here and hope you do too.

ABOUT THE CONTRIBUTORS

Megan Abbott is the Edgar award-winning author of the novels *Dare Me*, *The End of Everything Bury Me Deep*, *Queenpin*, *The Song Is You* and *Die a Little*. Her writing has appeared in the *New York Times*, *Salon*, the *Los Angeles Times Magazine*, *Los Angeles Review of Books*, *The Guardian* and *Best Crime and Mystery Stories of the Year*. She is also the author of a nonfiction book, *The Street Was Mine: White Masculinity in Hardboiled Fiction and Film Noir*, and the editor of *A Hell of a Woman*, an anthology of female crime fiction. She has been nominated for the Steel Dagger Prize, Hammett Prize, the Macavity, Anthony and Barry Awards, the *Los Angeles Times* Book Prize and the Pushcart Prize. *www.meganabbott.com*

Nathan Banks grew up in Muskego Wisconsin, where he currently resides while studying law enforcement. He graduated with his associate's degree in Criminal Justice in 2012, and is preparing to begin the police academy. In his free time, he writes, reads and converses with individuals all over the world through his hobby interest in ham radio. "The Muskego Long Count" is Nathan's first published work. He hopes there to be many more in the future.

Whether writing noir, historical fiction, urban fantasy, thriller, or traditional mystery, **Dana Cameron** draws from her expertise in archaeology. Her fiction has won multiple Anthony, Agatha, and Macavity Awards and has earned an Edgar Award nomination. In addition to "Pattern Recognition," other Fangborn stories include "The Night

Things Changed," "Swing Shift," "Love Knot" and "Finals." The first of three novels set in the Fangborn 'verse, *Seven Kinds of Hell*, will be published in early 2013 by 47North. Dana lives in Massachusetts with her husband and benevolent feline overlords. *http://www.danacameron.com*

Called a "hard-boiled poet" by NPR's Maureen Corrigan and the "noir poet laureate" in the *Huffington Post*, **Reed Farrel Coleman** has published fifteen novels. He is a three-time recipient of the Shamus Award for Best PI Novel of the Year and a two-time Edgar Award nominee. He has also won the Macavity, Barry and Anthony Awards. His essays, poetry and short fiction have appeared in *Brooklyn Noir3*, *The Lineup*, *Wall Street Noir*, the *Huffington Post*, *MulhollandBooks.com* and several other publications. Reed was the editor of the short story anthology *Hard Boiled Brooklyn*. He is a founding member of Mystery Writers of America University and an adjunct professor of English at Hofstra University. He lives with his family on Long Island. Visit Reed at *www.reedcoleman.com*.

Hilary Davidson is the author of *The Damage Done*, which won the 2011 Anthony Award for Best First Novel as well as a Crimespree Award. The sequel, *The Next One to Fall*, was published by Forge in February 2012 and the third book in the series, *Evil in All Its Disguises*, will be out on March 5, 2013. Hilary's short stories have been featured in publications including Ellery Queen, Thuglit, Beat to a Pulp and Crimespree. Hilary is a Toronto-born travel journalist who has lived in New York City since October 2001. She's also the author of 18 nonfiction books. Visit her online at *www.hilarydavidson.com*.

Sean Doolittle is the award-winning author of *Dirt, Burn, Rain Dogs, The Cleanup* and *Safer*. His latest book is *Lake Country*. He lives in western Iowa with his family. *http://seandoolittle.com/*

Greg Rucka was born in San Francisco and raised on the Central Coast of California, in what is commonly referred to as 'Steinbeck Country.' He began his writing career in earnest at the age of 10 by winning a county-wide short-story contest, and hasn't let up since. He graduated from Vassar College with an A.B. in English, and from the University of Southern California's Master of Professional Writing program with an M.F.A. He is the author of nearly a dozen novels, six featuring bodyguard Atticus Kodiak and two featuring Tara Chace, the protagonist of his Queen & Country series. Additionally, he has penned several short-stories, countless comics and the occasional non-fiction essay. In comics, he has had the opportunity to write stories featuring some of the world's best-known characters—Superman, Batman and Wonder Woman—as well as penning several creator-owned properties himself, such as *Whiteout* and *Queen & Country*, both published by Oni Press. His work has been optioned several times over and his services are in high-demand in a variety of creative fields as a story-doctor and creative consultant. Greg resides in Portland, Oregon with his wife, author Jennifer Van Meter, and his two children. He thinks the biggest problem with the world is that people aren't paying enough attention. *http://www.gregrucka.com/wp/*

J.M. Edwards is a pseudonym for an author who has participated in MMM in the past, but who prefers to remain anonymous.

Andrew Grant was born in Birmingham, England in May 1968. He went to school in St Albans and attended the University of Sheffield where he studied English Literature and Drama. After graduation, Andrew set up and ran a small independent theatre company. Following a critically successful appearance at the Edinburgh Fringe Festival, Andrew moved into the telecommunications industry as a 'temporary' solution to a short-term cash crisis. Fifteen years later, Andrew became the victim/beneficiary of a widespread redundancy programme. Freed once again from the straight jacket of corporate life, he took the opportunity to answer the question, what if...? Andrew is married to novelist Tasha Alexander and divides his time between Chicago and the UK. *www.andrewgrantbooks.com.*

Ted Hertel, Jr. is a Wisconsin attorney whose publications include an essay on Linda Barnes (St. James Guide, 1996), two essays on Ellery Queen: *Queen's Gambit* (The Tragedy of Errors, 1999) and *The American Detective Mystery* (CrimeSpree, 2004). He assisted in editing *The Adventure of the Murdered Moths* (2005), a collection of Queen radio plays and authored *The Alphabet Crimes of Lawrence Treat* (Crime Spree, 2005). He was a contributor to the Anthony and Macavity Award winning *Mystery Muses* (2006). *My Bonnie Lies...* (The Mammoth Book of Legal Thrillers, 2001) received Anthony and Macavity nominations, winning the Robert L. Fish Edgar Award. *It's Crackers to Slip a Rozzer the Dropsey in Snide* (Small Crimes, 2004) received an honorable mention in the Sternig Short Fiction competition and was nominated for an Anthony. His latest publications include *The Town at the End of the Road* (West Coast Crime Wave, 2011) and *The Name of the Dame* (Murder & Mayhem in Muskego, 2012). Hertel reviews for Deadly Pleasures, co-chaired Bouchercon '99 and chaired Local Arrangements for Eyecon '95. He was president of the Midwest Chapter of Mystery Writers of America and served for two years on its national board.

Chris F. Holm was born in Syracuse, New York, the grandson of a cop who passed along his passion for crime fiction. His work has appeared in such publications as Ellery Queen's Mystery Magazine, Alfred Hitchcock's Mystery Magazine, and *The Best American Mystery Stories 2011*. He's been an Anthony Award nominee, a Derringer Award finalist and a Spinetingler Award winner. Chris' Collector series (*Dead Harvest*, *The Wrong Goodbye*) recast the battle between heaven and hell as Golden Era crime pulp. You can visit him online at *www.chrisfholm.com*.

Brad Parks is the only author to have won the Shamus Award and Nero Award for the same novel. That book, *Faces of the Gone*, introduced Carter Ross, the sometimes-dashing investigative reporter, who has gone on to star in *Eyes of the Innocent* and *The Girl Next Door*, which reached No. 3 on the Baker & Taylor Fiction/Mystery Bestseller List. The series, which Shelf Awareness called "perfect for the reader who loves an LOL moment but wants a mystery that's more than empty calories," has earned starred reviews from *Library Journal* and *Booklist*. It will continue with *The Good Cop* (due March 5, 2013) and a fifth, as-yet-unnamed installment. Parks is a graduate of Dartmouth College and spent a dozen years as a reporter for *The Washington Post* and *The (Newark, N.J.) Star-Ledger*. He is now a full-time novelist who lives in Virginia with his wife and two small children. His and his zany interns can be found at *www.BradParksBooks.com*.

Gary Phillips' recent work includes being editor and contributor to *Scoundrels: Tales of Greed, Murder and Financial Crimes*. an anthology from Down & Out Books. His paperback original *Warlord of Willow Ridge*, about crime and mores in suburbia, will be out soon from Kensington, and he has a short story in the upcoming *Heroin Chronicles* from

Akashic. Please visit his website at: *www.gdphillips.com.*

Kat Richardson is the author of the bestselling Greywalker paranormal detective novels. She lives on a classic yacht in the Seattle area with her husband and a lunatic pit bull named Bella. You can learn more about Kat, her books, and her dog at: *http://katrichardson.com/.*

Marcus Sakey has worked as a landscaper, a theatrical carpenter, a 3D animator, a woefully unprepared movie reviewer, a tutor and a graphic designer who couldn't draw. In 2007 his first novel *The Blade Itself* was published to wide critical acclaim, and thank god, because nothing else seemed to be working. His five novels have been nominated for more than fifteen awards, named to multiple "Year's Best" lists and translated into numerous languages. Three are currently in development as films. Marcus is also the host and writer of the acclaimed television show *Hidden City* on Travel Channel, for which he is routinely pepper-sprayed and attacked by dogs. His website is at *MarcusSakey.com*, or you can follow him on Twitter or Facebook, where he posts under the clever handle *MarcusSakey.*

Tom Schreck is the author of five novels, including *On the Ropes, The Vegas Knockout* and *Getting Dunn.* He graduated from the University of Notre Dame and has a master's degree in psychology—and a black belt. He previously worked as the director of an inner-city drug clinic and today juggles several jobs: communications director for a program for people with disabilities, adjunct psychology professor, freelance writer, and world championship boxing official. He lives in Albany, New York, with his wife. *http://tomschreck.wordpress.com/*

Zoë Sharp is the author of the bestselling Charlotte 'Charlie' Fox crime thriller series. She opted out of mainstream education at the age of twelve and wrote her first novel at fifteen before becoming a freelance photojournalist in 1988. She became a crime writer after receiving death-threat letters in the course of her work. Her fiction has been nominated for the Edgar, Anthony, Barry, Benjamin Franklin and Macavity Awards in the United States, as well as the CWA Short Story Dagger. Zoë says she hopes people will like her, or at least that they will respect her, but failing that she will settle for their fear. More info can be found on *www.ZoeSharp.com*. Zoë also witters on Twitter *(@authorzoesharp)*, fools about on Facebook (*www.facebook.com/authorzoesharp*) and blogs on Murderati (*www.Murderati.com*) and Hardboiled Collective (*www.HardboiledCollective.blogspot.co.uk*).

When he's not slinging fish, **Bryan VanMeter** is devouring books with the ferocity of a rabid dog who stumbles on a fresh steak. This is his first published work of fiction. You'll typically find Bryan enjoying the witty, intellectual company of his family and friends whenever possible. He is a native of Milwaukee, Wisconsin and can often be found in a library, bookstore or Bryant's Cocktail Lounge if you'd ever like to buy him a drink.

L.A. native **Jeri Westerson** has been a journalist, a theology teacher and graphic artist, among other things. She combined the medieval with the hard-boiled and came up with her own brand of medieval mystery she calls the Crispin Guest Medieval Noir novels. Amid the dark plots and medieval setting is her brooding protagonist, Crispin Guest, a disgraced knight turned detective on the mean streets of fourteenth century London, running into thieves, kings, poets and religious relics. She writes on a variety of topics for short stories (a Japanese-themed short called "Noodle Girl" in the anthology *Shaken: Stories for Japan*; a 1930s comic book re-do short called "Mesmer Maneuver" for the upcoming serial anthology *Night of the Insurgents*), writes a medieval caper series called *Oswald the Thief* and the Skyler Foxe Mysteries, a gay contemporary series written under the name Haley Walsh. Jeri is vice president for the southern California chapter of Mystery Writers of America and is also vice president of Sisters in Crime Los Angeles. When not writing, Jeri dabbles in gourmet cooking, likes fine wines, cheap chocolate and swoons over anything British. She herds two cats, a tortoise and the occasional tarantula at her home in southern California. *www.JeriWesterson.com*

Jon and Ruth Jordan are fans of the mystery genre going WAY back; they met each other at a mystery convention in 1999. Since becoming a couple they have taken the love of all thing mystery to new levels and have each hosted a Bouchercon, Ruth in 2008 with Judy Bobalik in Baltimore and Jon in 2011 in St. Louis. They also help organize the annual Murder and Mayhem in Muskego held each November. When not running things Crimespree related, they like movies, live music and travel, though these things usually end up being related to crime fiction as well.

OTHER TITLES FROM DOWN AND OUT BOOKS

By J. L. Abramo
Catching Water in a Net
Clutching at Straws
Counting to Infinity
Gravesend

By Trey R. Barker
2,000 Miles to Open Road
Road Gig: A Novella
Exit Blood (*)

By Richard Barre
The Innocents
Bearing Secrets
Christmas Stories
The Ghosts of Morning
Blackheart Highway
Burning Moon
Echo Bay (*)

By Milton T. Burton
Texas Noir

By Reed Farrel Coleman
The Brooklyn Rules

By Don Herron
Willeford (*)

By Terry Holland
An Ice Cold Paradise
Chicago Shiver
Warm Hands, Cold Heart (*)

By David Housewright & Renée Valois
The Devil and the Diva

By David Housewright
Finders Keepers

By Valester Jones
The Pimp and the Gangster (*)

By Bill Moody
Czechmate: The Spy Who Played Jazz
Fair Trade (*)

By Gary Phillips
The Perpetrators
*Scoundrels: Tales of Greed, Murder
and Financial Crimes* (Editor)

By Lono Waiwaiole
Wiley's Lament
Wiley's Shuffle
Wiley's Refrain
Dark Paradise

(*)—Coming Soon